Goodbye Woodstock:

The Last Reunion

by

M. H. Sullivan

Romagnoli Publications

Goodbye Woodstock: The Last Reunion
by M.H. Sullivan

Second Edition

ISBN-13: 978-1-891486-08-1 (paperback)
ISBN-13: 978-1-891486-15-9 (eBook)
ISBN-13: 978-1-891486-18-0 (hardcover)

Library of Congress Control Number: 2026913972

Romagnoli Publications
Manchester, NH, USA

email: romagnoli.publications@gmail.com
website: www.romagnoli-publications.com

"Alone, we can do so little; together, we can do so much."
Helen Keller

Table of Contents

Chapter 1

Ceil walks the Labyrinth Trail

Love & Peace Commune, Brookings, OR
Friday, August 9, 2019, early morning

After breakfast and a quick chat with Jade, the greenhouse master, Ceil strode across the commune compound in her purposeful gait. Her long brown hair, streaked with gray, lapped against her back at each step. She was so absorbed in her thoughts that she barely noticed the morning quiet around her. She had to find Sky to find out whether he'd heard from his doctor yet.

He'd had a bunch of tests the day before and they were waiting to find out definitively whether his cancer had returned. Lately, he'd been complaining of a bone-weary fatigue and some abdominal pain and she was worried. While not a doctor, she was a certified midwife. For decades she had been the only medically-trained person at the commune, and over the years she'd learned a lot about health and illness. They called her "The Healer," which both humbled and pleased her. She was as passionate about her vocation today as she had been five decades ago, when she had welcomed her very first newborn into the world.

She came out of her revelry and noticed the sun was just beginning to seep between the branches of the trees around her, dappling the leaves with touches of sunlight. At this time of the morning, she could usually find Sky in the forest, walking the commune's labyrinth trail which wound among the gigantic trees in the hidden grove of sequoia redwoods. He had been making it a daily practice and said it brought him peace. She sighed. He could use some peace, that was for sure.

Oh, Lord, what will I do without Sky? She tripped over the uneven ground and caught herself. *Life without Sky?* The phrase itself felt unreal. After nearly five decades together, she couldn't imagine life without him. And what about the commune? He was the glue that held it all together.

As she neared the center of the compound, the only sound was the ceaseless buzz of insects. Where was everyone? Of course, they must be over at the greenhouses, she decided. They would be packing this week's vegetable harvest onto the trucks bound for Portland to make the weekly deliveries to their upscale restaurant clients.

She could see the rounded roof of one of the greenhouses above the trees. Two of the three greenhouses had been built from old Quonset huts, and they now contained the commune's livelihood, their organic produce business. It always amused her they had recycled these massive military Quonset huts and put them to such a green and peaceful use. "Swords into ploughshares," she liked to think. It was both Biblical and satisfying. She was proud of the commune's flourishing food business, but it had required long hours of dirty, tedious work. And now, with the summer harvest upon them, it was an especially hectic time.

Although she welcomed the success of the business, she also knew that the more prosperous it became, the harder it was to sustain. With the commune now mostly filled with aging Baby Boomers, how much longer could they continue to keep up with it all? *Heck, where was the next generation of hippies?* She smiled wistfully. Times certainly had changed. It was 2019 and the country seemed to be—not just out of control—but possibly heading off a cliff.

She shooed the negative thoughts away. After all, there were always challenges in life, and sometimes things looked bleak, but you couldn't wallow in the darkness. Times had been bad back in the '70s, too. Nixon was in the White House then, and the Vietnam War was raging. Politics, war, and the changing culture were dividing the American people back then, too. It wasn't so different from now. Except, she thought wryly, *This time, I'm on the other side of the generational fence. What goes around, comes around, huh?*

As she passed the central fire pit, she saw tree branches strewn across the bricks. She would have to find Archer later to ask him to clean up the area before people started arriving for the big end-of-summer Woodstock Reunion next week. She wanted everything to look great.

The commune always timed the celebration to coincide with the dates of the original Woodstock Festival: August 15 to 17th. But this year was going to be extra special. It would not only be the 50th anniversary of Woodstock but also the 45th anniversary of the commune. They were expecting twice as many returnees as usual, plus families and other guests. Her thoughts turned bittersweet when she realized that if Sky's cancer had returned, this might be his last reunion.

As she stepped into the trees, she paused and took a deep breath, filling her lungs with the aroma of verdant pine and woody ash. She loved that smell. It was the reassuring scent of nature. She looked ahead and could just make out the ink-black outlines of the big trees—the special ones—just beyond the stands of pine and ash. There they stood, the commune's silent sentinels, their grove of giant sequoia redwoods.

The huge Goddess Tree marked the beginning of the first twist of the labyrinth trail. Before stepping onto the path of the labyrinth, Ceil rested her hand on the trunk of the tree. The Goddess Tree was the oldest and the largest sequoia in the grove. Ceil caressed the thick grooves of the reddish bark; the hand-to-bark connection was familiar and reassuring, like reaching out and touching a friend's shoulder. Then she started walking and soon the peace of the trees enveloped her. As was her habit, she cleared her mind while slowly letting the smells and sounds of the forest fill her. Gradually, time receded.

Soon she was rounding the last curve of the labyrinth trail and just up ahead was the center of the grove with its group of sequoia redwoods that they called the Peace Grove. The trees stood directly above a huge peace sign made from white river stones which were laid out on the ground.

Immediately, she spied Sky and smiled in relief. He was lying on the ground, his head resting on his backpack, with one arm draped over his eyes. The other arm lay slack at his side, palm up, fingers relaxed and gently curled. He was wearing his favorite pair of ratty-old cut-offs. They were white from age and bleached by the sun. His legs were deeply tanned, with stringy muscles, now slack and at rest.

She sat down beside him and then leaned over to kiss his forehead. "Hey, how are you feeling?" she asked softly.

Sky moved, and his arm fell away from his face. His eyelids fluttered as he glanced up and squinted. "Hey, babe," he mumbled, smiling with contentment, and stretched. "Geez, I must've fallen asleep. When I reached the center of the labyrinth, I laid down in this tiny patch of sunlight. It felt so good and cozy."

Ceil leaned back against the tree. "You looked so comfortable I almost didn't have the heart to wake you," she said. She reached over and stroked his hair, pushing the sweaty strands of gray away from his forehead.

He smiled. "I'm glad you're here," he said, pulling himself up to sit beside her. "Want to climb a tree with me?"

"What? You mean, now?"

"I'd like to go up to the top one more time, while I'm still able to climb these giants."

Ceil studied him. "Are you sure you feel up to it?"

He nodded. "I do. Come on," he said as he got up and pulled her to her feet.

She looked down at her clothes. "I'm not exactly dressed for a climb." True, she was wearing a pair of jeans, but she was also wearing one of her nicer tops because she was planning to go into town to see her mother at the nursing home. If she got it dirty, she didn't have many alternatives to change into.

"You look fine. I've got some micro-spikes and a couple of those hard-foam climbing helmets in my pack, plus an extra harness, too." He reached down and picked up the backpack and started pulling out the climbing gear.

"Are you sure about this, Sky?"

He paused and looked at her. "Yeah. I've been thinking about it for a while and I'd really like to climb one more time with you," he said and added, "like old times."

She smiled remembering all the times they'd climbed these wonderful old trees. It started back when the commune rallied to protect them from the timber companies. For months, they used to take turns camping in the canopies of the trees. "OK, then," she said. "Like old times."

They quickly donned the harnesses and pulled on the micro-spikes over their hiking shoes. When they were ready, Ceil untied and tugged on one of the climbing ropes that dangled from the Peace tree nearest her. "Should we do Peace Tree 1?"

He looked up at the tree and nodded. "Perfect."

Ceil studied him thoughtfully. She was feeling a little anxious. Did he have the strength to climb these huge trees anymore? His energy levels were erratic lately. Some days he was his old self; unstoppable. But there were other times she thought he looked exhausted and used up. "Sky, how about if you go first and I spot you, then I will follow you up?"

He squinted, trying to read her expression. Then he shrugged. "Alright. I'll try not to be a male chauvinist about it."

She chuckled and it eased the tension.

He checked his gear with easy assuredness, hooked his harness to the rope and threaded it expertly through the pulley.

Ceil checked her harness and climbing gear, too, then held the rope taut as Sky started climbing. Using the friction hitches and pulley, he made his way up the tree. He went more quickly than she had expected. Did that mean anything? *Maybe he's feeling better than I thought.* The notion eased her anxiety a bit.

Soon he was waving down to her from his loft in the branches and she took the rope and began her own climb. She didn't have his upper body strength, but the hitches and pulley system gave her the extra edge she needed. Even so, she was breathing hard by the time she pulled herself onto the platform.

Sky was already sitting on the wooden plank platform the commune had built years ago. He was leaning back against the main trunk. At the time they constructed the platforms, they were in the fight of their lives against the timber companies that wanted to chop down all the big trees and ship them south to satisfy consumer demand for redwood decks, fences, and furniture. To protect the trees, the commune created a team of tree sitting sentries in all the largest trees in their grove, and they took turns sleeping in the trees. Eventually, the timber companies gave up and moved on.

She crawled over to Sky and sat next to him.

"So why were you looking for me today?" he asked, squinting his eyes against the beam of sunlight coming through the branches above them.

"You heard from your doctor about those tests, didn't you?" she asked quietly.

He paused, looked out at the world of treetops surrounding them, then glanced over at her. "It's like we thought, babe. Not good. He says the tests show I'm not in remission anymore."

She closed her eyes and felt a stab in her heart. Even though she'd known deep down—she guessed it a while ago—it was still hard to hear him say it out loud. She looked at him and nodded slowly.

They were quiet for several long seconds. Then she sighed and reached over to take his hand. "Not very good timing with everyone arriving this week."

He let a breath out and smiled. "The Woodstock Reunion. I am really looking forward to it, though."

She shook her head in amazement. "It's crazy that we've been doing this thing for so long, huh?"

"I know! Remember when we started it? We didn't mean it to be any big deal. It was just supposed to be a blowout, end-of-summer celebration; a party for the poor suckers going back to jobs in the straight world." He chuckled and then coughed.

At the sound of his cough, she felt another stab in the heart. She asked quietly, "Sky, are you going to feel up to it?"

He shrugged. "S'pose so. I'm not on death's door yet. Heck, I just climbed a frickin' redwood, didn't I?" He met her eyes and she saw a lot less bravado in them. He finished more gravely, "Come on, Ceil. I don't want to be a downer for everyone, OK? I mean it, babe. Chances are I probably won't make it to Christmas, so just let me focus on having this last big party without people pitying me or standing around weeping and wailing."

"You think people are going to weep and wail for you? Really? You must think a lot of yourself, huh?" Her voice broke a little, and she could feel her eyes welling. For a second, she looked away. She pressed her lips together to keep the tears from spilling down her cheeks. She wished she was better at hiding her emotions from him. She wanted to help him feel better, not worse.

He reached up and touched her cheek with his index finger. "It's OK, Ceil. We have a lot ahead of us in the next month or two. Let me have this last Woodstock Reunion without all that depressing stuff hanging over us, OK?"

She nodded and swallowed, hoping her voice would be steady. "I plan to make sure you have a great Woodstock Reunion. I promise you that!"

He patted her arm. "Thanks, babe. It means a lot to me."

She hesitated then gently reached over and touched his stomach with her hand, her fingers spread wide.

He immediately covered her hand and kept it from moving over his belly. "You can't heal this thing, Ceil. You know that, right?"

She closed her eyes in frustration. "Sky, I can sense it. It's right there." She squeezed her fingers into a small, rounded shape. "It's like a nasty little black thing in my mind's eye. Evil."

Sky laughed. "Really? Did you just say it's 'evil'? Now you're beginning to sound more like a witch than a healer."

She batted his shoulder, knowing that he didn't mean it. "Stop it! I am not a witch! Besides, you know how much this frustrates me. I'm supposed to be a healer, Sky. Why can't I heal this thing?"

He touched her hand. "Because you can't heal everyone, Ceil. Some people's illnesses are beyond your capabilities. Who knows why? You should not be making it about you, anyway. Maybe it's something I must go through that is tied up with my karma, not yours. We all walk our own paths. You know that. Apparently, I need to walk this one. It has nothing to do with you, babe. I'm learning to accept it; you should, too. Besides, I've lived a glorious life, Ceil. All my regrets are small ones."

"You have regrets?"

He grimaced. "Of course. Everyone does."

"What regrets?"

He thought for a minute. "Well, I never went to China, for one," he said.

She sat up and snorted, "Really? You wanted to go to China?"

"Sure. I wanted to see the Great Wall. I also never climbed Everest." He paused, then chuckled. "OK, even on my best days, I never had the skill or the stamina to do that. So, maybe that's not a solid regret." He shrugged. "I probably would've died trying, and that would've just been ironic."

They were quiet for a moment. She said, "Sky, there's something else we should talk about."

But he interrupted her, "Hey!" He squinted and pointed upward to the top branches above them. "Look at all the butterflies!"

Ceil glanced up. He was right; there was a swirl of dozens upon dozens of blue butterflies above them. The two of them watched the graceful flutter, mesmerized, for several long moments.

"I'm going to do that," Sky said in an awed whisper.

"Do what?"

"I will swirl around these trees on my blue butterfly wings, just like that." He looked at Ceil. "Babe, when I'm gone, you'll know I'm fine when you look up and see a kaleidoscope of butterflies swirling over your head like this."

She met his eyes. "Promise you won't dive-bomb and scare the shit out of me, OK?"

"Scout's honor," he said, putting three fingers over his heart.

"I'll hold you to that." Their eyes met and she realized with a start that this was the first time they'd talked about a world that he wouldn't be in with her. A deep sadness settled over her but she reminded herself that all anyone ever has is today. She knew she would need to remind herself of that in the coming weeks.

They sat on the platform silently looking out at the world of treetops around them. There were tufts of the bushy green canopies of smaller trees extending, like a green ocean, far into the distance where the mountains started. After a while, Ceil noticed the heat haze from the rays of sun streaming through the branches.

"Oh, geez, it's getting late. I need to get back," she said. "I have to go into town to visit Esther at the nursing home."

He touched her arm. "Thanks for coming up here with me, Ceil."

She smiled. "This was nice, wasn't it?"

He nodded.

They crawled to the edge of the platform and reached for the climbing rope. Soon they were on their way down—a much easier task than climbing up—although Ceil found that it took a lot of concentration not to go too fast. She knew it would be folly to take the chance of a misstep by not paying enough attention. She could end up with rope burns, strained muscles, or even worse. She didn't need a reminder that the older she got, the longer it took to heal even from the most minor mishaps. *Getting old sucked. No two ways about it.*

Chapter 2

Kate in the Timestream

Timestream, Pacific Crest Trail, Oregon
Friday, August 9, 2019, dawn

Kate Truford was confused. She assumed she must be waking up from sleep, but every one of her senses jangled, and the world seemed topsy-turvy. Something was definitely wrong and her thoughts couldn't seem to catch up. She opened her eyes and glanced around trying to get her bearings, but her surroundings seemed blurry, like she was looking through a cloudy lens or out-of-focus binoculars. Where was she? The last thing she remembered was falling asleep in the tent with Cody next to her. But where was the tent? Where was Cody?

She felt lightheaded, like she was flying. Flying? So then, I'm not awake, right? The confusion frightened her, and instinctively, she reached out to grab onto something solid. But there was nothing solid around her, there was nothing...but air. Her stomach lurched. Then all thoughts were forgotten as she glanced downward.

Far below, she could plainly see a city with its streets laid out in a grid. After a second, she recognized the place: it was Portland. With horror, she realized the skyscrapers in the downtown were swaying unnaturally in the early morning mist. Low river fog rose from the Columbia River as it flowed past the city on the last leg of its journey to the Pacific. Each highway bridge that spanned the river seemed to be hovering not over water but over a thick cloud. Or was it smoke?

She recognized the I-5 bridge. She could see that it was shaking, and the pavement rippled, causing the cars and trucks to skitter and slide across the expanse. Some ricocheted sideways and piled up against the railing, which appeared to be the only thing stopping them from a plunge into the river below. In the distance, past the parallel runways of Portland International Airport, the bridge carrying I-205 traffic was split down its center lane, and the two halves buckled separately. Pieces of metal fell away, and a small blue sports car tumbled over the edge. She watched the car as it dove through the fog in a graceful metallic swan dive and then it was gone.

Kate reached out as if to stop the destruction, but her hand swam futilely through the empty air. She covered her mouth in dread but couldn't seem to look away. Smoke and clouds of dust rose from the multi-storied buildings below. After a moment, the haze cleared, and she noticed people scrambling from their cars and then running uncertainly down the middle of the street. Others raced out of the buildings but quickly stopped, hunched over, and covered their heads as protection from falling debris. She could see several bodies lying motionless on the sidewalk.

Next, she heard a deep rumbling, like a passing freight train. The sound was a growl so deep she could feel its reverberation in the pit of her stomach. Next, there was a flash in the sky to the northeast that looked like a tongue of fire rising from Mount Adams on the Washington side of the Columbia River.

"Oh, no," she breathed but still found it impossible to look away. Mount Adams wasn't the only volcano in the Cascade Mountain range. There were nearly twenty of them lined up from British Columbia, through Washington and Oregon, and down into Northern California. Most were still considered active volcanoes, although there hadn't been an eruption since Mount St. Helens in 1980.

Kate felt herself falling, and she involuntarily paddled her arms as if she could swim through the air. Finally giving up, she squeezed her eyes shut, anticipating a swift and final plunge to the earth below. But instead of instant death, her left wrist hit something hard, and pain instantly shot up her arm. She opened her eyes and quickly looked around, trying to take in her new surroundings. She was relieved to see she was back on solid earth, at least. In fact, she was sprawled on a sandy riverbank near the lapping edge of a wide stream. Could I have sleep-walked here? Maybe I tripped and that's what woke me up. As she sat up her arm throbbed in pain. Still, pain was a good thing. It meant she was really awake, didn't it?

Was any of it real? Was there an earthquake in Portland? Or was it all just a very realistic nightmare?

Kate glanced around, trying to get her bearings. She saw that it was growing light out, so it must be morning, and she was on the edge of a thick pine forest. It was still dark under the canopy of the trees. There was a boulder to her left and another to her right. She could hear the gurgling splashing sounds coming from the stream nearby. There were birds chirping in the branches of a tall lacy willow tree bowed low over the opposite bank of the stream. Its green tendrils bobbed gently in a soft breeze. She squinted and thought she could just make out a footpath just beyond the willow tree.

"Kate?" Like an apparition, Cody appeared on the footpath. He was staring at her from the other side of the stream with a stunned expression.

"Cody?"

"Kate? Are you OK?" he asked. He frowned as he glanced down at the wide stream flowing between them. He looked from her to the stream and back again several times, then he squinted. "What are you doing over there? How did you get across the stream?"

Kate shook her head. "Cody, I just had the weirdest...uh... dream." She stood tentatively and slowly stepped down the embankment towards the edge of the water until she was directly opposite him with a span of about fifteen feet of flowing water between them.

"Kate," he repeated, "I don't get it. How did you get over there? I woke up in the tent and you were gone."

The tent. The hike! It came back to her. She and Cody were hiking the Pacific Crest Trail. They'd been on the trail for a few weeks, doing the trail's Northern California and Oregon sections.

It had not been going well, which was probably her fault. For one thing, their strides were different. They'd be on the trail and inevitably he'd get way ahead of her. His legs were longer so to keep up, she had to take a step and a half for each of his steps, which was exhausting. Eventually, she'd end up lagging behind a bit and when she'd catch up with him, he'd have a disgruntled look on his face, like she was intentionally trying to slow him down.

She was trying hard to be the outdoorsy hiking girl for him because she knew hiking was important to him. But, it was obvious that she was failing miserably and it didn't make sense because she enjoyed hiking in the mountains, and of course, she enjoyed being with Cody. But no matter what she did, she couldn't seem to please him.

She watched as Cody waded through the knee-deep water. When he got close to her, he started to reach out, but he suddenly stopped and just stared at the pant legs of her jeans. "Hey! You're not even wet. How did you get across the stream without getting wet?"

Kate looked upstream and downstream, but she didn't see a bridge or stepping stones across the water nearby. Then she looked down at her jeans for some kind of explanation and that's when she noticed she was wearing her moccasins. That was odd. She never would have left the tent without changing into her boots.

She met Cody's eyes, then shook her head and repeated. "I had the weirdest..." but mid-sentence, she stopped. "Cody, I have to go to Brookings to talk to my grandmother about this."

"What!" he exclaimed, stepping back and nearly losing his footing in the water. "Are you kidding me? You want to go see your grandmother, the hippie, now? Kate, that's insane!"

"I know it probably sounds crazy. But this whole dream experience has been...really strange."

"I thought your dad forbid you to visit the commune. Anyway, we're way north of Brookings now. We're halfway to the Columbia River. Why the rush to see your grandmother all of a sudden?"

"Because she used to have strange experiences like this. She told me about some of them. So she'll know what it means. She'll know what I should do. Don't you see? It's like I've been shown the future. It could be a message or something." She looked up at the sky, noticing the crystal blueness and the fat puffy clouds barely moving. She looked back at him. "Cody, this is important. I know it is. This dream or vision or whatever it was...my grandmother will know what it means."

"Kate, you had a bad dream. Everyone has them. What can your grandmother do about it? You are not making any sense." He tried to pull her into his arms, but she held him off with a palm on his chest.

"Cody, I'm serious. I think it's a warning. Something awful may happen. It's important. I can't just ignore it." She shivered as if she'd felt a cool breeze.

He gently brushed his hands down the length of her arms and said, "This is important too, Kate. This hike. You know it means a lot to me."

She nodded even before he finished. "I know. I didn't mean that you need to get off the trail. I only meant that I do. I have to get to Brookings. I'll hike with you to the next road and then hitch a ride to the coast. It shouldn't take me long to get there. A day or two, tops."

"I thought this hike was important to you too," he said petulantly.

She could hear the hurt in his tone and touched his arm. "It is, Cody. It was. But this thing...I don't think this can wait." As she said the words, a flutter of butterflies took wing from the tall grass along the stream bank and swirled around their heads, and then suddenly whirled up into the sky.

"Oh, my God," Kate said in an awed whisper. "Look at all the butterflies! You know, butterflies are supposed to represent rebirth and renewal," she said to Cody, but when she turned, she saw that he was already heading back across the stream. His head was bent, his shoulders stiff, and his gait determined as he sloshed through the shallow water.

She let out her breath with a sigh as she sat down to take off her moccasins to cross the stream. She paused as she watched Cody step onto the opposite bank. He didn't even turn to look at her. She rubbed her left wrist and winced. It was tender and sore and she saw the beginnings of a nasty bruise. *It wasn't just a silly dream.* She was sure of that.

She stood up with the moccasins in one hand and walked slowly along the bank of the stream towards the willow tree that had long tendrils bobbing over the water. The stream seemed a little less turbulent there and when she moved the willow branches aside, she saw a series of flat stepping stones breaking the surface of the water. She rolled up the cuffs of her jeans, just in case, and stepped onto the first stone. She was pleased to see that the water didn't cover any of the stones. Her feet were dry when she climbed up the bank on the other side.

She glanced around to see if Cody was nearby watching, but he was gone.

Chapter 3

Ceil & Sky in the Redwood Grove

Love & Peace Commune, Brookings, OR
Friday, August 9, 2019, early morning

Ceil and Sky were soon back on the ground at the foot of the tree again.

"Sit with me for a couple more minutes, Ceil, OK?" Sky asked, patting the spot next to him. "We haven't meditated together in weeks."

He was right. It'd be good to relax a few minutes before she headed into town to see her mother. She sat down next to him, and he leaned back, relaxing against the tree.

"Whew, that climb tired me out a little." He blew out a long breath. "But it was great being up there again with you."

She nodded and then reached over and gently kneaded his shoulder. He moved a bit so she could reach both of his shoulders more easily.

"Mmmm, that feels good," he said, closing his eyes.

They were quiet for several minutes, taking in the sounds of insects buzzing in the ferns around them and the calls of birds in the trees above.

She pulled her hands back and leaned against the tree. She tried to slow her breathing and to clear her thoughts, but it wasn't working. She was filled with a melancholy about Sky that felt like a black curtain at the edges of her consciousness. It wasn't grief. Not yet. But it was an acknowledgment that grief was heading her way. Pre-grief, then?

After a moment, she said, "Sky, there's something I need to talk with you about." But when he didn't answer, she glanced at him and realized he'd fallen asleep. She took a deep breath. *My poor tired Sky.*

She had such wonderful memories of this man. She had met him at a concert at college on the side of a hill in Montana. That whole afternoon, they had talked non-stop. They discovered they had similar ideas about the purpose of higher education. They both believed college courses should be filled not with job skills but with exciting and idea-sparking knowledge. They also found out they agreed on what it means to live a good life, that it should be full of community and giving back. That's when she knew they would stick together.

And they had stuck together. First, heading to San Francisco after graduation and eventually traveling north to Oregon, where they had settled with their friends on this commune that they named "The Love & Peace Commune." At its height back in the 1970s, young people had crowded into the commune. They were all part of the back-to-the-land movement, a social movement based on the idea of living a self-sufficient life close to nature. Back then, nearly a million people throughout the United States left the cities for the countryside, hoping for a better, simpler life.

Times had changed in the decades since. Many friends had returned to the cities. Still, the commune had thrived, although with a less frenetic intensity and with a lot more focus and intention. They had been back-to-landers, and the land had been good to them.

Ceil felt so connected to this place. She remembered that it was the first time in her life she had felt that way about a place. She had spent her childhood, the daughter of an Army colonel, living on one Army base or another around the world. She had had a nomadic lifestyle way before the 1960s when the hippies had made it seem cool. The commune was where she finally put down roots.

They had settled the property like homesteaders of previous generations. Surrounded as they were by state and national forest lands, the remoteness of the location had given them privacy and a real, rely-on-each-other togetherness. The remoteness had also probably accounted for the commune's longevity. Without any near neighbors, their bohemian lifestyle wasn't a threat to anyone.

At night, the soft snores and dream sighs of her friends would mingle with the forest night sounds of a hooting owl or the buzz of insects. Like a comfortable blanket that protected them, the natural world lapped lazily around them. Ceil remembered her last thoughts before falling to sleep most nights was that she never wanted this way of life to end. *Nobody should leave, nobody should change, nobody should grow old, and nobody should die. Please, God, Amen.* Silly. A child's prayer, she realized now, but she still felt the wistfulness and the soul-deep desire in it.

Looking down at Sky now, she sighed. He was her life partner, even though they'd never formally married. They hadn't felt the need for the government's stamp of approval. But, more than that, for her part, she believed that marriage was jury-rigged in favor of men. She didn't judge other women for submitting; but she knew it wasn't for her.

Just then, Sky moved his head and opened his eyes. "Did you feel that?" he asked groggily.

"Feel what?" She looked around and noticed the ferns nearby were quivering in the still air. She glanced up. The trees towering over her seemed to sway against the sky and it made her dizzy. Then she heard a deep rumble like the earth was groaning way down beneath them. An earthquake.

"Was that... a... an earthquake?" Sky asked as he sat up and looked around. But the forest seemed back to normal and soon the insects were humming again.

"How odd," Ceil whispered. "Usually when we have an earthquake, I hold my breath, and I wonder if this one will be the 'Big One.' But this time, the only thought I had was of our granddaughter, Kate."

He glanced at her in surprise. "Katie Rose?"

"She's hiking with her boyfriend, Cody, on the Pacific Crest Trail. Remember? Just now... I just had the weirdest feeling about her."

"What kind of weird feeling?"

"Huh. I'm not exactly sure yet. I guess I need to keep her in my thoughts and it'll become clear." She smiled, reaching to cover his hand with hers. "She's fine, Sky. I'm sure of it. Don't worry. It's just that I think there's something going on with her."

He looked at her for several long moments. "If you say she's fine, then she's fine." He breathed out. "I sure miss that little girl."

"Little? Can you believe she will be a college senior this fall?" She nodded. "I miss her too." She paused thoughtfully. "You know, Sky, I've got a feeling we're going to be seeing her soon."

He beamed. "Now, that's a feeling I want to come true! It'd be great to have her here for a visit, wouldn't it?"

She studied him and felt her shoulders fall a bit. *How many more times like this would she have with him?*

Maybe she was just feeling a little rattled by the earthquake, and now these strange thoughts of Kate were spinning around in her mind. She stood up. "I'd better get back so I can get into Brookings to the nursing home. Do you want to come with me?"

He shook his head. "No, you go on. I think I'm going to stay out here a little longer. I'd like to soak up some more of these forest juices. I think it does me good."

"OK. I'll see you this afternoon when I get back. Maybe we can talk more then. Do you need anything in town?"

"Nah, I'm fine. Go on now. Have a pleasant visit with your mother."

She grimaced, and he chuckled at her reaction.

She turned to leave and as she started back on the labyrinth trail, she thought again about the earthquake, then of Kate. Thoughts of her granddaughter naturally led to wondering what was happening with Kate's mother, her daughter Summer?

She sighed remembering that she would need to call Summer to tell her about the return of Sky's cancer. If Summer wanted to spend some time with him, she needed to come soon, while he was still feeling good. *Should I call and invite her to come for the Reunion?* Many friends would be asking about Summer, as they always did, and it'd be gratifying to be able to say that she was back at the commune, even if only for a little while.

Ceil mulled it over. She admitted she had mixed feelings about her daughter coming for a visit. On the one hand, she did want to see her—it'd been nearly two years since the last time Summer had been to Oregon. But their relationship hadn't been great for a long time now. Whenever Summer was around, Ceil always ended up feeling betwixt and between.

She shook her head. The truth was, Summer had baffled her from the day she was born, and that was 42 years ago! She was proof that the Universe has a sense of humor. Otherwise, how could a committed hippie like herself produce a daughter like Summer?

She had arrived in the world a cynic—a real straight-as-an-arrow, facts-are-facts type of person. Summer had turned her nose up at meditation, mindfulness, astrology, ESP, and anything else she couldn't see, touch, taste, smell, or hear. Their interactions from the very beginning had been like mixing oil and water.

But they were both older now, and they had Sky to think about. Ceil knew she needed to fix things between herself and Summer. But where did she start?

Well, that was easy: first, she had to finally tell Summer that Sky isn't her biological father. She'd kept that secret all these years and she knew it wasn't right or fair, was it?

But, if she told Summer, she'd have to confess it to Sky, too. She felt a stab at her heart. *Could she do that? Would he hate her?*

Chapter 4

Ceil meets Spencer at the nursing home

Brookings Healthcare Facility, Brookings, OR
Friday, August 9, 2019, early afternoon

Ceil's drive into the town of Brookings from the commune took a half-hour. She arrived at the Brookings Healthcare facility in the early afternoon. She thought it'd be a good time of day to visit her mother because, over the past year, she had noticed that Esther was usually less agitated after lunch.

Ceil had always had a strained relationship with her mother. She was pretty sure that Esther had never been thrilled to see her when she visited, even before her mind had become so clouded. Esther was ninety-four, and dementia seemed to have relentlessly dismantled her personality, layer by layer. There was a time when Ceil occasionally saw a flash of recognition in her mother's eyes; but now, she rarely did. Of course, her mother had always been stubborn; so she might be intentionally refusing to acknowledge her. There was no question that Esther could be obstinate. As her memory faded, she had become more childlike, but unfortunately, it wasn't a sweet child that emerged. Instead, she threw tantrums and made incoherent demands in a whiny, high-pitched voice, like an unhappy toddler. Just last week, she had thrown a bowl of butterscotch pudding across the room, for no apparently reason. The sun had gone behind a cloud and the dimming of the light in the room seemed to bother her.

As Ceil entered the facility, she recognized the woman dressed in a gray uniform sitting behind the reception counter. "Hello, Janice."

Janice looked up from her computer screen and smiled at her. Even though Ceil visited nearly every week, Janice was a stickler about protocol and always formally checked her in. "How are you today, Ceil?" Janice turned the clipboard around for her to sign. "Oh, by the way, your mom has another visitor today."

"Really?" Ceil looked up in surprise. "Who?"

Janice turned the clipboard back around and ran her finger down the list of visitors. "Here he is. Spencer Rodgers. He said he is Esther's son. So...your brother, I assume?"

Ceil frowned. Spencer was here visiting their mother? What had brought him out to Oregon from New York? She looked up and saw that Janice was waiting for a response. Ceil cleared her throat and smiled. "Uh, yes, Spencer is my younger brother. I just didn't realize he was in town."

Janice nodded. "He's been here for about a half-hour. Go ahead back. Esther had her lunch a while ago, although unfortunately, she didn't eat much. Ceil, you should prepare yourself. She's fading on us."

"Doctor Gupta said as much last week when we talked."

Janice added sympathetically, "Esther's been pretty lethargic lately, too, sleeping a lot. We're keeping a close eye on her."

"Thanks, Janice."

Ceil knew that Esther's condition was deteriorating. She saw the little changes each week on her visits. One week her mother could sit up in her wheelchair, the next she was slumped a bit; the next, there was a tremor in the hand resting in her lap.

She walked down the long hallway to the right. The nursing home was located in a beautiful spot, on a hillside overlooking the harbor and the vast Pacific Ocean. Through the windows of the rooms she passed by, she could see there were whitecaps on the sea today.

Ceil slowed, and her attention shifted from the view outside to the aging residents in the rooms. None seemed to care about the view from their windows. Most were either sleeping or, if awake, had their faces turned towards the small TVs on the wall opposite their beds. How in the world could a daytime TV show compete with that view, she wondered, not for the first time.

Her mother's room was the second door from the end. Beyond it was a sunny atrium, just steps away. A few elderly residents were sitting in rocking chairs in the atrium, and a small group in wheelchairs gathered around a table playing a card game and laughing quietly in high, reedy voices.

She glanced into her mother's room and saw that she was awake and propped up in her wheelchair by the window. Maybe the nurses thought it'd be pleasant for her to have lunch by the window? The sun was streaming in from behind her, so her face was in shadow; but for a second, Ceil thought that her mother was smiling at her, and she felt her heart swell. Then, as she stepped into the room, she realized her mother wasn't looking at her at all. She was staring at the other occupant of the room, Ceil's brother, Spencer, who was sitting rather stiffly in the uncomfortable wooden chair by the door.

He glanced up at her as she entered and rose to his feet. "Hello, Ceil." He leaned in to kiss her cheek. "Good to see you. It's been a long time," he said perfunctorily.

"Hello, Spencer. I had no idea you were in Oregon. To what do we owe the pleasure?" Without waiting for a response, she walked across the room to where her mother was seated, bent over, and kissed her on the cheek. "How are you, mother? Did you have a nice lunch?"

Her mother stared up blankly at her, and as Ceil watched, the fog in her eyes lifted for a second and she seemed to recognize her. But then, the confused look returned, and her eyes darted here and there. Ceil couldn't be certain she'd seen the earlier spark of recognition or not.

Esther didn't respond, which wasn't surprising. She hadn't spoken more than one or two words at a time in over a year. It had become a chore coming for regular visits and asking questions that elicited no response. Sometimes Ceil would bring Sky with her so that the two of them could carry on a conversation to fill the void of silence in the room. She thought perhaps her mother enjoyed overhearing their conversation, but she couldn't be sure. It was frustrating, seeing and talking to her mother and getting very little response from her. She often wondered what her mother was thinking about or feeling?

Ceil glanced around and Spencer motioned for her to sit in the chair where he had been sitting. She hesitated but walked back across the room and sat down. He moved halfway between Esther and Ceil, standing with his hands in his pockets and rocking a bit on his feet.

"Is she always like this?" he asked, indicating Esther with a nod of his head.

Ceil glanced at her mother to see if she appeared to understand his words. She thought not. Esther's hands were in her lap, shaking with little tremors. Occasionally, she clasped them together as if to stop the spasms.

Ceil nodded in answer to Spencer's question. "She's been pretty far gone for months now. Her memory is unreliable and disappearing. Occasionally, I see recognition in her eyes, but she doesn't speak. I'm not sure she can put together sentences anymore."

"Yeah, she just stared at me when I came in. Like I was some kind of apparition."

"You probably looked like one to her. When was the last time you came out to visit her?" She couldn't control the tinge of disdain in her voice.

His voice turned cool. "I try to come out as often as I can. But let's face it, Brookings isn't an easy place to get to."

"Not for a busy man like you, I'm sure," she said dryly.

His mouth tightened. "Look, let's not forget that I'm paying for all this, and yes, as a matter of fact, I am a busy man. The New York real estate market is booming. We have Asian investors begging to unload huge sums of money in the city. Cash, mind you; not mortgage loans."

She felt the sides of her mouth pinch in a familiar way. She wanted to roll her eyes, but what would be the point of starting a fight with him? He was indeed paying for Esther's care, and besides, he was a Scorpio. There wouldn't be any use talking to him about money. That was the unspoken deal they'd struck–he handled their mother's finances while it was Ceil's responsibility to visit her, even though Ceil knew that Esther would've much preferred seeing her son instead of her.

Ceil and her mother had never gotten along well. She wasn't sure if it was a conflict of personality, temperament, or astrological sign. Her mother was a Pisces, and she was a Sagittarius, which might explain some of their difficulty. But Ceil knew exactly what year their relationship had gone over the edge–1971. She had been in college, and her father had just been forced to retire from the military after suffering a heart attack. Her parents had settled back in Boston, and her father had spent several months in and out of the hospital before finally dying of congestive heart failure that spring. In her anguish at losing her father, Ceil had fought continuously with Esther until finally, in a huff of fury, she had transferred from her mother's alma mater, Vassar, to attend the University of Montana. She was determined to be as far away from Esther as possible.

Esther, in turn, refused to speak to her for several years, not even acknowledging Ceil when she graduated with honors. By then, Ceil was living with Sky, and they were traveling like nomads all over the West Coast.

Esther had been born and raised in Oregon and her mother, Rosalie, Ceil's grandmother, had lived in Brookings. It was during a stop on the Oregon coast to visit Grandma Rosalie that Rosalie offered Ceil and Sky permission to homestead on some forest land that she owned. Back then, it had been a 25-acre slip of privately held land wedged between large tracts of Federal and State forest. Ceil's grandfather had bought it hoping to start a bidding war for it, but he died before he could do anything with it. Rosalie had no interest in selling the land, so she kept the deed and occasionally went out and camped on a pretty spot next to the river. When Sky and Ceil said they were looking for a place to settle, she gladly offered the land to them.

Ceil and Sky had returned to San Francisco, gathered a dozen of their closest hippie friends, and brought them to Oregon to settle on Rosalie's land. Over the years, the group had cleared part of the land for an organic farm that eventually blossomed into a successful produce business, and they built their cabins, raised their children, and they lived, as Ceil always described it, "a life of peace, love, and freedom." Rosalie's allowing them to homestead on the land was a gift that Ceil could never repay. Still, she liked to think that the success of the commune was a living tribute to Rosalie and that her grandmother had become a kind of guardian angel watching over them.

As for Esther, when she discovered that her mother had permitted Ceil to homestead on the land with her slovenly hippie friends, she was furious at Rosalie. She felt that Rosalie was giving away Esther's inheritance to Ceil and her friends.

After Rosalie died, Esther moved from Boston to Oregon and settled into Rosalie's house in Brookings. She soon took over the management of the other properties Rosalie owned, sold the timber rights, and let the lands be stripped of vegetation and minerals, banking the profits, and living well. As time passed, she made it abundantly clear that when she passed on, she would leave all of the family inheritance to Spencer, not to Ceil. For Ceil, it wasn't the money that bothered her; it was the feeling of being excluded.

Ceil looked over at her brother, and it struck her suddenly how much older he appeared. His hair was gray now; there was even a little white in his sideburns. He'd always be her little brother, so it was a shock to see that he was aging along with her. He looked tired, too, and the stiffness in his features made her wonder when the last time he had laughed. Suddenly she felt sorry for him. "Never mind, Spence. I appreciate your taking over her power of attorney and paying her bills. It's just that she might've wanted to see you a bit more than she did me. You know?"

"If you wanted to please her, you should've stayed at Vassar, like she wanted you to." He smiled.

"Yeah, she liked being in control of things, and people." Ceil added dryly, "I guess I messed up things by being a bit of a hellion, huh?"

"Hellion? You were a 'damned drugged-out hippie.' And that's a direct quote from her highness." He nodded at Esther.

As they turned to look at her, Ceil saw that Esther had fallen asleep. Her head sagged back against the headrest, and her mouth hung slack and open. Ceil could hear the murmur of her soft snores.

Spencer looked speculatively at Ceil, then pointed to the door. "Do you have a few minutes? I want to discuss something with you." He glanced up and down the hallway from the doorway and then nodded to the atrium. "Let's go in there."

"Sure," she said, though she was mystified by what he might want to discuss that couldn't be said in front of their sleeping mother.

As they entered, Ceil saw that the room was now empty. Spencer walked over to the windows and looked out towards the deep blue expanse of the Pacific Ocean in the distance. "They wasted this view on a nursing home," he commented. "Too few of these old farts are with it enough to appreciate what they have, huh?"

Ceil shrugged. "Some can, I suppose." She watched him and waited.

"I wanted to talk to you about the land."

She frowned. "What about it?"

"I was wondering what your plans are."

"Plans?" she said, shaking her head. "Well, next week, we have our annual Woodstock Reunion. But that's about it for plans."

"Woodstock..." he repeated with a slight roll of his eyes. "I'm not talking about your damn parties. I'm talking about your plans for the future of the land."

Ceil stared at him for several moments, then shook her head. "Spencer, I still don't get what you are asking."

"Ceil, come on. You and I both know that when our mother dies, she will not leave that land to you. I was wondering what you planned to do...you know, in that eventuality...."

Ceil took a deep breath, then she let it out in a huff. "Spencer, you know that Rosalie gave the land to me. She gave it to me to live on with Sky and our friends so we could farm it and make it our home. That's still my plan, Spencer. That's always been my plan."

"You're living in a dream world, Ceil. You always have," he said dismissively. "You are aware that Grandma Rosalie died without a will, right? So whatever she said or didn't say is moot. Everything she owned automatically passed on to Esther."

"Except Rosalie gave the land to me." She looked at him for several long moments, trying not to blink. "Anything else, Spencer? I need to get back."

He looked at her speculatively for another second. Then, without saying anything more, he turned on his heel and walked right past Esther's room, down the hallway, and through the double-doors to the reception area.

Ceil watched him leave. Then she walked slowly back to Esther's room, where she saw her mother was still fast asleep in the chair. She gathered a light throw from the foot of the bed and brought it over to the chair. She tucked it around her mother's shoulders and whispered, "Night, Mom. See you next week."

But her mind wasn't on her mother or next week. Instead, she was still thinking about Spencer.

Chapter 5

Kate meets Rob Manyrivers

Pacific Crest Trail, Oregon
Friday, August 9, 2019, morning

Back on the trail, Cody was sulky as they hiked northward. He would only give her abrupt one-word replies to questions, and his expression was sullen. It reminded her of dealing with her mother's moodiness in the months after her father had asked for the divorce. During the split-up, Kate had spent most of her senior year of high school living out of her backpack as she shuttled on the MBTA between her father's condo in Boston and her mother's house in the Boston suburb of Chestnut Hill. Two days in one place, three in the other, and then alternating weekends.

What should've been a fun senior year was instead a commuting nightmare. Graduation and college couldn't come fast enough, and Kate stubbornly refused to apply to any college on the East Coast. The further away she could get from both of her parents, the better. Oregon, with its comforting childhood memories of summers spent with her hippie grandparents at the commune, was the only place she would consider. Eventually, her father relented, particularly after she got accepted and even scored a small scholarship to the University of Oregon, but he had one condition: that she stay away from the commune.

That was nearly three years ago, and she had held up her side of the bargain, pretty much. She hadn't physically visited the commune. But she regularly emailed and called Ceil and Sky, and for their part, they drove up to see her as often as they could manage. Of course, she didn't share that information with her father.

Kate was so tired of straddling the divorce divide between her parents. She felt she owed her father something. He was paying her tuition, room and board, and all of her expenses. But mentioning that to her mother was like pouring fuel on a fire. All Kate got in return were angry outbursts or passive-aggressive silence.

Cody's backpack shifted up and down with his steady gait as she caught sight of him through the trees. Kate would've liked to give in and tell him she would stay on the hike. But once she had said that she needed to go to Brookings out loud, she knew it was true. It was the one place she truly needed to be right now.

Cody's voice broke into her thoughts, "Once you talk to your grandmother, will we meet up again?" He'd stopped and was waiting for her in a small clearing. He reached for his water bottle in the mesh pocket on the side of his pack and eyed her as he tilted it towards his mouth.

She pulled out hers too and tipped it up, swallowing several long draughts of water. When she lowered the bottle, she adjusted her headband and looked at Cody. He had one booted foot propped up on a small boulder, but he wasn't looking at her now. Instead, he was staring out through a break in the trees down to a tranquil small pond below them.

Kate cleared her throat uncomfortably and said, "I'll talk to my grandmother and decide then. How will I get a hold of you to let you know what's going on?"

He glanced over at her and, after several moments, said, "You've got the list of the resupply spots, right? You could stop by or call any one of them and leave a message for me. It's simple: if they say our stuff is gone, it means I've already passed through."

"That'll work. Will you have your cell phone on at any point? Maybe I could call and actually talk to you."

He shrugged. "Hard to say. I've heard that coverage is non-existent for most of the trail and spotty even where it crosses roads. Besides, you know I leave it off to conserve the battery. But, go ahead and call and leave me a message. I'll check it from time to time. If I receive a message from you, I'll try to call you back the next chance I get."

"OK." She took another drink of water. "Cody, this is something I have to do."

He looked at her without expression. "Whatever."

She felt like she'd been slapped. She screwed the top on her water bottle and shoved it in the side pocket of her pack. Then she heaved the backpack onto her shoulders. After adjusting the weight and cinching the buckles on the belt, she glanced over at him. "You ready?" she asked coolly.

"Go on ahead. I have to pee. I'll catch up with you," Cody said, and he turned away from her.

She stared at his back for a second. "OK."

She stopped a few times to wait for him, but he didn't catch up with her until an hour later. It was just before they came to a road crossing. They stopped at the point the trail came out of the dense woods and sat on the ground to wait for a car to pass. Neither of them spoke. Maybe there was nothing more to say, Kate thought.

It was another fifteen minutes before they heard a car engine approaching. Kate stood and immediately put her thumb up; she was pleased when the car slowed and pulled to a stop.

She jogged up to the passenger window and leaned in. There was just the driver in the car. At first glance, she thought he looked normal enough, a young guy with dark hair and eyes, probably not much older than she was. "Hi," she said. "I'm Kate, and I need to get to the coast. How far west are you going?"

"Hi, there!" he responded with an easy smile. "Name's Rob. Rob Manyrivers. To the coast, huh? Lucky you! I'm heading to Port Orford. Will that work?" He had longish black hair tied back with colorful threads around a short stubby ponytail.

Kate smiled. "Port Orford? That'd be perfect!"

Cody reached them. "Hi, I'm Cody Brennan." He put out his hand to shake Rob's hand. He continued, "My girlfriend, Kate, is heading to Brookings to see her grandmother. We appreciate your helping her out."

Kate nodded uncomfortably. Cody was sending a not-so-subtle message to Rob that she was his girlfriend and not to mess with her. Kate suddenly felt like a chattel from the Middle Ages, which both amused and irritated her. She looked at Rob, "I appreciate your giving me a ride."

"No problem. You can throw your stuff on the backseat," Rob said, pointing to the seat that already contained several open boxes filled with file folders and books, a large backpack, a suitcase, and a tall plastic cooler. He shoved two of the boxes over to make room for her backpack.

"Thanks," Kate said. She peeled off her pack as Rob got out of the car and came around to open the back door so she could put her backpack in. "You moving?" she asked, indicating the boxes.

"Yeah, temporarily. I'll be working on a research project for a month or two, so I'm renting a cabin just north of Port Orford."

Rob glanced at Cody. "What about you? Do you want a ride into the next town or anything? I can move my stuff around a bit and squeeze you in...."

Cody shook his head. "No, man, that's fine. There's still a lot of daylight, and I want to eat up as much of this trail as I can before I make camp." He turned to Kate, but they already seemed out of sync and it became awkward. "I'm going to miss you, babe," he said, but as he leaned down to kiss her she had already turned to get into the car. When she realized, she stopped, but by then, he was moving away.

She hated to leave him like this; it gave her a hollow feeling in the pit of her stomach. Hoping to lighten the mood, she quipped, "Don't have too good of a time without me." But when his expression didn't change, she felt worse.

She slid into the front seat alongside Rob, and Cody stepped forward and pushed her door shut. He reached through the open window and touched her shoulder for just a second, then he stepped back and put a hand in the air and gave a lackluster wave as the car pulled away.

Kate watched Cody's figure recede in the side mirror. He looked rugged and healthy but very alone. Was she wrong to be leaving him like this? She let the question linger in her mind. Finally, she shook her head. She knew she must see her grandmother. Something was coming. She could feel it. Her experience this morning was a warning and only Grandma Ceil would be able to tell her what it meant.

Chapter 6

Ceil tells Sky about seeing Spencer

Love & Peace Commune, Brookings, OR
Friday, August 9, 2019, evening

Ceil had been busy all day. After returning from her trip to Brookings, she worked for a while on billing and accounts at the computer in the lodge until the cooks and set-up crew showed up to start preparing for dinner. Dinner was their usual communal affair. Nearly all of the community came to the lodge to share a family-style dinner each night. A chore list was posted in the kitchen once a week, indicating whose turn it was to cook, set up the tables, serve, or do clean-up afterward. All jobs rotated through the group.

Dinner was over now, and the place was pretty empty. Some of the communards would gather at the bonfire in the compound later after dark. The rest usually returned to their cabins to put their children or grandchildren to bed, enjoy a joint, a beer, or glass of wine, and relax.

Ceil and Sky took their coffee mugs and sat opposite each other at one of the long tables closest to the kitchen in the lodge's main hall. It was their first chance to talk since earlier that morning in the forest. Sky spent the day setting up wireless speakers in trees throughout the compound and in the greenhouse buildings in preparation for the Woodstock Reunion. As usual, he was in charge of the playlist and set up his audio command center in the loft of the lodge. Ceil knew he took the job seriously and intended that the great groups of Woodstock would be heard throughout the commune, even in the depth of the forest.

Sky pulled his steaming coffee mug closer and cupped it between his hands as if he was drawing warmth from it. Ceil wondered if he was feeling cold but knew better than to ask. He hated when she observed his illness too closely.

"How did your visit with Esther go?"

Ceil leaned forward. "You won't believe it! Spencer was there! Not that my mother seemed aware of his presence."

Sky snorted. "Too bad, huh? She would've appreciated him visiting her. Heck, she would've been elated."

Ceil knew that Sky was right. Her mother would've been thrilled that Spencer was there. "She hardly seemed to notice, so he won't even get credit for the visit." She paused and frowned. "He asked me something surprising, Sky. He asked me what I planned to do with the land."

"The land?"

"Apparently, he was referring to our land, the land that Rosalie gave us for the commune."

"What did he mean by what you planned to do with it?" Sky asked, a frown creasing his brow as he took a sip from his mug.

Ceil shrugged. "He seems to think that it belongs to Esther and that he will inherit it when she passes. I think he was asking if we have a contingency plan in case that happens."

"I wonder why Spencer think it's Esther's land?"

Ceil shook her head. "I don't know. You were with me when Rosalie gave us the land to settle on. Maybe he's just assuming?"

Sky looked thoughtful and took another sip of his coffee. "Rosalie did die without a will."

"Yes, but if Esther had inherited the land back when Rosalie died, wouldn't she have thrown us off it long ago?"

"True," Sky agreed. "Unless something's changed. Maybe Esther's lawyer told Spencer something."

"I guess that's possible. But why didn't Spencer just say that? Why is all this coming up now?"

"Who knows? I've never been able to figure out Spencer. It's like he's a different species or something."

Ceil took a sip of coffee and nodded, "True. He's been a different guy ever since high school when he attended that fancy prep school. I swear he was a normal kid before that."

"Turned into a preppie monster, huh?"

Ceil laughed. "I wish I knew what happened to him there. He was such a sweet boy when he was little."

They were quiet for several minutes as they sunk into their own thoughts. Finally, Sky picked up his mug and blew on his coffee before taking a sip. Then he settled back in his chair.

Ceil looked over at him. "Do you want to go to the bonfire tonight?"

He shook his head. "Nah, you go if you want. I think I'll stay here and read for a while."

Their eyes met, and she waited, biting her lip rather than asking how he was feeling.

He sighed, apparently, reading her mind. "I'm just tired, Ceil, that's all. I had a busy day putting up the speakers around the compound. I feel okay otherwise. Alright?"

"It's OK. You relax and read. I'll go find Nia and see what she thinks about this Spencer thing."

"Time for some girl talk, eh? The two of you will pull the mystery apart and figure it all out?"

"Or...we'll just bad mouth my brother for a while. Either way, good times!"

She came around the table and laid her hands on Sky's shoulders and rubbed them playfully for a second. "I won't be late. Promise."

"If I've gone to bed, wake me if you want to talk," he said, touching her hand with his own.

"Okay," she said, but she knew she wouldn't. If Sky was asleep, she would let him be. He was tired a lot these days.

Chapter 7

Ceil & Nia - girl talk

Love & Peace Commune, Brookings, OR
Friday, August 9, 2019, evening

Ceil stepped out of the lodge and quietly pulled the heavy door closed until it latched behind her. Tim Hardin's rendition of "If I Were a Carpenter" played from the speakers nestled in the trees. Sky must have set up one of his many playlists for the evening.

It would be sunset in another hour, but it was already dark in the trees. There would be stars in the sky later on, but no moon. She could feel the thick August air around her and hear the crickets and other insects starting their soothing thrum. It was all so comforting and familiar.

She saw that no one had lit the bonfire in the central fire pit at the center of the compound yet, but as she drew closer, she could hear the soft laughter and murmured discussions of several friends sitting on the benches near the fire pit.

"Hey, Ceil! Is Sky coming out tonight? The music sounds great!" Jade, the greenhouse master, said, her voice high and almost squeaky, just as it had been forty years before when she was twenty and Ceil had first met her.

Ceil shook her head. "No, he says he wants to relax and read a while. But don't worry, he has the music set up to play for a few more hours, I think."

Jade's voice grew soft. "He's feeling OK, isn't he?"

"Yeah, so far, so good."

"Well, it's too bad he's not here because I wanted to tell him how well the new herbs are doing since we moved them to the southwest corner of the Love building."

"So, moving them made a difference?"

"Sure did. That and having Wilder and Vijay chanting Tibetan growth mantras over them," Jade added with a laugh. "I'm thinking of branding them as 'Intentionally Good' – what do you think?"

"Not bad, except I'd hate for customers to think everything we grow isn't intentionally good. Heck, we want everything to be intentionally GREAT!" Ceil said, and the others laughed along with her. She looked around. "By the way, have any of you seen Nia?"

Marigold, a copper-haired woman sitting cross-legged on the ground, faintly cleared her throat. "I think she is trying out a new bread recipe in her cabin."

"Ah," Ceil said. "I think I'll go see how that's coming along. See you guys later." She turned towards Nia's cabin, which sat on the edge of the forest at the far end of the compound. It was at the quiet end of the commune, and it was so like Nia to pick an out-of-the-way spot where she could have her privacy but still keep tabs on nearly everything that went on. In the distance, Ceil could hear Ravi Shankar's three-song set playing as she reached Nia's cabin.

"Hey," Ceil said as she pushed open the door and let herself in.

She found Nia in the kitchen, her hands and apron covered with a fine dusting of flour. Her hair was pulled back in tight corn-row braids but a few curly black strands had escaped and surrounded her face. She looked up and grinned. "Ceil! Come and see," she said, nodding at the butcher block surface in front of her. On it were seven small mounds of bread dough sprinkled with a mixture of honey, seeds, and ground-up nuts.

"Wow, those are darling," Ceil cooed. "What are they?"

"I'm calling them 'mini-sun loaves.' What do you think? I made them from wheat germ, flax, and sunflower seeds. But the crust is going to be sweet and crunchy with a mixture of honey and nuts and lots of other good stuff. If they taste as good as I hope, I'll make a big batch for Sunday brunch."

"Yum, that sounds good."

Nia eyed Ceil for several seconds. "So, you went to see Esther today?"

Ceil nodded. "Spencer was there."

"No way!" Nia's eyebrows shot up in surprise. "When did he blow into town?"

"He never said, nor did he say how long he'll be here. But he did say something that left me feeling a little queasy."

Nia slowly wiped her hands on the edge of her apron. "What did he say?"

"He wanted to know whether we had plans for the land."

"Plans for the land?" she repeated with a frown. "Wait! THIS land?"

"Crazy, huh?"

"But he knows that Rosalie gave it to you."

"Yup. But Sky thinks Rosalie's dying without a will may have changed things."

Nia paused, then she shook her head. "Nope, that doesn't make sense. If Esther somehow inherited the deed to the land after her mother passed, she would've tossed us off this land so fast our heads would've spun."

"You're right about that. So, what do you think he meant?"

Nia frowned. "Rosalie never gave you the deed, right?"

Ceil shook her head. "I always figured she kept it for safekeeping."

"Did she keep her important papers at her lawyer's?"

"I dunno. But Rosalie and Esther had the same lawyer, a guy named Crandall in Brookings. He is currently Esther's lawyer and Spencer's too, at least, when it comes to matters relating to Esther."

Nia looked thoughtful for a moment. "Maybe the lawyer has the deed, and he said something to Spencer about it."

Ceil looked unconvinced. "If he had the deed, he would've told Esther that she owned the land back when Rosalie died. And, if that had happened, as you so graphically put it, our heads would still be spinning."

"No doubt about that!" Nia chuckled as she turned towards her oven and set the temperature for baking the mini-loaves.

"He definitely sounded like he would inherit this land, though. So, what changed to make him think that?" Ceil asked in exasperation. "Do you think maybe the deed suddenly turned up?"

"Or maybe it hasn't...maybe he was feeling you out to see whether you have it."

Ceil's eyes widened. "Oh my God, you might be on to something there. It would be like him to bait me to find out what he wanted to know. If I did have it, I would've said I did, just to shut him up." Her shoulders drooped. "So, I probably told him exactly what he wanted to know, that I don't have it."

"But we still don't know what his game is, and why now?"

Ceil looked at Nia. "I assume it has to do with Esther's deteriorating condition."

They both sat quietly for several minutes, staring off into space. Finally, Nia looked up and asked, "So have you called Summer to tell her about Sky yet?"

Ceil shook her head. "Not yet. But I do need to convince her to come for a visit while Sky is still feeling good."

"I'd love to have Summer back here for a while."

"Yeah, it'd be good having her here again." She stared off into space for a second, thinking.

Nia patted her hand. "It'll be fine, Ceil. Summer's a grown-ass woman now. She can manage things for herself."

"Yeah. I just never know what she needs from me," Ceil said plaintively. "Know what I mean?"

"Yeah. You always had everyone else in the palm of your hand, except Summer. She had a mind of her own, even as a toddler. Remember?"

"Yeah. Boy, she was a handful! Thank God I had Sky to broker the peace between us. I never would've survived her teen years otherwise."

Nia squeezed her shoulder. "Hon, maybe you never saw it, but she's just a chip off the old block if you ask me." She turned back to her loaves and patted them a little.

Ceil was quiet for several minutes, watching Nia as she finished shaping the little loaves and sprinkled more of the ground nut mixture on the tops. Then she asked, "Nia, did you feel the earthquake earlier today?"

"Sure did! It scared the shit out of me, to be honest. Every earthquake scares me these days. Ever since I read that piece in *The New Yorker* a couple of years ago about Oregon and the 'Big One.'"

"Me, too. But this time I had a queer feeling that the earthquake was somehow connected with Kate."

Nia glanced up in surprise. "Summer's Kate?"

"Uh-huh. Sky and I were in the grove when we felt the earthquake this morning. When it stopped shaking, I just couldn't stop thinking about Kate."

"You don't think anything has happened to her out there on that hiking trail, do you?" Nia asked, touching Ceil's arm.

"No, I think she's fine. But I felt the earthquake was like...like a sign or something." Ceil shook her head, unable to describe the sensation.

"Oh, boy, I don't like it when you start sensing things and seeing signs."

"Well, anyway, we'll know soon enough. I'm pretty sure she's going to show up here."

Nia grinned. "Really? That'd be amazing! I'd love to see that little girl again. Hey, you should see if you can get Summer to visit at the same time!"

Ceil looked skeptical. "It's been a long time since they were both here at the same time."

"Remember how Summer used to leave Kate with us when she was little? Little Katie would stay with us while Summer and Peter traveled. It was so great having her here. That little girl fit right in, didn't she?"

"She certainly did. And you're right. It'll be good to see her again. Phone calls are just not enough for me."

"Well, she's a busy college girl now, and she said that her father doesn't want her to spend time here at the commune. He thinks we're a bad influence, you know," Nia said, rolling her eyes.

"That's just Peter getting back at Summer, I think. But, heck, when was the last time Summer was here anyway? She was supposed to come last year but couldn't make it at the last minute. It's probably been two years since we've seen her in person."

Nia nodded. "Well, when you call her, tell her to get out here soon. Sky will be thrilled to see her. And she should come while he's still feeling good."

"Yeah, that's what I think, too."

"By the way, speaking of visitors. Sky mentioned that Zeke is coming to the Reunion."

Ceil smiled. "I can't wait to see him again."

"Hmm, I bet you can't," Nia said, her voice teasing. She wiped her hands on her worn-out tie-dye apron.

"Its been a while."

Nia sat down on the stool next to Ceil. "So? Are you finally going to tell them then?"

Ceil shrugged. "I have to, don't I?" Her face fell a bit. "Now that Sky's cancer is back, I may be running out of time."

Nia reached out and touched Ceil's hand. "You know you didn't do anything wrong, don't you? Times were different back in the '70s when you got pregnant with Summer. Everyone was loving everyone back then, and no one really cared." She sighed wistfully. "Those were the days, huh?"

Ceil nodded.

"But even so, you still should've told Sky from the beginning that he wasn't Summer's papa." Nia shook her head. "Nothing good comes from secrets." She paused for effect, and then continued, "And as for Zeke...no question he should've had some say in deciding things. And heck, girl! He's Sky's best friend. So, yeah, now's the time. No more secrets."

Ceil was silent. After a minute, she let out a breath and glanced at Nia. "I know you're right. But after all this time..." She sighed and looked almost pleadingly at Nia, then seeing the hard look on her friend's face, she finally said, "OK, OK. I'm going to make it right with Sky and Zeke first chance that I get, and with Summer, too."

Nia's eyebrows rose. "Wait. You're going to come clean with Summer, too?"

"She deserves to know, doesn't she? I mean, Zeke's her biological father. Besides, once I start unloading all this on Sky and Zeke, how is she not going to hear about it?"

"True." Nia nodded. "So then, what about Kate?"

Ceil looked dubious. "I don't know. Shouldn't I leave it up to Summer to decide if she wants to tell her?"

Nia shrugged and rose to her feet. "Fair enough." She went over to the oven to check the temperature, and paused looking kindly at Ceil. "You're going to feel so good once you've got this off your chest, honey. It's gonna be hard, but it's really bad karma to let Sky pass without his knowing the truth."

Ceil looked grim. "Yeah, and there's more than enough bad karma floating around these days already."

"True enough," Nia said with a smile.

Chapter 8

Kate meets Sowi

Alsea River Lodge Restaurant, Tidewater, OR
Friday, August 9, 2019, evening

As Rob drove towards the coast, Kate quickly discovered they had a lot in common. It turned out they were both currently students, although he was in a graduate program and she was still an undergrad.

"So, what are you studying exactly, Rob?" she asked him.

He took his eyes off the road for a second to glance at her and smile. "I'm a doctoral student in geology at Oregon State in Corvallis. I'm doing my thesis on the Cascadia subduction zone. Have you heard of it?"

"I think so. It's under the ocean near Vancouver, where the earth's plates meet, right?"

"Yeah, sort of. It stretches from British Columbia along the Pacific coastline all the way down to northern California, including the entire length of Oregon's coast."

"And it's where they say the next 'Big One' will originate, right?" she asked, with the morning's vision of Portland's swaying skyscrapers suddenly filling her mind.

"That's what everyone thinks. But, believe me, calling it the 'Big One' hardly does it justice."

She frowned. "What do you mean?"

"Well, for one thing, I've heard some pretty credible predictions that it could be a magnitude 9.0 earthquake, and possibly even stronger. Think Japan's 2011 earthquake ... only way worse."

Kate's skin tingled, and she felt slightly nauseous. "And you think it's a sure thing?"

He glanced over at her, and his smile faded. "Hey, are you OK, Kate?"

She took a deep breath and let it out. "I guess it's just been a long day."

Rob reached and picked up his cell phone from a cubby hole above the console and checked the time. "Oh, geez, Kate. Sorry. I didn't realize it'd gotten so late. You must be starving. Let's stop and have some dinner. What do you say?"

"Sure, that sounds great! I am hungry."

"You should've said something sooner." He looked thoughtful, "I know a good place not too far from here. A close friend runs a bar and grill that's just a mile or so off the highway. It won't take us too far out of our way, and I think you'll like it there. But, it's up to you. If you'd rather we find something in the next town we come to, we can do that."

Kate knew she didn't know him well, but so far, he'd been nothing but friendly and accommodating. Her gut was telling her that she could trust him. "I think I'd rather go to a place you recommend than take a chance on one of the cowboy bars in these little towns out here. Is the food good?"

""You bet!" he answered. "I should also mention that it'd be a good place to crash for the night, if you're tired. My friend rents rooms out to tourists and hunters. I'm sure she'd be glad to help us out if she has any rooms available."

"Let's eat first and talk to your friend. We can decide then, OK?"

He nodded. "Sure, that sounds good to me. I'm fine with pushing through to the coast after we eat, too, if it works out that way."

Rob drove on and turned off the highway onto a smaller, local road. After a few minutes, Kate saw some lights up ahead. The place was a large log building, possibly a former hunting lodge. She read the sign lit up above the massive front door: "Alsea River Lodge." Under the name, it said simply "food, drinks, and rooms."

There was an upper floor with a few lights on in the windows, and dormers indicated a possible third floor above that. A few cars were parked out front and there was a dirt driveway leading to the back.

They walked in, and several heads turned towards them. Kate felt grubby after days of hiking and wished she could've taken a shower first. She knew she must look pitiful. Did she stink? She was relieved that Rob didn't seem put off by her. He smiled reassuringly at her as if he knew what she was thinking and led her to the bar.

A large woman with thick black braids came around the bar towards them. She was wearing a leather-skin Native American dress, apparently, in keeping with the Native American theme of the restaurant. Kate guessed she was in her early 20s, just a bit older than herself. She glanced up and looked at them, and suddenly her face brightened. She exclaimed, "Robbie!" and threw her arms around him in a warm hug. "It's been weeks! Where have you been? How come you haven't stopped by to see me?"

"Hey, I'm here now!" Rob grinned and nodded towards Kate. "Sowi, I want you to meet Kate. She's taking a break from hiking the PCT, and I'm giving her a ride to the coast."

Sowi turned to Kate with a welcoming smile. "Any friend of Rob's..." she said, with a laugh.

"Thanks. Your name is 'Sowi'? That's a different sort of name."

Rob said, "It's short for "Soft Wind" – 'Sowi' is a Native American nickname."

"Oh," Kate said. "Are there still many tribes in Oregon?"

Sowi nodded. "Oregon has nine federally recognized tribal groups, and it's been a messy history, as you can imagine. Robbie and I were lucky, though. We didn't live on a reservation. Instead, we grew up just outside Coos Bay. Our mothers were childhood friends who married a couple of hippies. She grinned at Robbie, who returned the smile.

"Really?" Kate said with increasing interest. "My grandmother lives on a commune outside of Brookings."

Sowi looked at her with excitement. "Really? Brookings? Would that be the L&P?"

"Yes!" Kate said with a smile. "That's the one! Do you know it?"

"Oh, sure! My parents took me down there a few times when I was little. The place was known for having epic parties. I only wish I was old enough back then to enjoy it." She led them over to the bar. "What's your grandmother's name?" she asked as she pointed to the large wooden captain's chairs for Rob and Kate to sit.

"Her name is Ceil ... Ceil Rodgers," Kate answered as she settled into the comfortable seat. She noted that the seat cushion was decorated in a colorful intricate woven design.

Sowi went around to the other side of the bar, but when she heard the name, she stopped and stared at Kate. "Ceil, the Healer, do you mean?"

"Ceil the Healer?" Kate repeated. "Huh. I hadn't heard her called that, but it would be apropos. She's got the healing touch, for sure. She's a certified midwife and takes care of everyone's medical needs down there."

"They say she has a great spirit."

"A great spirit? How do you mean?"

"She's like one of our shamans. That's what my aunties used to say about her."

Rob looked at Kate with new interest. "So, your grandmother is the Healer, huh? Small world."

Kate looked around the room to take it all in. There were Native American wall hangings covering the log walls, and above the huge stone fireplace hung a large oil painting depicting a tribal ceremony with the participants colorfully dressed, faces painted, and all wearing elaborate headdresses. On either side of the painting were the furry heads of two gigantic elk, with their massive antlers reaching upward toward the ceiling. On the lower ceiling above the bar area, dream catchers hung and gently swayed and twisted sending spiderweb shadows onto the floor and surrounding walls whenever the light hit them just right.

Sowi dished out heaping bowls of chili, along with thick-crusted bread, warm from the oven. Kate was ravenous and ate everything set down in front of her plus several slices of the delicious bread before her appetite was finally satisfied.

They talked into the evening. Sowi occasionally went around and checked on the other patrons to see if they needed anything, and as it grew later, the other people in the bar began to leave. Eventually, it was just the three of them in the place. Kate found their stories about growing up half Native American with a counter-culture hippie lifestyle fascinating. As she listened to them and asked the occasional question, she could see that Sowi and Rob were very close friends.

"You guys seem to finish each other's sentences, and it's obvious you care about each other, so I don't get why you have been out of touch for so long. You said it's been weeks since you've seen each other."

Sowi reached over and patted the back of Rob's hand. "He's in school, and I'm busy with this place. Besides, we don't need to see each other. We're connected to the same source."

"Huh? What does that mean?" Kate glanced from one to the other.

Rob spoke up. "She means we always just know how the other one is doing. If something terrible happened to her–God forbid!–I'd feel it, and I'd be there as soon as I could. Same with her. Right, Sowi?"

"It's true," Sowi nodded. "Hard to describe, but to give you an example, once Robbie and a friend of his were in a car accident over on 101. They nearly plunged off a cliff into the ocean. She looked at Robbie. "We were what? Seventeen, maybe?"

He nodded.

She said to Kate. "I was at my girlfriend's house, at a sleepover. Suddenly, I knew in my heart something was wrong. I made such a fuss that my friend's father agreed to drive me up Highway 101. It was such a strong feeling that something bad had happened to Robbie." She closed her eyes for a second. "His friend, Benji, had been driving, probably stoned. I don't remember. And when we found them, both of them were both unconscious. We called 911."

Kate put her hand over her mouth. "Wow! Somehow, you just knew?"

Sowi responded, "Always have. It's like we are twins. Like our souls are intertwined or something. That's the way I think of it."

Kate stared at her. "It sounds comforting to have that kind of connection with someone."

They both nodded. "It is. We're never alone. Ever."

Kate thought of Cody back on the side of the road and how solitary he'd looked to her. Were their souls intertwined the way Sowi described it? If he were in trouble, would she feel it? Kate didn't think so. And yet, there were times when she felt she could read his mind and he, hers. Was that the same thing?

Rob and Sowi were leaning toward each other, talking quietly.

Kate sat up, yawned, and stretched.

Rob asked, "Kate, do you want to crash here for the night? You look beat. Sowi says she's got a couple of empty rooms upstairs and a decent shower."

Kate blushed. "Oh, God! I DO stink, don't I? You should've told me about the shower before we ate dinner!"

"I don't know. You seemed pretty darn hungry. I thought we'd better feed you first."

Kate grimaced and felt her cheeks grow pink. She turned to Sowi. "Do you mind? I'd love a shower and a night in a real bed. Of course, I'd be happy to pay for my room."

Sowi shook her head. "No, it's fine. You're a friend of Robbie's and the grandchild of The Healer. I think the karma from that is payment enough."

Kate smiled but she would find a way to pay Sowi back. She turned to follow Sowi towards the stairs.

"I'll show you where everything is, and then you can get your pack from the car and scrub some of the trail off yourself. By the way, there's a washing machine out back. Do you need to do some laundry too?"

Kate shook her head. "I do, but I'll wait until I'm down at my grandmother's. There will be plenty of time to do it then."

"OK but let me know if you change your mind. You're welcome to use my washer and dryer."

While Rob went out to the car, Sowi took Kate upstairs to a small bedroom that was plain but clean and adequate. The shower was down the hall. In the bedroom, there was a single bed with a white coverlet, an old oak nightstand, and a matching oak dresser. At the foot of the bed was a folded woolen blanket, decorated with elaborate Native American designs. It looked old and treasured.

Rob returned, carrying her backpack up the stairs. "Yikes, how did you manage hiking with this thing? It weighs a ton."

"It's not too bad once you get it adjusted just right. You have to use the hip brace and tighten the waist belt to keep the weight off your shoulders."

He brought it in and set it on the floor next to the bed. "You can have the bathroom first," he said. "Go ahead and enjoy your shower. I'm going to go down and help Sowi close up the place. I'll see you in the morning."

"Thanks, Rob," she said as she hoisted the backpack on to the bed. "I'll take a quick shower. I know you must be tired, too." She loosened the straps at the top of the pack to look for her shower gear and a change of clothes. "By the way, what time do you want to be on the road?" she asked as she saw him turn away to head downstairs.

"No hurry. Go ahead and sleep in if you feel like it." He waved over his shoulder. "Good night, Kate."

"Night. And thanks for everything, Rob. It's been a fun evening."

Kate started pulling clothes out of her pack and her thoughts turned to Grandma Ceil. How strange that the people who were helping her should know her grandmother. Ceil, the Healer. Indeed. Everything seemed so interconnected.

Chapter 9

Kate's 2nd Visit to the Timestream

Timestream, Tidewater, OR
Saturday, August 10, 2019, early morning

Kate woke Saturday morning, feeling like she was coming out of meditation, not sleep—a sort of restful yet alert sensation. She took a deep breath with her eyes still closed, and slowly let her senses awaken to her surroundings. But, almost immediately, she knew something wasn't right. Even with her eyes closed, Kate felt an open expanse around her, and she smelled the salty air of the sea. Damn! She was outdoors! She cocked her head and listened. She could hear seagulls squawking in the distance. The sound grew louder as they came closer, and it was a chaotic, dissonant sound as if they were fighting or were terrified.

Kate opened her eyes and immediately her eyes darted around, as she tried to figure out where she was this time. Why did she keep waking up in these strange places? She noticed a grove of short, twisted fir trees nearby, contorted from the vagaries of harsh wind and weather. Beyond the trees, Kate could see the dark blue of the ocean and way out on the horizon, the sea seemed to be in turmoil.

She rose to get a closer look and moved through the trees. As she emerged from the tree line, she realized that she was on an outcropping of rock above the churning surf. Just offshore were several craggy 90-foot sea stacks that were being battered by huge waves. The water sprayed up as the waves exploded against the rocky ledges.

The gulls circled and squawked angrily above the sea stacks wanting to land but unable to. Then the ground began to shake, and she turned her head in time to see the side of the mountain, perhaps a quarter mile away, sheer off and slowly slide across the highway and then tumble down into the ocean below. The highway? "Oh my God," she whispered. A portion of it was buried under rock and debris. Her heart raced.

A deep roar rose up behind her, and she spun around to face the sea again. What she saw next took her breath away. Way out on the horizon, a gigantic wave seemed to stand up and curl without breaking as it rippled in towards her. The St. George's lighthouse, that had been visible a moment before on the horizon, disappeared as it was swallowed up by the massive wall of water. Tsunami. The word came into her mind unbidden as she watched in growing horror as a series of giant waves, one behind the next swept towards her.

Her knees buckled and she sank to the ground. She reached out with her left hand and wrapped her arm around a gnarled tree trunk nearby and held on. She could smell the bitter pine scent from its needles. She stared, mesmerized by the undulating wave as it approached.

She must have passed out because her last memory was looking up at the water, as it hung over her. Then the next moment she was opening her eyes and she was in a completely different landscape. No ocean cliffs, no waves, but oddly she could still smell the sharp scent of pine. She glanced down and saw that she still held a handful of pine needles clenched in her fist. She released them, and they fluttered to the ground.

Kate looked up and before her was a vine-draped spiral staircase. She hurried over to it, convinced that by climbing it, she'd be safe. Her heart pounded in her chest, and she was breathing hard. She grabbed the railing, and bent over, hoping that she wouldn't pass out.

Where was she? She glanced around but nothing looked familiar. A white mist billowed along the ground. It was like being in the center of a cloud. "Hello?" she called out. Her voice sounded raspy and dry. She cleared her throat and tried again, "Hello?"

"It's OK, Kate." Rob was suddenly there next to her, a step above her on the staircase.

"Rob!" she said in relief. "Where are we?" She instinctively moved closer to him. After spending hours in the car talking and getting to know each other, she realized he was like the big brother she had always wanted. She found the warmth emanating from his body reassuring and she was so grateful not to be alone in this place.

"It's OK, Kate. It's just that I ...Wow! I'm amazed that you're here!" He grinned. "You don't know how awesome this is."

She looked at him uncertainly. "Awesome?" she repeated. "Where are we? How did I get here? Rob, I'm so confused. Is this a dream?"

Rob put an arm around her shoulders and pulled her close. "It's OK, Kate," he said for the third time. "I've heard it called the timestream or the dream space. Different cultures call it different names."

"Timestream?" Was she dreaming? Or had she been swept away by that wave after all? She whispered, "Rob, am I dead?"

His eyebrows shot up in surprise, and he laughed. "No, Kate! Of course not. This is the place between waking and dreaming."

Kate took a slow, deep breath, and the anxiety and panic started to recede. It didn't make sense to her, but Rob didn't appear concerned. She nodded to the stairway behind him, "Where do the stairs go?"

He looked up. "Deeper in, I guess."

She turned towards the horizon. No ocean here. She could make out a snow-capped cone of a volcano in the distance and billowy white clouds drifting across a deep blue sky. Then she noticed a hawk circling above. The hawk's wings were outstretched wide as it glided effortlessly on the breeze, scanning the ground. She could feel its weightlessness, the wind brushing through its feathers and making its body bob. *Such freedom!* And in a second, she was floating, drifting in a circle in the air, her arms outstretched like wings. She looked down, and saw Rob watching her from far below. He waved. *Wait! Was she flying? This must be a dream.* She relaxed and decided to fly back to the vine-covered staircase, and she was there in an instant. She reached out and touched the vines. They felt vibrant and alive. *But do dreams let you feel the texture of vegetation and smell the earth?*

"Be careful," Rob said. He was just below her now. He reached up and held her wrist gently. "Baby steps, Kate. You need to take baby steps."

She frowned. "What?"

"You're new to all this. Take it in slowly. It can be overwhelming until you get used to it. Every level of consciousness has its own rules."

There were rules? How would she learn them? Before she could ask more about the rules, she looked down at herself and saw that she was now wearing a light brown flowing robe similar to her high school graduation robe. "Where are my clothes? Where did this robe come from?"

"You can wear whatever you can imagine. Try it."

When she went to bed, she had been wearing one of Cody's concert tees. She looked down, and it was back, along with a favorite pair of dark gray yoga pants that she was sure she'd left at her dad's place in Boston.

She peered at Rob. "What's going on here? Did you and Sowi drug me?"

He looked surprised. "Drug you? Oh, I see. This probably does feel a bit like tripping, doesn't it? But, honest, no, we didn't drug you." He leaned back and was watching her with the expression of a proud teacher, both gratified and entertained.

"Is this a hallucination then?"

"No, it's real. The three of us are here in the same dream space."

"Three?" she repeated. Then she turned her head and with amazement, saw Sowi walking towards them.

"Hey, cool! Kate's here?" Sowi said to Rob as she reached the staircase. Sowi was wearing a loose-fitting blue cotton caftan blouse with intricate mosaic designs, over a pair of jeans.

"Awesome, huh?" Rob said. "It turns out, she's one of us!"

"Wow!" Sowi said. "This is a first."

"I know!" He turned to Kate. "You are the first person we've been able to bring here."

"Rob, I feel...weird," Kate said, closing her eyes.

"Uh oh." He put his arms around Kate and held her. "We're going to wake you up now, Kate. Ready?"

She frowned in confusion. "Huh?"

And the next moment, she and Rob were sitting side-by-side on the single bed in her room back at Sowi's place. The bedspread hung loosely over the unmade bed. She spread out her hands, feeling the rough texture of the bedspread beneath her fingers. It seemed real enough, and everything looked the same. Her dirty hiking clothes from yesterday were in a pile near her pack on the floor, her boots lay just as they landed when she pulled them off the night before.

"You OK?" Rob asked.

Kate nodded. The room was dark, but it was indeed the room she'd fallen asleep in the night before. A glow of morning light was just brightening the edges of the curtains.

Rob looked at her. "It's amazing that you were able to go to the dream space with us. Have you ever had that kind of experience before?"

Kate told him about the previous morning on the trail when she woke up over Portland during an earthquake.

"And that's why you're going to see your grandmother in Brookings?"

Kate nodded. "She used to have a lot of weird experiences. I remember her telling me stories when I was little."

"Hey! I can't believe you were there with us, Kate!" Sowi said from the doorway.

"Kate's been in the timestream three times—once yesterday morning and twice this morning. I think it means something is going to happen soon."

Sowi asked Kate, "What did you see in the first two?"

"An earthquake in Portland yesterday and then a tsunami hitting the coast this morning," Kate said.

Sowi whistled. "Yikes, that sounds pretty dire. It must have been scary for you." She touched Kate's shoulder.

Kate agreed, "It was terrifying."

"Listen, I'll drive you down to the commune today," Rob said. "I don't start work until Monday, so I have the time. Besides, I'd like to meet your grandmother."

"I wish I didn't have to work today. I'd go too," Sowi said wistfully.

"Maybe you and I can go down later in the week and visit," Rob said to Sowi.

"Yeah, let's do that!" Then Sowi asked, "You guys ready for breakfast? I can whip up some pancakes if you're interested."

"Yum, that sounds wonderful." Kate grinned.

"Coffee?" Sowi asked.

Kate started to nod but then shook her head. "No, actually, I think I'd prefer tea if you have it," she said. Hmmm, did she just hear herself ask for tea? She wasn't a tea drinker, but today it appealed to her. *Something is going on with my body, that's for sure,* she decided.

"Coffee for me," Rob said.

Rob was heading towards the door when he turned back to face Kate. "Sorry if this has gotten weird for you. I keep forgetting this kind of stuff doesn't happen to other people."

"It does to you?" she asked.

"Synchronicity, timestream, crazy dream spaces, sharing a soul source with my best friend, yeah, all that and lots more. I'm not sure what any of it means, but I believe that everything happens for a reason. Or maybe everything is random, and we are just charged with making sense of it...but, either way...." He shrugged. "Eventually, we'll find out what all this means."

He closed the door gently, and Kate stood up and stared at the door for several long seconds. "What does all this mean?" she whispered. *And what if Grandma Ceil doesn't know either?*

Chapter 10

Ceil welcomes Kate

Love & Peace Commune, Brookings, OR
Saturday, August 10, 2019, morning

Ceil was standing in the kitchen area under the loft, leaning over the big farmer's sink, peeling onions. She heard the squeal of the lodge's double doors opening as someone entered, and then light footsteps as they crossed the large room.

"Hi, Grandma Ceil," Kate said from the doorway.

Ceil turned and wiped her eyes carefully with the back of her hand so as not to get onion juice into her eyes. She sniffed loudly and then smiled broadly at Kate through watery eyes. "Oh, my God! Katie Rose! You're here! I don't know why but I've been thinking about you non-stop for the past two days!" She nodded her head toward the onions. "I'm not crying, just peeling onions," she added with a sniff and a laugh.

Kate hurried over and gave Ceil's shoulders a hug. She leaned in. "It's good to see you again, Grandma Ceil. It's OK that I'm here, isn't it?"

"OK? Are you kidding? It's way more than OK! Oh my God, it's a dream come true, sweetie. And I'll give you a big hug to prove it as soon as I wash this onion juice off my hands." She stepped over to the sink, not taking her eyes off Kate's face. She turned on the faucet, ran her hands under the water, and then reached down and wiped them on her apron, once brightly tie-dyed with a giant orange peace sign, now rumpled, and stained with age and cooking. Done with that, she hurried over to Kate and wrapped her in a warm hug. "It is so good to see you, Katie. I've missed you more than you'll ever know."

Kate kissed her on the cheek. "Making soup?" she asked, indicating the onions on the butcher block counter. There were several peeled onions lined up in a row.

Ceil nodded. "Good timing on your part, sweetie. I know onion soup is one of your favorites. So how long are you staying? At least for dinner, I hope?"

"If it's OK with you, I'd like to stay for a bit. I need to talk to you, and I thought it'd be better in person." She exhaled slowly. "It's about...well, about some weird shit that's been happening to me."

Ceil blinked and then eyed her granddaughter. "Maybe that's why you've been on my mind lately. But what 'weird shit' are you talking about? What's happened?" She looked at Kate with concern.

Kate leaned against the counter, folding her arms across her chest. "To be honest, Grandma Ceil, I'm not sure where to start."

"At the beginning?" Ceil suggested. She faced Kate, mirroring her stance, folding her arms across her chest. "OK, I'm ready. Tell me what's up." She brushed an errant loose lock of hair behind an ear.

Kate paused, then plunged ahead. "OK. Here goes. When classes let out at the end of the spring semester, I went south to California with my boyfriend, Cody."

Ceil nodded. "Your mom said he seemed like a nice kid."

"I've been hiking the PCT with Cody for the last month. Then yesterday, we were halfway to the Columbia River, and I had to quit the hike."

Ceil frowned. "Why? Did you twist an ankle or something?"

Kate shook her head with a grimace. "No, nothing like that. I had a very odd experience. I knew I had to get off the trail and come down here to talk to you about it. You seem to understand weird experiences."

"And what about Cody?" Ceil asked, her eyebrows raised.

"He continued with the hike. I got a ride down here from a guy named Rob. He's outside. You can meet him later. I told him to have a look around while I came in to talk to you. He's anxious to meet you, by the way. He said you're pretty famous and known far and wide as 'The Healer.'"

Ceil looked at Kate in surprise. "Geez, I didn't think I was... you know, famous." She put her hand to her cheek. "But that can't be what you wanted to talk to me about."

"No, I wanted to talk to you about the weird stuff that's been happening to me over the past two days."

Ceil gestured towards the table just outside the kitchen area. They took seats opposite each other, sitting in the same seats they once sat in many summers ago. When Kate was little, she would spend part of the summer with her grandparents, so her parents could travel without her. Back then, the place had been filled with the children of the other hippies who lived in the surrounding treehouses of the commune or in the tents and cabins along the riverfront.

"So, tell me: what weird stuff has been happening to you?"

"Well, for one thing...Do you know anything about the Cascadia subduction zone?"

"Oh, sure. We have an evacuation route map and all the prep information for this area. We all know the drill: when the earth shakes, get to higher ground immediately, and all that. It's one of those things you deal with when you live near the Oregon coast, honey. However, we're pretty far inland here, so we aren't overly concerned about a tsunami. That is unless the earthquake is truly the 'big one' they keep saying is coming. If that's the case, all bets are off. But the average tsunami will make the river rise, and we might lose a few tents and cabins along the riverfront, but I think we'd be fine."

Kate said, "You know, it won't be just a tsunami, right? When it happens, it'll be preceded by earthquakes starting with a massive one – magnitude 9.0 – a truly colossal earthquake."

Ceil shuddered and nodded. "And then a tsunami fifteen or twenty minutes later. Yup, I'm familiar with the predictions. For us, here, the concern is more about the earthquake and the potential for landslides."

"It's going to happen," Kate said quietly.

"Sure, I know. The scientists say it's inevitable and overdue. It could happen ten minutes from now, in ten years, or in a hundred years."

Kate shook her head. "No, I mean, it's going to happen soon, Grandma Ceil. Maybe even within weeks ... or...or possibly days."

Ceil went quiet as she stared at her granddaughter. She cleared her throat, and the sound filled the quiet building. "Tell me, Katie. How do you know that?"

The blood left Kate's face. She closed her eyes. "Because I saw it."

"You..." Ceil started, but then shook her head, "No, you need to tell me yourself. What do you mean when you say you saw it?"

Kate laid her hands in front of her on the table. The fingers of one hand gripped the fingers of the other hand. She leaned forward. "I felt like I was there watching as the earthquake hit Portland, seeing the buildings swaying, the bridges buckling. Then, early this morning, I saw...no, not just saw, I felt like I was actually on a staircase that rose into the clouds, and it was in the middle of... well, I don't know where exactly...outside somewhere. It was so strange that I thought maybe Rob had slipped something into my beer. It was like I was Dorothy waking up in Oz, you know?"

Kate continued, "The first experience was on the hike, and Cody and I didn't have any weed or anything else with us, and before the second experience, I'd only had two beers the whole evening."

Ceil frowned. "Tell me exactly what you saw, and especially tell me what you felt."

"It was early morning yesterday. I saw the city of Portland. My perspective was from above it, like a bird's view of the city. When I started to fall out of the sky, I woke up next to a stream near our campsite on the trail."

Kate paused, then continued, "The second time was early this morning, and I found myself on the Oregon coast. I was standing on a jut of land looking out at the sea. I could see the St. George's lighthouse on the horizon. Highway 101 was just to my left – I could make out the black asphalt, but there were no cars. The ocean was turbulent all the way out to the horizon like it was boiling, and, at the horizon, I could see this huge mass of water forming and rising. Then St. George's disappeared under the surge. When the wave finally hit, I blacked out and woke up in another place. It was a sandy plain with rocks and bushes all around. In the middle of this place was a vine-covered spiral staircase leading upward into the clouds. Rob was standing on one of the steps. Sowi showed up, too."

Ceil, stared at Kate, open-mouthed. "Were you there? Or were you just dreaming that you were there?" she asked.

"I... I don't know. At the time, I felt like I was there, not that I was there now, but rather like I was there in the near future. Do you know what I mean?"

"You can't actually BE somewhere in the future. You know that, right, honey?"

"That's the thing. I had the feeling that I was in the future, and it was so real, Grandma Ceil! I could feel the vegetation around me and smell the pine needles." Kate looked into Ceil's eyes for several long seconds. "Oh my God! Wait! You know what I'm talking about. You've experienced it, too, haven't you? I remember when I came here years ago, and you asked me if I'd ever traveled in time. Of course, I thought you were being metaphorical." She shook her head. "No, actually I thought you were on something and tripping."

Ceil nodded. "So, you have it too, then? I always wondered. I sort of thought so when you were really little. You always had such an imagination, such interesting invisible friends. Your great-great-grandma Rosalie guessed it, you know, when I took you to see her before she died. She looked into your eyes and said it must skip generations because we both knew that your great-grandmother and your mother didn't have the gift."

Kate repeated, "The gift?"

"That's what Grandma Rosalie called it. I've always figured it was some kind of Irish thing. She was full of talk about rainbows, pots of gold, and leprechauns..."

The door opened behind them, and they both jumped.

Sky stood at the door, looking from one to the other, with a grin. "Hey, sorry. I didn't mean to scare you two, but I saw the car, and that guy, Rob, out there said my little Katie was in here with her grandma."

Kate stood up as Sky crossed the room and took her in his arms in a warm hug that lifted her off her feet.

"It's so good to see you again," he said into her hair. "I hoped I'd see you this summer." His eyes met Ceil's for a second over

Kate's head, then he pulled away and looked Katie up and down. "So, what's up, kiddo? You OK?"

"I'm fine, Granddad. I just needed to talk to Grandma Ceil."

"I just met Rob and he said you were hiking the PCT when he picked you up. If you wanted to quit that hiking thing, I'd understand. Don't get me wrong. I think it's great to get out in nature. Spend some time in a mind-meld with old Mother Earth and all, but I never understood the whole long trail thing. It just seems...I don't know...so militaristic, regimented, and bloody overzealous." He shrugged. "But, hey, that's just me."

"It's definitely you, Sky," Ceil said. "No one's going to tell you where to walk or how far," she added with a laugh. Then, she stood up, returned to the butcher block, picked up an onion in one hand and the knife in the other, and began peeling the skin off. "Kate was just telling me that she thinks she has the gift."

Sky stood very still and looked at Kate. "You do?"

"You know what that is?" Kate asked, looking from him to Ceil's back.

"Sure. Ceil used to scare the willies out of me with some of the things she saw."

Ceil turned and met his eyes but didn't say anything.

"How is it I'm the only one who knows nothing about this gift thing?" Kate asked plaintively.

"It wouldn't make sense to mention it unless you had it, and if you had it, you would eventually say something or ask about it, then we'd know and could talk to you about it."

"Mom doesn't have it, does she?"

They both shook their heads.

"What about you? Do you have it, Granddad?" Kate asked.

He shook his head again. "Nope."

Kate asked, "Do these things always come true?" she asked carefully, again looking from him to Ceil, who turned to face her.

"Not always. No," Ceil said in a measured way.

Kate sat down at the table and breathed out with a whoosh. "What a relief! How do we know if it will or won't happen then?"

"Well, first of all, everything you see, or experience DOES happen," Ceil corrected. "It all happens, but it happens in its own timestream; it's just one of many possible futures."

"Possible futures?"

Sky sat down next to Ceil, opposite Kate. "It's because of the whole free will thing. Every choice creates a different cause and effect..." he said. He looked at Ceil for confirmation.

Ceil glanced at Sky. "Well, you're right up to a point. But it's not just our free will that creates the future." She turned to Kate. "Every animal, insect, and tree has a life will too. So, the whole lot of us; we ALL create the future together."

"So, what is it that I'm seeing when I... you know...when I see some future event?" Kate asked.

"You're seeing one of the many possible outcomes of everything that has happened up to that point."

Ceil saw the look of confusion on Kate's face and thought for a moment. "OK, let me try a metaphor on you. It's like our life is a moving river. We think of it as linear, moving from upriver to downriver. Right? From the past to the present and on to the future."

Kate nodded. She leaned back and she looked off into space as she listened to Ceil.

"Supposing you are on the riverbank, and you look into the water right in front of you. That's the present. Everything is as it is at this moment. But if you look back up the river, you see the past flowing toward you and becoming the present. All the decisions made in the past are set and unchangeable, but any decisions you make now in the present moment can alter the future. When you look down the river in the direction it's moving, that's the future and there is a multitude of possibilities—all the rivulets represent choices that haven't been made yet, and each one of those choices will cause the flow of the river to move into a slightly different channel, an alternative future, so to speak. Throw a pebble in, and it changes the river. The past determines where you are today and what you decide today determines what will happen tomorrow."

Kate leaned forward. "So, can we change where it's headed?" Kate asked.

"I think so. The choices we make, the goals we set all influence the future, for sure."

"But if I saw something really awful, could we change the course the future takes? Make it not happen?"

"What did you see?" Sky asked, leaning forward.

"The subduction zone nightmare," Ceil said to Sky, then turned to Kate for confirmation. "Right?"

Kate nodded. "I didn't know what to call it, but yeah, it was a series of earthquakes, each stronger than the one before. It turned the ground into quicksand; landslides buried roads and houses, buildings cracked and split in half, and bridges toppled into the water below. And the ocean!" she said, putting her hand over her eyes. "The tsunami – it's not just one wave but a series of powerful waves, a tide that just comes on and on. The waves came flooding in over the broken houses and swept away the cars and people, pulling them far out into the sea."

No one spoke.

Sky pushed away from the table and stood up and began to pace. He ran his fingers through his long graying hair. "Yup, that's the nightmare, all right." He looked at Kate. "You said you saw this...when?"

"Over the past couple of days. Each time was slightly different, but the extent of the disaster was the same." She looked at Ceil. "Grandma Ceil, can it be stopped?"

Ceil stared at her. "We can only make choices that affect our own futures. For us here, we could save ourselves, run for high ground or go to the airport and get on a plane headed for the East Coast. So, yes, we can change our own future, but to stop the earthquakes and tsunamis from happening? Wow, natural forces aren't affected by our free will, so you'd be trying to change Nature itself. And let's say you could put it off temporarily. For how long? I mean, these continental plates are relentlessly moving a few inches every year. The geologists tell us that they fire off and relieve that pressure every – what? – every five hundred years or so? The region is way past due for one of those corrections."

Sky stopped pacing and shook his head slowly as he thought about what Ceil had said. They were quiet for another long minute. Then Ceil said, "Are you sure what you saw was now? Not something ten years from now or some other time in the future?"

Kate looked at her and considered. "It's hard to say. The cars and buildings looked familiar like they belonged to the present time." She was quiet for another moment, then she sighed and added, "No, I feel pretty positive that it was going to happen soon. I don't know exactly why, but it felt...soon."

"You feel positive? How so?" Sky looked at her with interest.

"I can't explain it, but somehow I knew when I saw it that it would be happening soon."

Ceil reached across the table and took Kate's two hands in hers and squeezed reassuringly. "I know what you mean. I always had a sense of the when too. I could always tell if I was seeing something immediate."

Sky looked at her and, after a moment, said, "That's true. And it usually happened right away, I think."

Kate leaned back and her shoulders dropped. "A group from the local tribe up there – Klamath or Moduc, I can't remember which – anyway, Rob said that they have already headed for Crater Lake to get away from the coast."

"Crater Lake?" Sky said thoughtfully. "That makes sense. It was considered a sacred place for many of the Northwest tribes. Interesting choice, huh? An extinct volcano and all."

Kate blinked. "Volcanoes...oh my God, I forgot about the volcanoes. They were part of it too. The whole string of them started rumbling." She looked from one grandparent to the other.

"Did you know there are a LOT of volcanoes here in the Pacific Northwest?"

"The Ring of Fire," Sky said. "The most active geologic region in the world. 90% of the world's earthquakes happen in the rim around the Pacific; at least, all the big ones certainly."

"Geology 101?" Ceil teased.

He smiled in acknowledgment.

Kate shook her head in exasperation. "So, what can we do? I mean, should we warn people?"

Sky stared at her for a second. "How do I say this, honey?" He shook his head. "No one will believe you. Think about it. Did you ever see the cartoon guy carrying the sign saying: 'The World's Going to End'? Do you think his warning caused anyone to prepare?"

Ceil added, "Actually, warning them might even make it worse because then you'll have all those minds THINKING about it, imagining it, some even getting excited about the novelty and adrenaline rush of it. So that could end up drawing it to us even quicker."

"Drawing it to us? What do you mean?" Kate asked with a frown.

"Well, you know. Thoughts draw things into being. It's like prayer, meditation, ESP, or any other psychic mode. We're all just energy beings within a vast universal force field. That means we can communicate with all other beings at some level. We don't usually do it, but we could."

"How?"

"Well, take, for example, prayer circles. You know, groups of people are praying for someone's health or the success of a risky operation or whatever. I don't happen to believe in the whole Christian-personal-God paradigm. You know, the God-that-will-fix-my-personal-problems. But I believe there is an underlying life force, and sometimes we get the wavelength just right and, bang, our prayers have a real-life effect, and change happens. So, I guess some people would interpret that as God's intervention; but I think it's just us tuning in to the life force."

"Could we do that to stop the earthquake?" Kate asked.

"Us? You mean the three of us?" Ceil shook her head even before saying, "No, three people just wouldn't have enough... enough...uh...." She looked at Sky questioningly as she searched for the right word.

"Juice?" he asked.

"Yeah, enough juice...no, uh...enough psychic energy," she amended.

"But you mentioned prayer circles sometimes work. How many people would you need to have an impact?"

"Well, there are many Native American myths about rituals and ceremonies designed to affect the weather, give a good harvest, or assist warriors in battle, or assure good hunting," Ceil said.

"Like doing Rain Dances to make it rain," Sky said.

"And what about earthquakes?" Kate asked, looking from one to the other.

Ceil's face suddenly brightened. "You know they do have a mythology about the Thunderbird coming down from the high mountain to fight with the Whale who supports the earth on his back. In the Whale's struggle to overcome Thunderbird, Whale shakes the entire earth."

"Ah, and creates an earthquake," Sky said with a nod.

"Could the Native Americans control the Thunderbird?"

"The shaman was supposed to be able to placate the Thunderbird," Sky said. 'They'd have a sacred ceremony and get high on mescaline or cannabis, and in their ritual dances, the spirits would enter the shaman's body, and he was the only one who could deal with these gods or beasts."

"A shaman, eh?" Kate perked up. "Well, we're in luck because I think I know where to find one."

Chapter 11

Ceil & Sky show Rob the Commune

Love & Peace Commune, Brookings, OR
Saturday, August 10, 2019, late morning

"This is some place you have here," Rob said as he, Kate, Ceil, and Sky left the lodge for a walk around the commune. He turned to Sky, "Kate said some of the people here live in treehouses."

"Yeah, that's true! The treehouses are in the forest mixed among the big trees. But technically, they're not really treehouses. More like stilt houses built around the trunks of the trees rather than up in the branches." Sky made a circle with his hands. "A real treehouse would've been impractical, since the lowest branches on some of those trees are hundreds of feet up."

He pointed toward the forest opposite them. "The treehouses in the woods over there are mainly used by the communards who live here year-round. Although a few belong to former members who return regularly for visits in the summer or on long weekends. We also have some dorm-style cabins on the other side of the greenhouses." He pointed towards the top of the greenhouse, which could be seen above the treetops. "Those cabins are mostly used by the contingent workers who come and help at harvest time."

Rob looked in the direction Sky was pointing. "They must be pretty well camouflaged because I can't see any cabins from here at all."

Ceil stood next to Rob and looked towards the forest. "That's by design, Rob. We wanted everything to blend into Nature. We feel strongly that we should serve the environment, not the other way around."

"Back over that way by the river," Sky said, turning and pointing, "are another seven cabins along the riverfront. They're just one room log cabins with a bunkbed and minimal furniture inside. We reserve those for our summer visitors. We also have some tent camping sites just beyond the cabins along with a small shared communal bathhouse."

Before Sky could say any more, there was the revving of an engine and the squeal of brakes.

They all turned and looked towards the lodge just as an SUV swung in. There was the sound of loud rock music—it sounded like Jimi Hendrix to Sky—was pouring from the open windows of the SUV.

An older guy slowly emerged from the driver's seat. He was dressed in blue jeans and a gaudy vest with no shirt underneath. He yawned loudly and as he stretched, they could see the pale white skin of his arms iridescent in the sunlight. When he turned towards them, Ceil saw that his belly—soft and pink—sagged out below his vest and hung over the waistband of his jeans. She grimaced. "Damn," she said under her breath, "Pell Mel is back."

She looked at Sky and saw his shoulders sag for a second, but then he pasted on a tight-lipped smile.

Pell Mell slowly made his way towards them, weaving and then catching himself as he came. Ceil guessed he was either drunk or stoned.

"Hey, Mel," Sky said in greeting without much enthusiasm.

The man stopped and studied Sky for a long second and then glanced over at Ceil, and back again at Sky. "Oh, hey, Sky, Ceil! I gotta tell you we had quite the trip down from Portland."

"We?" Ceil repeated, looking back at the SUV.

Mel turned around and continued turning until he had completed a full circle. He came to a halt and stared blankly at the SUV for several long seconds.

"Did you come down alone, Mel?" Sky asked.

"Nah," Mel answered. "Tulip's in their somewhere. She must've fallen asleep." He snorted as if he was telling a funny story. The others just stared at him.

"Did you reserve a cabin or are you camping this year?" Ceil asked, hoping to bring him back to the conversation.

Mel looked at her and then seemed to pause for the meaning of her words to become clear. When he realized everyone was waiting for an answer, he said, "Uh, what'd you just ask me?"

Kate and Rob grinned at each other and had to turn away as Ceil repeated her question. Finally, she shook her head and pointed towards the greenhouse. "Mel, how about you go over and see Jade in the office. She'll let you know where you can bunk. OK?"

Mel nodded, then spun around again, nearly losing his balance, then he stumbled back to the SUV.

"You need help?" Sky called after him.

Mel shook his head. "Nah, I'll wake up Tulip. See what she wants to do." He waved a hand in the air. "Later."

Ceil looked at Sky and blew out a breath, closing her eyes for a second.

"Pell Mel?" Kate asked, with a twinkle in her eye.

Sky sighed. "He used to live here. It might've been after your time, Katie. Let's just say, he was never a good fit for communal living."

"In what way?" Rob asked, a grin still playing on his lips.

Ceil shook her head. "Mel was a stoner and obviously, he still is. Let's just say that when he left, he wasn't missed."

"Huh. I thought nearly everyone here was a stoner at one point or another," Kate said in mock seriousness.

Sky combed his fingers through his hair. "Yeah, well, you know when they say a little kid 'doesn't play well with others?' That pretty much describes Mel. He would smoke everyone else's stash, never contributed anything to anyone, never worked, and never did chores. Mel was a slacker."

Ceil shrugged and changed the subject. "So tell us about you, Rob. Kate said you're from Coos Bay."

"Yeah, my mother is from the Coos tribe. She and her best friend, Lela, were the rebels who went away to college and came home married to hippies." He laughed. "It was a bit rocky for them for a while. You see, her father—my grandfather—is on the tribal council for the confederated tribes of the Coos, Lower Umpqua, and Siuslaw Indians of Oregon."

"Tom Manyrivers?" Ceil asked with interest.

"You know my grandfather?"

"It's been a while since I've seen him, but we did each other a favor many years ago. I remember him as a very wise and generous man. When you see him next, please give him our regards, would you?" Ceil said, touching Rob's arm.

"Grandma," Kate said slowly, "I was actually thinking Rob's grandfather might serve as the shaman we're looking for."

"Yes! That's a great idea, Kate! " Ceil turned to Rob. "I don't know if Kate has said anything to you, but we need someone to lead us in a battle with Thunderbird."

Rob looked from Ceil to Sky, and then laughed out loud. "Fighting Thunderbird, huh?" He slowly shook his head in appreciation. "Kate told me what she saw in the timestream, but I have to admit I never thought about fighting the vision." He paused and then shrugged. "Look, I'm planning to visit my grandfather tomorrow. I'll present the idea to him and find out if he would be willing to come down here to try it. If he agrees, we'll probably need a few others for the drumming and other parts of the ritual. I'll see who I can round up."

"Based on what Kate's told me," Ceil said, "I don't think we have a lot of time. So, the sooner, the better."

"Yeah," Sky said, "Next week's our Woodstock Reunion weekend, so it's going to get really nuts around here."

"Woodstock Reunion?" Rob repeated.

Sky explained, "We have an end-of-summer reunion every year and we always hold it during the week of August 15 – 17th to commemorate the original Woodstock Festival. This one is going to be the best yet! It's the 50th anniversary of Woodstock and the commune is forty-five this year. Hard to believe it's been that long!"

"It makes me feel ancient," Nia said as she walked up to the group. "I was nineteen back in 1969 when the Woodstock Festival took place. You should've seen me with my big-ass Afro!" She snorted "Just as proud as you please!"

Rob glanced at her. "Did you go to Woodstock?"

She shook her head, "Nah. I was down in San Francisco the summer of 1969. But Sky went."

Rob looked at him, impressed. "Wow! I mean, Woodstock!"

Nia added, "He and his friends hitched from Montana to New York for it."

"So how was it? That must have been so cool!"

Sky laughed. "You got that right! It was incredible! Well, except for the rain and sloshing around in the mud, and oh, let's not forget the massive traffic jams." He paused, and then his voice took on a more serious note. "But, yeah, the music, the great vibes of the crowd—it was one of the most amazing experiences of my life. I believe I came back a different person after it."

"Different, how?" Rob asked.

Everyone turned and looked with interest at Sky as he responded.

"Hard to put into words, but I felt connected to the world in a way I never had before. For that weekend, I was a part of a crazy, wonderful Woodstock community, with people who came from everywhere. I felt intimately connected to my country and to our planet in a way I never experienced before. Like I belonged here, in this country and on this planet. I think it's what made me decide to live in a commune."

Ceil smiled and took his hand. "You were lucky to have experienced it, Sky. But, still, I hope we don't get the Woodstock weather next week."

"Fingers crossed," Nia said. "And speaking of the coming celebration, Ceil, we need to do some meal planning for next week."

Ceil nodded. "Yeah, we'll have quite a crowd to feed."

"Do you guys need any help?" Kate asked.

Sky shook his head. "Go ahead and show Rob the rest of the compound. They'll be lighting the bonfire in the center fire pit later on. You should check it out. I think you'll find some old friends, Katie."

As Rob and Kate walked away, he asked, "Do you think anybody'd mind if Sowi and I come to this Woodstock thing?"

"Rob, that'd be great! Consider yourself invited," Kate responded. "In this place, it's always been 'the more, the merrier.' Plus, I'd love to spend some more time with you...uh, and Sowi, of course," she corrected. She quickly pointed towards the greenhouses. "Over here is our oldest greenhouse...."

* * *

Rob texted Kate late that night, confirming that he, his grandfather, and a few others from the tribal council would be at the commune the next afternoon to attempt the Thunderbird ritual. Kate was glad to hear from him but felt a little disappointed at how short and impersonal the text was, but even so, she was looking forward to seeing him again.

Chapter 12

Ceil - Sunday Brunch & Dylan

Love & Peace Commune, Brookings, OR
Sunday, August 11, 2019, morning

The following day was Sunday, and the lodge was buzzing with activity beginning before dawn as Ceil, Nia and the Sunday crew set up the tables for brunch. As the sun rose, the campers began to trickle into the lodge, groggy and asking for coffee. Ceil and the others welcomed everyone and pointed them to the urns of coffee and the lines forming in front of the nearby serving tables laden with food.

Over the morning hours, more people flowed in and out of the lodge. The weather couldn't have been more cooperative. It was sunny and warm but not sticky humid, and there was even a rare breeze through the trees.

Ceil could see that once again Nia was at the top of her game, decked out in her cleanest apron over a long billowy sari skirt. Nia's long, braided dreadlocks were tied back with a silky kerchief. She stood in the center of the kitchen, commanding her cadre of helpers like a general at her battle station. She directed the first wave of diners through the buffet and had them sitting down at the long family-style tables in no time. Then after a decent pause to let the folks eat, she sent a team to go from table to table to wipe them down and start setting up for the next wave of hungry diners.

Ceil watched with satisfaction from the back of the room, holding her coffee mug and raising it in easy greeting to some of the recent arrivals. She enjoyed the surprise of familiar faces of old neighbors and friends and the hum of happy voices.

When she heard some excited squeals coming from a table of children in the back of the room, she went to investigate and saw that one of the little boys, Dylan, a rambunctious four-year-old, was standing on the bench seat with a fork in one hand and a spoon in the other, swinging the flatware in the air before him as if he were conducting an orchestra. The other children egged him on, and Ceil could see him contemplating a climb up onto the table.

Ceil looked around but didn't see his parents, Meadow and Gage, so she hurried over and grabbed one of Dylan's arms just as he lifted his foot to step up. Gently, but firmly, she turned him around. She brought her face close to his and waited for him to look squarely at her before she spoke. "I can see you're having a lot of fun, Dylan," she said with a smile. "Have you finished eating?"

His chin lowered and he bit his lower lip. He dropped his eyes as he shook his head.

"OK, then," Ceil said brightly. "Have a seat here next to me because I have a game I want to play with you." He looked up at her with a little hesitancy as she continued. "I want you to take one bite of everything on your plate and tell me which food is your favorite." She sat beside him and gently guided him back to sitting in his booster seat attached to the picnic bench. The other children watched with interest. Ceil glanced at the other children. "Now, while he's tasting everything, I want each of you to try to guess which food Dylan likes the best, but don't say it out loud yet. OK?"

They nodded eagerly, now wholly captivated by Ceil's game.

Dylan grinned, enjoying being the center of attention once again. He looked up at Ceil, and she nodded as he stabbed a bite of potato from his potato salad, put it in his mouth, and chewed. He beamed.

"OK, that's the first bite," Ceil said approvingly. "What will you choose next, Dylan?"

He pointed to a small chunk of carrot from the mixed vegetables, stabbing it, and popped it in his mouth, grinning broadly as he chewed.

The other children laughed.

"I think he likes that one," a little girl of about seven said with delight.

"You may be right, Crystal, but wait until he's tested the other two dishes," Ceil said to her.

Dylan was now enjoying himself, and he hovered his fork over several bites of food and looked up at the other children for their reaction. Then, he chose a small piece of apple from the apple-and-walnut salad, slowly raised it to his mouth, and dramatically bit into it. The children clapped and giggled.

Ceil shook her head with a smile. "You are something of a ham, Dylan," she said, patting his head.

"I've got one more bite, right, Ceil?" he asked, looking up at her with his large brown eyes.

She nodded. "Last one," she said.

Dylan looked at his plate and made a face, "But I don't really like that one," he said, pointing with his fork to the small serving of egg omelet.

Ceil raised her eyebrows, "Really? It's a cheese omelet. It's one of my favorites. I bet you might like it as much as me if you took a bite. Do you know why?" she asked.

He looked thoughtful and shook his head.

"Because it's made with cheese, and cheese makes the eggs taste cheesy!"

He laughed at the word "cheesy" and repeated it several times. Then he looked up at her. "I like cheese."

"So do I," she said. "Hmmm, I wonder if you would be able to taste the cheese in this omelet?" she shook her head as if considering it.

He stabbed the smallest piece of the egg dish that he could find. Then, he put it in his mouth and seemed to be thinking about it as he chewed.

Ceil watched him, as did the other children.

"So, can you taste the cheese, Dylan?" Crystal asked him.

He looked at her and grinned. "I did! I tasted the cheese!" he announced. Then, he looked up at Ceil, and she smiled.

"Good for you," she said. She started to get up when the little girl, Crystal, stopped her.

"Can I tell you which food I think Dylan likes best?" she asked Ceil.

"Sure! Which do you think is his favorite, Crystal?"

"I vote for the apple!" she responded.

Ceil went around the group and asked for everyone's opinion. "Now, we should ask Dylan." She looked at him. "Which did you like best, Dylan?"

They all looked at him as if he was announcing an Oscar winner. "I think my favorite is...." He paused dramatically and then laughed, "the cheesy egg!"

Everyone laughed with him, and Ceil grinned and got up. She put her hand on his shoulder. "Good job, Dylan! I'm proud of you for learning to taste your food. Do you all know what that is called?" she asked, looking at each of the children in turn.

They shook their heads and waited.

"Mindful eating! And this table is the best at it!"

They clapped and giggled happily.

Ceil walked away, wishing she could spend the day just being with the kids and their parents and enjoying the camaraderie. However, she knew that the Thunderbird ritual would be soon and she needed to prepare herself.

Chapter 13

Kate & the Thunderbird Ceremony

Love & Peace Commune, Brookings, OR
Sunday, August 11, 2019, afternoon

Just after the brunch, two vehicles—Rob's sedan and an old
green pickup truck—drove up to the lodge. In the front seat next
to Rob was one of three large tribal elders; the other two sat on
either side of Sowi in the backseat, towering over her so that she
nearly disappeared between them. The elders were an incredible
sight, sitting solemnly in their ceremonial finery. Their vests
were covered with intricate brightly-colored beadwork, and were
edged by a soft leather fringe. People were drifting back to their
cabins or down to the river to swim or relax on what looked to be

a lazy Sunday afternoon. As they walked by, they stopped to gawk at sight.

A group soon surrounded not just the car but the pickup too, where they stared into the truck's bed, which contained several drums and an elaborately decorated shaman's shaft with eagle feathers and charms clinking together from beaded leather straps.

After a moment, the front passenger seat of the pickup opened, and Rob's grandfather, the tribal shaman Tom Manyrivers, slowly stepped out. He wore a butter-brown leather tunic over matching bead-embossed breeches. All the Native Americans were adorned with face paint, including Rob and Sowi.

Kate, Ceil, and Sky came out of the lodge when they heard the hum of excited voices.

"Wow!" Sky said, whistling appreciatively as he caught sight of the decked-out tribal members.

"This is going to be good," Ceil said to no one in particular.

Twelve of them would participate in the ritual: Rob, Sowi, shaman Tom Manyrivers, the three elders, Ceil, Sky, Kate, and three other commune members—Harmony, Arlo, and Vijay. As the group walked towards the woods, Kate watched as Ceil and Tom Manyrivers leaned together to confer in low voices about what would take place. Rob carried a backpack containing various ceremonial items, including the special cannabis, and smoking pipes, for the ritual smoking before the meditative labyrinth walking and dancing.

They walked into the woods and, as they reached the Goddess Tree, the group stopped. Grandma Ceil gathered everyone around, and she told the story of the old-growth trees, the labyrinth, and the commune's rituals and meditative practices. Her soothing voice and air of quiet command set a tone of solemnity for the ceremony to come.

When she finished, Tom Manyrivers signaled to Rob, who removed his backpack and began to take out the pipes, a small reed bowl with a tight-fitting lid, a candle, and other paraphernalia. He laid everything carefully on the ground in front of the Goddess Tree and ceremoniously lit the candle. The elders sat down with their drums placed before them. They silently listened to the shaman as he said a prayer over the group.

"What is he saying?" Kate whispered to Ceil.

Rob, who was in front of Kate, turned and murmured, "He's asking the Great Spirit to guide us in this ceremony."

When Rob turned back, his grandfather was done and his eyes were closed. When he opened them, he looked at Rob indicating it was time to light the large pipe that Rob had been carrying. When all was ready, the drummers began beating the drums in a steady rhythmic beat. The pipe was handed around and each person took a turn sucking in the smoke and passing the pipe, one to the next.

As soon as she drew in the smoke, Kate realized that this was indeed potent weed. Almost immediately, she felt a change, like she was suddenly viewing the world through thick aquarium glass.

"Oh, boy," she whispered, or did she? She wasn't sure if it was something she thought or something she said out loud.

Grandma Ceil must have noticed because she came over and put an arm around Kate's shoulder, then leaned in and whispered, "Breathe shallowly next time, Katie Rose, or we may have to carry you out of here."

Kate looked at her grandmother. "Agreed," she said. Her voice sounded strange and stilted, but she saw that Ceil heard her, and she was relieved since she felt very disconnected from her voice, as if it were something separate from her.

Sky stood close by, and Kate heard him say to Ceil, "I'll keep an eye on her. You go ahead and get things started."

Ceil seemed relieved. She turned to the shaman and bowed slightly and said, "Let's walk the labyrinth. We can set up the drums when we get to the center. There is a peace sign made of river stones on the ground there. It will be a good place for the ritual to commence."

Tom Manyrivers nodded and spoke in his native tongue to the others. Soon they were all slowly walking the labyrinth, spaced a bit apart and following singly one after the other. The elders began a chant, and soon they all joined in. It sounded like solemnly repeated holy words to Kate even though she couldn't understand them, but on some level, she realized that she also felt wholly connected to the others through the chant. The sound alone seemed to gather them and harmonize their movements. Soon each foot fell in time with the chant, and she was no longer sure whether her step was precipitating the chant, or the chant was triggering her to take the next step. She understood at a gut level that the spell created by the chant bound her.

Kate became so immersed in the chanting and following the weaving path of the labyrinth that she was surprised when the elder in front of her came to a stop. She was confused for a second until she realized they had reached the center of the labyrinth. She looked around at the familiar grove and followed the group into the center space, just large enough for twelve people to sit knee to knee in a circle around the peace symbol on the ground.

When everyone was seated, they passed around the pipe, person to person. An elder sat on one side of Kate, and Sky was on the other. The elder passed the pipe to Kate, and she took it and remembered Ceil's advice to "breathe shallowly" this time. She took a quick hit, kept most of it in her mouth and, breathed in through her nose, then let the puff of smoke out of her mouth. Even so, she felt slightly higher and was glad they were no longer walking. In fact, she wasn't sure she could comply if someone asked her to stand up, let alone to walk. Instead, she stared at the peace symbol and noticed with wonder that it looked like a rocket ship and thought about how it symbolized peace, not just for her planet but for the entire universe. How odd it was that all these things seemed so clearly interconnected to her right now for the first time. She passed the pipe to Sky.

A while later, he nudged her with his knee, and she glanced at him. He nodded for her to look at her grandmother. Ceil was looking intently at her, and in response, Kate wanted to communicate that she was fine, so she decided to send the message telepathically. Ceil smiled, and Kate felt sure that Ceil had received the message. Telepathy was so much easier than texting on a smartphone, she thought. Kate wished she could send messages to Cody like this. But then, why couldn't she? Of course, she could! So, she turned her thoughts to Cody. She realized then that she wasn't sure what she would want to say to him. Did she miss him? She hadn't thought much about him in the past couple of days. Even though she'd like to see him, to touch him, and to be with him, she didn't feel like she missed him. Huh. Was that normal?

The drums started up, and Kate found she could no longer control her thoughts. It was as if they were scattering into the air around her, like white dandelion floaties. She thought of Cody and oddly, it made her think about Rob. She looked around to find him as a new chant began, and then her attention was on the shaman who stood in the center and slowly began to dance, wheeling around, shaking the eagle shaft, but always keeping in time to the drumbeat with each step he took. Rob and Sowi joined him, as did one of the drummers. Arlo and Harmony got up and, with closed eyes, swayed while Vijay spun slowly in place. Kate thought she heard Arlo muttering 'Om,' and Vijay was reciting some Vedic prayer. It all blended with the Native American chants as if they were repeating the same thing but in a Babel of languages.

Kate had no idea how much time had passed–the shaman began to wail, and he extended his long, decorated pole into the air and kept time to the drumbeat with it as the chants grew louder and more insistent. Then, suddenly, he spun in place, and just as abruptly, he stopped. He extended his arms up towards the sky and talked aloud as if praying or beseeching someone. *God? The Universe?* Kate watched him so intently that she wasn't sure if she was even blinking. She could see that his eyes were glazed, and she wondered what he was seeing. Could he see the Thunderbird?

Hear the roar created by its flapping wings, see the lightning bolts shoot from its eyes? Was he in battle with the Whale that shook the earth and caused tsunamis?

She began to see that vision. She could see the fight of the great bird and the whale, feel the earth tremble beneath their struggle, and hear the deafening roar of the coming waves. She'd seen the destruction before and now she was reliving it again. We can't stop it, she thought. We can't stop it.

"You OK?" Sky whispered as he took her arm in his and pulled her closer.

The drums had stopped, and the shaman and the others turned to look at Kate. She glanced at Sky but couldn't see more than a blur of his face through her tears. She shook her head. "We can't stop it," she said quietly, her voice breaking with profound sadness.

Ceil stood up and came over to kneel directly in front of Kate. "You saw it, didn't you?" she asked gently.

Kate nodded, tears streaming down her face. "What are we going to do, Grandma Ceil?"

Ceil reached out and took Kate's shoulders in her hands. She lowered her face until she was right in front of Kate's, practically nose to nose. "We'll survive this, Kate. If we can't stop it, we'll do everything we can to lessen its effect on us."

Kate nodded.

"Are you OK, sweetie?" Ceil asked.

"We're fine," Kate answered.

Ceil's brows furrowed, and she glanced at Sky and then back to Kate again. "We?" she repeated.

Kate shrugged. "I... I'm pretty sure...."

Ceil sighed and breathed out. "Ah, yeah, that makes sense."

Sky leaned forward. "It's true then? Katie Rose, are you pregnant?" He turned to Ceil. "It's just like you said you saw in the timestream." His voice filled with awe. Then he smiled and said happily, "Damn!"

They stayed in the woods a while longer. Kate had no idea how long. She'd lost all track of time. Sky and Ceil stayed close by and she felt safe and protected.

Eventually, everyone got to their feet and the shaman gathered them together around the peace symbol. He said some kind of benediction in his native tongue, his arms raised high and his eyes focused upward, far beyond the leafy canopies above them. When he grew silent, it was clear the ceremony was over.

Chapter 14

Ceil's mother Esther has passed

Love & Peace Commune, Brookings, OR
Sunday, August 11, 2019, afternoon

Ceil led the group back to the lodge. They'd been meditating and dancing for several hours, but it seemed even longer under the influence of what she guessed was some very high-octane weed in their pipes. She would have Jade ask for some of the seeds. Maybe they could mix a new blend to sell.

As they came out of the trees near the river, she saw Nia, looking worried and loping across the compound towards her with her arms waving in the air. "Ceil!"

Her braided dreadlocks bounced off her shoulders and down her back. She was wearing a voluminous t-shirt over a pair of sun-bleached cut-off jeans. By the time she reached Ceil, she was out of breath.

Ceil rubbed Nia's back soothingly. "Take a moment and catch your breath, hon."

Nia put a hand over her heart as she gulped air. "Geez, I'm in terrible shape, aren't I?" She took several deep breaths. "Oh, my! I came to tell you that I just answered a call on the landline in the lodge. It was the nursing home, Ceil. I'm so sorry, but your mom has passed."

Ceil closed her eyes for a second, then sank to the ground. Nia immediately sat down next to her and put an arm around her. Ceil looked at her friend with a tired smile and a single tear ran down her cheek. She wiped it away with the back of her wrist and sighed. "I shouldn't be surprised, you know. Esther's been doing poorly for months."

"It's always hard when you lose a family member, honey," Nia said comfortingly.

Kate arrived as Ceil and Nia were getting to their feet. She'd overheard what Nia had said. "Grandma Esther is dead?"

Ceil glanced at her and nodded. "I'm sorry, Katie Rose. It would've been nice if you'd been able to see her one more time before she died."

Sky had overheard the conversations and pulled Ceil into a hug. "Sorry, babe."

"Her timing isn't good, is it?" Ceil said dolefully, her voice muffled by Sky's shirt.

He smiled bleakly. "She never was much for being accommodating." Then shook his head as if to reprimand himself. "Sorry. I shouldn't speak ill of the deceased."

Ceil shrugged and stepped back, with one arm still around Sky's waist.

"Anything I can do, Grandma Ceil?" Kate asked quietly.

Ceil looked around and noticed Rob and the group now coming out of the woods. "Could you take care of Rob and his people for me? See if they want to stay for dinner."

Rob overheard and shook his head. "I've got to get them back up to Coos Bay, so we'll be on our way. But thank you, Ceil."

"Another time, then," Ceil said and then thought for a second. "Rob, ask them if they'd like some fresh vegetables to take back with them." She turned to Kate. "Could you take them to the greenhouse and tell Jade to let them have whatever they want. It's the least we can do." She faced Rob and took both of his hands in hers. "And thank you for bringing them here today, Rob. I don't know if the Universe heard our plea, but I feel like we at least gave it our best shot."

Rob gave her a warm hug. "Ceil, the labyrinth is amazing. My grandfather was in awe."

"Tell him he can come and walk it any time he wants. He's a welcome guest here, as are you."

"I'll tell him. And thank you."

Chapter 15

Kate & Rob

Love & Peace Commune, Brookings, OR
Sunday, August 11, 2019, afternoon

Kate and Rob waited for his grandfather and the others to make their way out of the trees. Rob quickly explained about the vegetables, and Kate led the group across the compound to the greenhouse.

As they walked, Kate suddenly put her hand over her mouth with a look of surprise. "Oh, no, I just realized that my mother will be here for the funeral."

Rob looked confused. "What's the problem? Don't you get along with her?"

"Oh, it's not that. It's just that it's been a while since I've talked to her, and she doesn't know I'm here. You see, I'm not supposed to be at the commune. It was the deal I made with my parents and one of the few things they seemed to agree on. They both believe that Ceil and Sky and their commune are a bad influence."

"You're kidding," Rob said. "Your grandmother is considered one of the greatest psychic healers in the Pacific Northwest, and Sky...well, just look what the two of them have created here."

Kate nodded. "Yeah, it's just that my dad has a thing about hippies. And my mom never liked being raised in a commune."

Rob looked bemused. "But I thought you said you spent summers here."

"Yeah, but only because my folks liked to vacation with their friends in Europe, and it was inconvenient to have a child along. As a last resort, they sent me out here for a few weeks in the summers. They probably figured I was too young to be unduly affected."

"Good times for you, I bet."

Kate grinned. "I loved it here. It was...magical."

"Well, it ought to get pretty magical around here in the next week, huh? Listen, if you need an escape, feel free to come and see me. I am renting a little cabin north of Port Orford near Cape Bianco." He brushed a hand through his hair.

Kate looked at him, not quite sure how to take the offer. "Uh, thanks, Rob. Hey, we'll be seeing you here for the Woodstock Reunion, right?"

"Oh, Sowi and I plan to be here, for sure," he said with a grin.

"Good. I'm looking forward to seeing you...uh, both of you. It starts at 5 p.m. on the 15th, by the way, and you might want to get here a little early. Sky really keeps to the original timeline."

"What does that mean?"

"You'll see." She smiled mysteriously.

Chapter 16

Ceil & Kate

Love & Peace Commune, Brookings, OR
Monday, August 12, 2019, morning

"Have you told Cody yet?" Ceil asked Kate early the following morning as they sat opposite each other at the dining table.

Kate shook her head. "I haven't taken a pregnancy test yet, so it's more just a feeling than anything real at this point."

"Even without a test, if you think you are, you probably are. You can't hide behind 'not knowing' forever."

Kate looked down, inspecting her nails.

"You want some coffee?" Ceil asked as she rose to get herself a cup.

Kate blanched, and Ceil saw the look on her face. "That, my girl, is telltale." She headed into the kitchen. She added, over her shoulder, "Just saying."

"What do you mean by 'telltale'?"

"Coffee or anything with a strong taste or odor upsets a lot of women early in their pregnancies. Some can't stomach coffee again until after the baby is born."

Kate grimaced. "I have been finding coffee a bit off-putting lately."

Ceil laughed. "I was the same way when I was pregnant with your mom. I had morning sickness starting in the second month and it lasted through the fourth month, then bam! It was suddenly over one day, and I felt fine. No, I felt better than fine. I felt great! And that lasted for the next two months. Then when I got to the sixth month, I began to feel like a beached whale. I used to wonder why pregnancy couldn't be just six months long. Nine months is at least three months too many." She found a clean mug and poured herself some coffee. "Do you want tea instead?" she asked.

Kate shook her head. "Nah, I'm fine."

"I still think you should tell Cody, but if you want verification first, I can give you a pee stick, or if you want absolute certainty, I could do a blood test."

"OK, give me the pee stick, but whether I am or not, I'm not ready to talk to Cody about it yet. I'm...just...not...sure...."

"About him?" Ceil asked, studying Kate.

"It's more that I'm not sure what I want from him. Do you know what I mean?"

"I assume you're talking about marriage?"

Kate shrugged. "Did you and Sky ever get married officially?"

Ceil shook her head. "Nah, we never felt a need to. When I got pregnant, we were both committed to raising Summer together. We didn't need any official blessing."

"Really? Because Mom said there was another guy...."

Ceil looked at her in surprise. But then, she heard her voice change ever-so-slightly, softening as she asked, "Summer told you that?"

Kate nodded.

"What did she say exactly?" Ceil asked. She held the mug of coffee between the palms of her hands.

Kate paused, then replied, "She said you had a thing for a guy named Zeke."

Ceil smiled. "Huh. Summer never let on that she noticed."

"Daughters don't miss much."

"And you're wondering what the story was, huh?" She tapped her fingernails lightly against the mug, thinking. Then she said, "OK, but I warn you that it's a sort of convoluted story." She paused, took a deep breath. "At the beginning, a group of us in San Francisco became quite close. We started a commune in an old house in the Haight-Ashbury section of San Francisco. One weekend, Sky and I came up here to Oregon for a breather and to visit my Grandma Rosalie. And that's when Rosalie offered us this land. So, we went back and moved the commune up here and we started building all this. The ten of us became the core group of communards."

Kate nodded and grinned. "What do you mean when you say you 'became quite close'?"

"I mean, we were all very good friends, and we loved each other, and yes, I think we were pretty indiscriminate about who we were sleeping with. But keep in mind that we were young, and we'd bought into the whole free love sexual revolution thing that was going on at the time. Thank God, it was before AIDS and HIV came into the picture." Ceil shook her head. She wondered if her cheeks were glowing pink. This was not a conversation she wanted to be having with her granddaughter.

"And what about Zeke? What happened to him?" Kate asked, leaning forward.

"Eventually, he left the commune and went home to Hawaii, where he started a very successful surfboard business, married his high school sweetheart, and ended up with a couple of kids, and later, divorced. He said he probably spent too much time on his business and not enough on his marriage. He was lucky to end up with a friendly divorce, and we're lucky because he comes back to visit from time to time. It all worked out in the end."

"But why'd he leave the commune?"

Ceil leaned back. "Commune life wasn't for him. He wanted to control his own life and build his own business. You know: be the 'master of my fate; captain of my soul,' that sort of thing. I believe he also secretly thought that communes were cop-outs. He believed we should be living our ideals out in the real world, where they might do some good."

Kate stared at her. "That seems a little harsh."

Ceil glanced at her. "He wasn't entirely wrong, you know. There's something brave about taking your ideals out into the world and fighting the good fight for them: win, lose or draw."

"But you created such a wonderful, nurturing place here. That counts for something, too!"

"It is, and it does. But it's for people who are open to sharing their talents, money, expertise, and love; sharing everything sometimes. You know, not everyone thinks that's a great way to live. Heck, not everyone can do it."

"He wanted you, though, didn't he?"

"He wanted a marriage. I wanted to stay here." She shrugged.

"Do you regret the decision?"

Ceil stared at Kate for a long second. "Honestly? No...but also yes. No, because I do love Sky and the life we've had together, raising Summer, building this commune and the farm, and making a success of the business it's become. But yes, I regret losing Zeke in the process. I don't know what that other life with him would've been like, but a part of me would've liked to have found out." She looked down and then at Kate. "Crazy, huh? To want it both ways."

Kate shook her head. "Not so crazy. No, I don't think it's crazy at all."

Chapter 17

Kate begins work at the greenhouse

Love & Peace Commune, Brookings, OR
Monday, August 12, 2019, morning

After breakfast, Kate hurried over to the greenhouse to begin working for Jade and her crew.

When Jade saw Kate, she welcomed her and immediately said, "Come on. I'll show you the office. Follow me." They walked the entire length of the greenhouse, past table after table covered with tender young plants—rows of starter strawberries in little green cardboard boxes, bright green cilantro, green onion seedlings. Kate took a deep breath of the fresh green smells of earth and plants. "This is fabulous!" she said.

Jade nodded. "Best place in the world to work! And probably the healthiest, too!"

When they reached the end of the aisle of plants, Jade stopped in front of a three-step ladder that led up to the office, which was a small, enclosed room built on top of a platform a few feet off the ground. Jade pointed up the short ladder to the office door, which was held open by a rope tied around the door handle and latched to a hook on the wall behind it. Jade led Kate up the stairs. "If you move some of the posters and stuff from this front wall here," she said, tapping the wall next to the door, "there's a window underneath, and it will give you a ringside view of the entire greenhouse."

"Why are there posters covering the windows?" Kate asked.

"Cooper was working in here and he put the posters up because he said looking out the windows from up here gave him vertigo." She shrugged and pointed to the desk. "In the desk drawer, there are a bunch of orders that haven't been put into the system yet. I think they are from the farm stands mostly, but a few are last minute orders from our restaurant clients. First, I need you to double-check to see if the order is already in the system. Then, if it's not, go ahead and enter it. I'll stop back later to see how you're doing. I've got to go check on my work crew that are transplanting broccoli into the field today." Jade paused and added, "Thanks for helping out, Kate. We really appreciate it! Any questions for me?"

Kate nodded to the dark computer screen. "The app is easy to find?"

"Yup. Just turn the computer on, the app will open automatically."

"Any password I need to know?"

Jade shook her head. "We're a trusting bunch, at least, within the commune community."

"I'll let you know if I have any questions."

"OK, then, See you later."

"Thanks," Kate said. She immediately started removing the posters and notices taped to the window and then tidied up the rest of the office before sitting down at the desk, which took up most of the floor space. On top of the desk was an old PC monitor with a separate tower containing an ancient data drive. She reached over and turned it on and wondered if she'd have trouble working on such an antique device. But, after several minutes of flashing lights and beeps as it booted up, the screen opened to a software order entry application. She was relieved to see the interface wasn't quite as ancient as she had initially feared. She settled back to get familiar with the software and when she decided she knew enough, she pulled the first file folder from the desk drawer.

It felt good to be doing something for the commune. This was her chance to give back a little. But before she got really involved with entering the invoices from the folder, she needed to text Rob.

Ceil had mentioned at breakfast that she wondered if we could get together with him to discuss how he and his grandfather thought the Thunderbird ceremony went. She pulled her phone from her back pocket and typed a message to him. She was surprised and pleased that he answered almost immediately.

> Sure. Glad to meet up again. I'm working tho. Can't do drive to you. Can you guys come here to Port Orford tomorrow?

Kate smiled and nodded as she responded. She'd let Ceil know when she saw her later. She was looking forward to seeing Rob again.

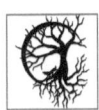

Chapter 18

Summer arrives at the Commune

Love & Peace Commune, Brookings, OR
Monday, August 12, 2019, afternoon

Summer arrived at the commune in her rental car. She pulled up next to the lodge and got out of the car and stretched as she took in the familiar surroundings. She paused, listening, and noticed that the place seemed quieter than she remembered.

There was no question that it had been a very noisy place when she was growing up here. There had been a lot of people coming and going and lots of chaos, with all the so-called adults acting like wild children perpetually at recess. So how much had it changed? She decided to walk around a bit to see for herself.

As she walked, she recognized some of the original treehouses built on stilts among the trees; "tree forts," she used to call them. Back in the day, there had also been dozens of temporary structures–tents and lean-tos with rain tarps thrown over–that were used during the summer months when the population would swell. In fact, when the commune was at its zenith, there had been a lot of people living here: adults, of course, but lots of children, too. That was one difference. Ceil recently mentioned that there were only about twenty children living at the commune year-round now. Sure, they'd get a crowd on summer weekends when the population would balloon with a bunch of 'part-time hippies.' They were the folks who showed up to party and smoke weed in order to forget their nine-to-five lives back in the straight world for a little while. But to Summer, they never counted as real communards.

The lodge building dominated the central part of the compound. It was an imposing structure and had been the largest building in the commune until the greenhouses were added years later. Summer had been born in the loft area above the main floor of the lodge. And her bedroom had been down the hall from Ceil and Sky's, in one of the several small bedrooms on the second floor behind the loft. The lodge loomed large in her life growing up here. It was where she ate nearly every meal and where she had been home-schooled along with the ever-changing array of children.

It was no secret that Summer hadn't enjoyed being raised in a commune. There had always been too many people around and way too much sharing. It's not that she wasn't a giving person, but they expected her to share everything–her clothes, her few toys, her bedroom, even her bed! When hippies with children arrived in the middle of the night with no place to sleep, Ceil would come into her room and whisper, "Summer, scoot over and let this little one sleep next to you. Just for tonight. We'll find a place for the family tomorrow." And Summer would grudgingly move over and let the child in. Most were dirty and had the funky smell of Peter Pan's Lost Boys from their irregular bathing and living outdoors. Sometimes they'd wet the bed, and she'd wake up with a start in the warm urine-drenched sheets. Summer shuddered. No, she wouldn't forget how glad she'd been to leave this place.

In fact, she believed that the best thing that had ever happened to her was leaving the commune to go to college, and the second best was meeting Peter and marrying him, because it had guaranteed that she wouldn't have to return home to the commune after college. She sighed. And yet, here she was at forty-two, divorced, and coming to the realization that the money from the sale of the house and the lump sum Peter gave her in the divorce agreement wasn't going to last indefinitely. She would have to get a job and start earning a living. She had been wallowing in her indecisiveness about what to do with the rest of her life for long enough. It was time to get on with it.

So, when Ceil called to ask her to come for Esther's funeral and to spend some time with Sky, Summer knew what she had to do. After the funeral, she would stay on at the commune while she looked for a job, hopefully one with a career.

Ceil and Sky would be thrilled to have her stay on, even though Summer cringed at the thought. It was her worst fears come true, after all–having to come back and live in the commune again. But she was determined to put a smile on her face. She would do this, and she would make the best of it. Then, as soon as she found the right job, she would leave and get on with the next chapter of her life. She didn't know yet what that life would be...or where, but she was sure it would be better than slowly going broke in Boston.

She turned and headed back towards the lodge to look for her mother and to broach the subject of staying on after the funeral. Just as she got close to the building, she saw Nia waving to her. She grinned and waved back. To Summer, Nia had practically been her second mother.

They greeted each other warmly with an extra-long hug. Nia stepped back and looked at Summer from head to foot. "You are still a very pretty young woman, Summer Rain."

Summer grimaced. "Not so young anymore, Nia. I just turned forty-two."

"I know. I was there the day you were born."

"You and Ceil," Summer shook her head. "What a pair you were."

Nia gave her a devilish grin of acknowledgement, then her face took on a more serious look. "Summer, I wanted to catch you before you talk to Ceil. She will need some help with this funeral thing and dealing with your Uncle Spencer."

Summer frowned. "Uncle Spencer?"

"Yeah. He was at the nursing home this past week when Ceil went for her regular visit. Him being there was very unexpected. He took Ceil aside and told her that we could lose all this," Nia said, her arm encompassing the lodge and commune. She frowned. "Personally, I think Spencer has wanted this land for years and now he believes he may get it. We have got to figure out how to stop him."

"But I thought Rosalie gave the land to Ceil. How can he take it?"

"Apparently, there's always been a question about who owns it. Your Great Grandma Rosalie inherited the land from her husband when he died and she let us homestead on it all these years. But Ceil never had the deed in her hand, and she doesn't know what it says. Rosalie often told Ceil she would leave the land to her–that was always her intention–but she didn't leave a will that anyone could find. You may remember that she had a stroke and died pretty suddenly."

Summer nodded. "Has the title turned up now that Esther is gone?"

Nia shrugged. "We don't know. Ceil and Spencer have an appointment with Esther's lawyer for the reading of the will on Friday morning. We'll know more then, I guess."

"What about Uncle Spencer? Is he still in Brookings?"

"I think he returned home to New York over the weekend. But he'll be back for the funeral. His wife, Audrey, left a message saying they were chartering a plane and would be here in time for the funeral on Thursday morning."

"Chartering a plane, huh? It sounds like he's already spending his inheritance, huh?"

Nia nodded, her lips pursed in disapproval.

"This is going to be a crazy week, isn't it?" Summer said.

"Yeah," Nia sighed. "First the funeral and then we have the Woodstock Reunion."

"Huh?"

"The Woodstock Reunion! Oh, come on, you can't have forgotten our end-of-summer bash. It's going to be a big one this year, too, what with it being the forty-fifth anniversary of the commune. So, it's a double-header—celebrating Woodstock AND celebrating us." Nia laughed.

"Oh, geez, I forgot all about that thing," Summer said.

"Tsk, I can't believe you forgot! It'll be the best one yet. Too bad we have the funeral right at the start of it, but," she shrugged, "life is strange like that sometimes, isn't it?"

Summer nodded. "Where is Ceil right now?"

Nia gestured towards the woods. "Walking the labyrinth. With Sky."

Summer caught her eye. "Ceil told me about his doctor's appointment. How's he doing?"

"He's tired a lot, but he doesn't complain. You know Sky."

"What's the latest on how long he has?" Summer asked, her eyes beginning to tear up. She blinked quickly to stop them.

Nia shook her head again. "Not sure. But when the Universe calls him, he'll be ready." She paused and looked at the ground. "I'm going to miss him so much, honey. I can't imagine this place without him."

"Me too." Summer bit her lip.

"Well, you go into the forest and bring them back. We've got lots of preparations to attend to. We've all missed you, Summer. Welcome home."

Summer felt a welling up in her throat, and her eyes grew watery again. She squeezed Nia's hand and turned to walk across the compound towards the forest.

She was nearly at the edge of the trees by the riverfront when she heard her name being called.

"Summer Rain?" a man's voice called to her.

Summer turned towards the tent sites at the river's edge, and after a second, she could make out Archer standing in a cleared area with a long broom in his hand. He must have been sweeping out one of the empty campsites. As she walked toward him, she noticed that he seemed a little more stooped, as if his body was slowly losing its struggle to stay upright. Sweet Archer. People underestimated him. Sure, Summer was aware that the drugs he'd consumed over the years had taken their toll, but she knew that he was stronger and craftier than anyone suspected.

She walked over to him, and he wrapped her in a warm embrace. He was so thin that she could almost count his ribs under his frayed jean jacket. "It's so good to see you, Archer! How are you?"

He studied her face. "Not bad now that I've seen you again. You look like a princess, Summer Rain. I knew you'd come floating back through here like a fairy-tale character."

"Some fairy tale," she said with a laugh. "My prince turned back into a toad, I'm afraid."

His smile faded. "I was sorry when I heard about that," he said as he studied the ground. Then he looked up and met Summer's eyes again. "Doesn't matter. You're still the princess I always knew you'd become."

"So, it's happily ever after anyway, huh?"

"The best stories end that way, don't you think?" he asked, and then he looked thoughtful as if the truth of the statement was only then becoming clear to him.

Summer loved Archer. He was one of her very best memories of living in the commune. He had been a sort of make-shift babysitter to her when she was very young. She'd heard others talk about how he'd follow her around when she was a toddler, keeping her out of trouble. And when she was older, he collected her and some of the other kids and taught them survival skills: archery, knot-tying, and even, climbing the big trees. But it wasn't all teaching and guiding; there were other times when he'd patiently let her braid his long hair, and then he'd join in with the kids and play dress-up and make-believe. He always seemed delighted and surprised at their imagination and their elaborate games of pretend.

When Archer returned from Vietnam, he could've gone back to live with his family in the Midwest if he'd wanted to. But he landed in San Francisco during the 1967's Summer of Love. Later, when he met Sky and Ceil and stayed at their San Francisco commune, he knew these were his people and that he'd found his forever home.

Summer remembered another hidden side of him. He had always had a dozen secret projects going on in the woods or behind the greenhouses that kept him busy. He tinkered with cameras and radios for fun, and turned fallen trees into fantastical forts, bird houses, and furniture. He was a man of many talents, and as a teenager, she had been one of his most willing apprentices. She wondered if he was still the secretive artisan of old.

"Have you seen Ceil and Sky?" she asked him. "I wanted to let them know I'm here."

He pointed towards the woods, and as if on command, Ceil and Sky strolled out of the dimness of the forest and into a circle of sunlight.

Summer told Archer she'd see him later and turned to watch her parents walking towards her. They were in the middle of some discussion and then Ceil looked up and smiled broadly when she recognized Summer. She waved excitedly. "Summer! Summer!" She grabbed Sky's hand and pulled him along.

There were long welcoming hugs from Sky and Ceil. Then, finally, Summer stepped back and eyed them. "You both look well," she said tentatively.

Ceil and Sky glanced at each other for the briefest moment, then Ceil nodded. "'So far, so good,' as they say. Thanks for coming so quickly, sweetie."

"Actually, I was planning to come and see you anyway, but Grandma Esther's funeral moved up my plans a bit."

Ceil looked at her quizzically.

"If it's OK with you guys, I may stay on a while after the funeral." She waited, letting the words hang in the air.

Ceil looked surprised. "Really?" She stared at Summer for a full second as if trying to decipher the reasons behind her wanting to stay on, then added, "If you're serious, honey, I think that'd be great." Then she nodded and broke into a smile. "Really! We'd love it if you stayed on a while."

Summer felt her shoulders relax. She could see that Ceil meant it.

Sky glanced from one to the other and then laughed. "All I can say is that it's great having both you and Katie here!"

It was Summer's turn to look surprised. "Kate's here? For the funeral, you mean?"

Ceil's eyebrows rose for a second, and then she looked down. "Well, actually, Katie's been here since Saturday. Apparently, she needed a break from her hiking trip."

Summer frowned. "She did? It's odd she didn't call to let me know," she said. She shook her head. "Peter will go ballistic when he finds out she's here. He specifically told her to stay away from the commune."

"Yeah, because we're bad influences on her. We heard about that," Ceil said and put her arm around Summer's waist to lead her back towards the compound. "Anyway, she needed to talk to us, so she came," she finished vaguely.

Summer walked with Ceil and Sky to the lodge in silence. When they got close, she asked, "So, tell me what's going on with Kate, Ceil."

Ceil's hands waved around as she said, "Oh, she's been helping out in the greenhouse...."

"No, I meant why did she come here in the first place?"

Ceil stopped and looked at Summer with a serious expression. "She had a weird experience on the trail and came down here to talk with us about it." She paused and added, "Summer, I really think you need to hear about it from her."

Summer's forehead wrinkled with concern, "A weird experience? What kind of experience?"

Ceil sighed. "She'll have to give you the details, but she woke up one morning with visions of tsunamis and earthquakes...."

She stared at her mother and Ceil stopped speaking. Summer closed her eyes for a second. "Oh, God! Now you're going to tell me this is that god-damned Gift thing, aren't you?"

Sky started to speak, "Honey...."

But Ceil interrupted, "Yes, Summer, as a matter of fact, Kate seems to have inherited 'The Gift'."

"Oh, Lord," Summer responded with a long sigh and dramatic rolling of her eyes.

Ceil ignored her response and continued, "Summer, get over it! Anyway, there's more. We had a Thunderbird ritual yesterday in the labyrinth. But we didn't get a chance to discuss it because we heard about your grandmother's passing just as we were returning from the forest. Kate's arranged with her friend, Rob Manyrivers, for us to meet up tomorrow to discuss how he and the shaman thought it went."

Summer stared at her mother for a second as she felt her anger bubbling to the surface. "Oh, for God's sakes, Ceil! Please tell me you haven't sucked her into a lot of your New Age mumbo-jumbo!"

Ceil's eyes' narrowed. "Hey, don't give me that look, Summer Rain. Just remember that you're on my turf now, so maybe you're the one who's out of step for a change, huh?" Her eyebrows raised as she stared Summer down. Then her voice softened slightly as she added, "Anyway, Kate is probably in the lodge helping Nia set up for dinner. Go and talk to her." Her voice changed to an irritating smug tone as she added, "You're her mother, after all."

Sky stepped between them and immediately changed the subject, "I tell you, Summer, we're really glad for Katie's help right now, too. Every day, more people are arriving. We're going to be bursting at the seams by the end of the week."

Summer sighed, trying hard to let go of her resentment. She didn't want to push her mother too far. Not yet. "The Woodstock Reunion," she said with a weary sigh.

"Exactly right." Sky waved a hand in the air. "Heck, it'd be hectic enough around here without having to throw a funeral into the mix."

Summer perked up. "Speaking of the funeral, when does Uncle Spencer get here?" she asked, glancing from Sky to her mother and back.

Ceil answered. "I called him to tell him about Esther's passing, and he said he'd be here for the funeral on Thursday. The crazy part is that he was just here last week! He was at the nursing home when I went for my weekly visit with Esther!"

"Nia mentioned that. She said he asked you about the commune's land," Summer said. She watched her mother's face for her reaction.

Ceil's head dipped. "Kind of presumptuous, I thought."

"But did Rosalie ever sign the title over to you?" Summer pressed.

"I never saw it," Ceil said as they reached the lodge. "But we have an appointment with her lawyer, Crandall, for the reading of the will on Friday. We'll find out then if Crandall has it."

"Good," Summer said, and added, "I'm coming with you."

Summer would have liked to get more details, but as they entered the lodge, she saw it was total mayhem with people milling around and whooping as they greeted old friends. Everyone seemed to be dressed in a flashback of 1960's hippie regalia—faded tie-dye t-shirts, peace medallion necklaces, cutoff jeans, granny dresses, and their hair adorned with daisy-chain headdresses. She smiled at the utter insanity of these alleged adults dressed like they were going to a hippie costume party.

She caught a glimpse of Kate in the kitchen hunched over a soup pot stirring and chatting with an older woman. Was that Fern? Yes, it was. Just then, Fern caught sight of Summer and waved at her with a huge smile. Fern was another of the original group who had been at the commune from the beginning. Summer had fond memories of her. One spring, when Summer was four, Fern taught her to write her name and to do some simple arithmetic. She remembered the pride and sense of competency she'd felt at having mastered tasks so innately meaningful.

Kate turned then and caught sight of her mother. Summer could see the uncertainty in Kate's eyes, and it gave a jolt to her heart. It was apparent that Kate wasn't sure how she would react.

"Ceil tells me you've been here since Saturday," Summer said, looking stern. "Does your father know you're here?"

Kate shook her head. "No, and please don't tell him, OK?"

"What happened on the hike? And where's Cody?"

"Mom, I'll fill you in later, OK? As for Cody, he's still on the trail."

"Alright. We need a good talk, huh?" She paused. "It's good to see you, honey." She squeezed her daughter's shoulders and she felt her daughter relax a little.

Kate turned and returned to the kitchen and Summer watched her daughter for several seconds and marveled at how easily she seemed to have meshed into life here.

This was going to be an interesting experience being back at the commune. But now that she was here, she wasn't sure whether she was looking forward to it or dreading it.

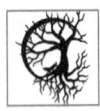

Chapter 19

Summer settles in

Love & Peace Commune, Brookings, OR
Monday, August 12, 2019, afternoon

Summer went upstairs, dragging her suitcase in one hand and balancing her backpack over her other shoulder. As she passed the open loft area, she noticed the music system that Sky would use to broadcast the Woodstock playlist. She smiled, thinking of his obsession with the exact time of each singer or group's performance. But, of course, that led to thoughts of Zeke because he was Sky's best friend and the two of them were nearly always in charge of the music.

Zeke. That was a name from the past. She knew he came back to the commune almost every year. After all, he was Sky's best friend and a close friend of Ceil's, too, which Summer had learned the hard way one summer when she was a moody thirteen-year-old.

Up until that summer, she hadn't been especially aware of Zeke. He'd left the commune years before and had moved back to Hawaii, so in her mind, he was just another occasional visitor, not a "real" communard. Thanks to him, though, she would never forget her thirteenth summer. How could she forget?

Back then, she and Ceil had been constantly at odds over just about everything, and Summer had been growing more and more rebellious. She was tired of homeschooling and wanted to attend the high school in town, but Ceil said she was dubious of its quality. Summer had wanted to wear make-up and shave her legs. But Ceil had just laughed at her and said she was too young, and besides, she had a naturally beautiful body, why spoil it? Summer had wanted to watch TV shows like other kids her age, like Saved by the Bell and 90201, that she read about in the teen magazines she borrowed from the library in town. But Ceil told her the commune's only TV set in the lodge was for news and special events only, not for inane sitcoms designed to sell them stuff that "no one in their right mind needed".

It was one thing after another until Summer spent half her time bickering with Ceil and the rest of the time sulking. Then Zeke showed up from Hawaii and everything changed. Summer was old enough to notice something was going on between him and Ceil. The proof came one afternoon when she was in the forest and overheard them talking and laughing together. She snuck up to investigate and caught sight of them kissing. She had been so enraged that she immediately raced off to find her father to report what she had seen.

Sky listened, and when she finished talking, he said quietly, "Come on, Summer Rain, let's go for a walk along the river. We need to talk about this."

She stared at him, wondering why he wasn't as infuriated as she was, but she followed him. They walked along the river's edge, and just beyond the last cabin, they found a large boulder next to the water to sit on. He took off his boots and then his socks and dipped his feet into the water. "Ah," he said, closing his eyes. He looked at Summer. "Take off your shoes and socks, honey. It feels so good."

She sat down and did as he suggested. After a few seconds, she pulled her feet out. "It's too cold," she said.

"Just wait and let your feet get used to it."

She put her feet back in and moved them around, splashing a little. She nodded and looked at him expectantly.

He took a deep breath. "I think you need to give Ceil and Zeke a break."

She immediately frowned. "Why?"

"Because Ceil has the right to kiss whomever she wants."

Her frown deepened. "But doesn't it make you angry?" There was real outrage in her voice.

"No, honey, not angry. But sure, I'd like it better if they didn't care quite so much for each other. But, then I remind myself that without Zeke, I wouldn't have you. And that makes me feel like it's not such a bad deal."

Summer looked at him in surprise. "Me? What do you mean?"

"Let me tell you a story, he said and paused, tossing a twig into the water. He looked at Summer. "When I was in college, you know, back in the Stone Ages...."

The corner of her mouth lifted into a hint of a smile.

"When I was in college, I caught the mumps virus," he said. "When a person has mumps as a little kid, it's not usually a big deal. The kid gets sick, stays in bed, and then gets well."

Summer nodded and waited.

"But it can sometimes be more serious when you're an adult. A couple of months after I had the mumps, my doctor did a test on me, and he told me that I would probably never be able to have children and that the mumps might've caused it." He stopped and just looked at her. They were both quiet for several seconds.

"Wait," Summer finally said. "I don't understand. But you're my dad, aren't you?"

"Of course, I am. I was there when you were born, and my name is on your birth certificate. Ceil and I are your parents, and we raised you. But, Summer, I'm pretty sure that Zeke is your biological father, and I believe it's thanks to him that we have you."

"He's my dad?" Summer asked in disbelief.

"No. He's your biological father," Sky corrected. "I'm still your dad."

"But how come no one's told me about all this before?"

"It's a little complicated," Sky said vaguely.

"Complicated, how?" Summer pressed.

"Well, first off," Sky held up a finger. "Ceil never knew about my having the mumps in college. It happened before I met her." He put up a second finger. "Secondly, when she became pregnant with you, she just said: 'Sky, we are going to have a baby.' And she clearly wanted me to believe I was the father."

Summer stared at the water for several minutes. "How can you be sure that Zeke's the father?"

"There wasn't anyone else it could be."

Summer looked at him for several long seconds. Then she looked down and stared at the water moving around her feet. "So why are you telling me this now?"

He blinked and stared at her, obviously not expecting the question. "Well, I guess because I don't want you to hate Ceil and Zeke."

"Why didn't Ceil tell me?"

He shrugged "Maybe she was afraid you'd tell me."

"OK, then why didn't you tell Ceil about your mumps thing or that you knew about Zeke?"

He looked down and grimaced, then nodded. "Yeah, I should have. Secrets aren't good between people who love each other. I think I was afraid to."

"Afraid of what?"

"Upsetting our lives and maybe losing you."

"Wait. How would you lose me?"

"I guess I thought if Ceil knew that I knew the truth, she might take you to Hawaii to live with Zeke."

Summer blinked.

They were quiet for a long time, both staring at the water.

Summer frowned again. "Well, even if I might like to live in Hawaii, I sure don't want to live there with them." She looked over at Sky. "She wouldn't try to take me now, would she?"

Sky shook his head and smiled. "No, Summer, not now. When she didn't tell me Zeke was the father, she obviously had already decided to stay here."

Summer looked relieved, then she frowned again. "So why didn't Zeke want to be my father?"

Sky's eyes widened slightly. "Ceil probably never told him. I figure she knew how she wanted it to be, so that's how it was."

"Yeah, that sounds like her." Summer's jaw tightened as she stared into the water.

Sky nudged her. "What about you? Are you going to be OK with all this, Summer?" he asked quietly.

She lowered her eyes and shrugged.

The two sat side by side, listening to the babbling water and the occasional chirping of a bird in the branches above them.

"You think about it for a while. Tell me if you have more questions, and we can talk about it again. But, try not to hate Ceil or Zeke, OK? They love each other and I love them both. You know we all love you, don't you?"

She nodded and looked out at the water again.

He paused. "Summer, don't ever forget that love is the currency of life; in the end, it's the only thing that really matters."

Summer opened the door to her old bedroom. She flipped on the light and stepped inside, pulling her suitcase in and closing the door behind her. She was still thinking about that long ago conversation with Sky and was a little shocked that he was so open and forthcoming about sex and adult relationships when talking to a thirteen-year-old child. She and Peter would never have been that open with Kate when she was that age.

But Summer knew that the hippies treated their children differently; they spoke to them almost as miniature adults. Sky and Ceil were convinced that everything wrong with American society sprang from its childish fascination and prudery about sex and nudity. As a result, Summer knew more about the human body from a very early age than was probably good for her. Although she may agree with their assessment of American culture, as a mother herself, she preferred to wait for her daughter to ask for information; that way, she could be sure that Kate was ready to receive it.

Summer glanced around her old bedroom and saw that Nia must have dusted and made up her old double bed for her. The place smelled clean and fresh. She looked at the posters hanging from the walls—the Rolling Stones, the Animals, Nirvana, Queen, and Alanis Morissette. The room was like a time capsule of memories and conflicting emotions. "A teenager's room," Summer thought.

There was a soft knock at the door. When she pulled it open, Kate was standing there, biting her lip, her shoulders slightly hunched.

"Did you want to talk now, Mom? Dinner won't be for another half-hour, I think."

"Sure. Come on in, honey," Summer said and, waving a hand at the posters, added, "I've just been admiring my teenage taste in music."

Kate smiled as she glanced around. "You definitely had classic good taste."

The only chair in the room was a stiff wooden piece pushed up next to the dresser and looked so old and dried up that it would probably leave slivers. Summer waved a hand at the bed. "Have a seat."

Kate sat and Summer lifted her suitcase onto the bed and opened it. She reached in to start unpacking when she noticed how quiet Kate was. She slid the suitcase over a bit and sat next to her daughter, studying her for a second. "What's up with you, Kate? Do you want to tell me why you came down to the commune last week?"

Kate looked at her mother and shrugged. "Cody and I were on the Pacific Crest Trail, and I had a weird experience as I was waking up one morning. I knew it was similar to experiences Grandma Ceil used to talk about. I wanted to discuss it with her. You know, to see if it was something to worry about...."

"And was it?"

"Yeah, Grandma Ceil and I think the vision I saw is all tied up with the Cascadia subduction zone and earthquakes and tsunamis."

Summer resisted the urge to roll her eyes; instead, she kept her expression impassive. Even though she could not accept this timestream silliness, she could see that Kate obviously did. "And then you all had this Thunderbird ritual in the forest, right?"

Kate looked at her in surprise.

"Ceil told me about that."

Kate nodded. "We're going up to see Rob tomorrow to find out what he and his grandfather, the shaman, thought about the ceremony."

"Rob's the kid who drove you down here last week?"

"Yeah. Mom, he's a really good guy. You should meet him."

Summer wondered about this Rob fellow. She wanted to know whether something was going on between him and Kate, for one thing. What did it mean for Cody? And why didn't Cody come with Kate?

Summer's mind was made up. "Yes, actually I'd like to meet Rob and hear more about all this for myself. I think I'll go with you and Ceil tomorrow." She paused and then reached out and touched Kate's arm. "For now, honey, why don't you tell me exactly what you saw and experienced." She added, pausing to hold up three fingers in a sort of Scout salute, "And I promise I'll try to keep my skepticism to myself."

Kate shook her head. There was a trace of a smile on her lips. "Mom, you were never a Girl Scout."

"True enough, but you were."

Chapter 20

Ceil, Summer & Kate meet with Rob

Love & Peace Commune, Brookings, OR
Tuesday, August 13, 2019, morning

On Tuesday morning, Ceil, Summer, and Kate sat on a bench overlooking the Pacific Ocean in Port Orford, on the coast of Oregon, about an hour north of Brookings. Ceil was at one end of the bench, Summer in the middle, and Kate on the other side of Summer. Every so often a large wave crashed against the craggy brown sea stacks further out in the small bay, and sprays of saltwater shot into the air making the sea birds, perched along the top of the rocks, nervous and quarrelsome.

"So, what do you think?" Kate leaned forward to ask Ceil.

Ceil looked at her, worried frown lines creasing the outer edges of her eyes. She shook her head as if to clear her thoughts. "Oh, honey, I think we'll be fine." She smiled unconvincingly. "But I'm curious what Rob's grandfather thought about Sunday's ceremony."

"We'll be fine if all your hocus-pocus works," Summer said, turning her head, giving Ceil a stern look.

Ceil lifted her eyebrows as she met Summer's gaze but didn't reply.

"Come on, get real, Mom! You know that Grandma Ceil and I aren't witches casting spells, for God's sakes." She tilted away from her mother, but Summer took Kate's elbow and pulled her closer.

"Look, Kate, I'm sorry if I don't buy into all this New Age nonsense. I understand that you and Ceil want me to believe you have some weird psychic power. But forgive me if I think it's nuts. You tell me that you have been meditating together for the past several days, and you even organized a Native American intervention to stop the Cascadia subduction zone from setting off earthquakes and tsunamis. Don't you hear how crazy that sounds? What should I think? I don't see how meditating and dancing around with a bunch of Indian medicine men can prevent anything. Give me some facts, some science, some proof. How about something meaningful? For instance, how will you know if any of these rituals and walking meditations have even worked?"

Ceil said, "When the earthquake doesn't happen, and the tsunami doesn't arrive you'll have your proof!" She let out a long breath.

Poor Summer had always longed to be conventional, Ceil thought with a sigh. It must've been so hard for her to be raised so differently when all she wanted was to fit in. Ceil nudged against Summer's shoulder. "I'm glad you're back, sweetie. It's good to have you here again."

Summer looked at her mother in surprise. "To be honest, this is not the year I thought I'd be having. But," she hesitated and added, "it has been good seeing everyone again."

"You're going to stay through Labor Day weekend, right?" Ceil asked.

"Yes, and then I'm thinking of heading up to Portland afterward."

"At least we'll be in the same state for a change. She looked over at her granddaughter. "What about you, Kate? What are your plans?"

Kate glanced at Ceil for a moment, then looked at her mother. "I'll be here through Labor Day, too."

"And after Labor Day?" Summer asked, her eyes narrowing. "You're going back to school, right?"

"I haven't decided. Daddy made me sign up for the Fall semester, but I... I'll see," she finished with a shrug.

Summer's brow furrowed. "Kate, you aren't thinking of dropping out, are you?"

"Not exactly, but maybe taking a break...I don't know yet."

Ceil interjected, "Let her decide for herself, Summer."

Summer looked as if she was going to say more, but she apparently changed her mind and sat back.

"Gorgeous view from here," a voice said from behind them.

The three women turned to see Rob coming down the hill towards them.

Ceil stood up. "Thanks for coming to meet with us on such short notice," she said with a smile. "I don't think you've met my daughter, Summer, Kate's mother."

Summer stood up and Rob stepped forward and shook her hand. "Glad to meet you, Summer. I've heard a lot about you."

"Kate mentioned you're working on a project for the university."

He nodded. "I'm a graduate researcher in geology at the university. They're paying me a stipend this summer to monitor readings at Cape Bianco on the movement of the subducting ocean plates off the coast."

"Plate movement," Ceil repeated thoughtfully. "So, I assume that involves monitoring underwater earthquakes?"

"Yeah, we have a seismometer that records all the seismic activity along and beneath the ocean just off the coast."

"Then you'll be the first to know if there's a sizable tremor offshore, right?" Kate said, glancing at Ceil.

"I recall hearing that if there's a big earthquake offshore, we'll have about fifteen minutes before the tsunami hits," Ceil said.

"Give or take," Rob answered. "The size of the tsunami would depend on the size of the tremor. The last massive one took place over 300 years ago, in 1700. We now believe it was an eight or possibly even a nine-magnitude earthquake. It was so powerful that the energy traveled across the Pacific and caused a tsunami on the coast of Japan."

"If we had another big earthquake like that, how large a wave would the Oregon coast experience?" Summer asked.

Rob said, "It'd probably be 80 to 100 feet tall depending on how strong the earthquake was."

Kate shivered. "That's what I told you I saw."

Summer locked eyes with her and then patted her arm in acknowledgment. She turned to look at Rob. "You may as well know, Rob, I'm not a believer in this Thunderbird mumbo-jumbo that was supposed to prevent this catastrophe somehow. But I am still interested in knowing what we could do to prepare for it, if it does occur."

"The problem we have along the Pacific Coast is a lack of an early warning system." He shook his head. "Coastal towns have invested in sirens, particularly after the 1964 Alaskan earthquake that caused a small tsunami along our shores, and there was a lot of renewed interest after the Japanese earthquake in 2011, which caused a lot of damage in Crescent City south of here on the other side of the Oregon-California border." He sighed. "But, there's nothing automatic about the sirens sounding at the first sign of a major tremor." He began pacing as if he were giving a lecture. "In most cases, a town official must receive word from the state and they, in turn, must order the sirens to be set off. If the earthquake takes place in Japan, there are hours to prepare. But if it's shaking in the Cascadia subduction zone, there won't be hours; it'll be just minutes." He stopped and shrugged. "And that's too short a time to evacuate people. It will inevitably mean some people will not have sufficient time to get to higher ground quickly enough."

They were silent as his words sank in. The only sound was the birds wheeling around the sea stacks.

"Minutes?" Summer said. "But you could warn us, right?"

Ceil looked at him. "Could you?"

Rob rubbed at his jaw. "Well, sure, if I saw it on my monitors or got word from the research center. Heck, all the alarms up and down the coast would be going off at that point."

"Yeah, but not at the commune they won't," Summer said dryly.

Rob nodded. "Oh, I see what you mean. Sure, passing a warning to you folks is doable. I have the commune's landline number and Kate's cell number. If it happens in the next month, I can notify you right away."

"Thanks, Rob, that'd be a huge relief. If we can't stop this thing, it'd be great if we at least have enough time to evacuate."

"So, you don't think the ritual worked last Sunday either, huh?" Summer asked.

Rob shook his head. "My grandfather said the Whale was too strong a foe. He could hold him, but he couldn't defeat him."

Kate hung her head. "That's what I was feeling too...We can't stop this thing."

Summer rolled her eyes. "OK, I know you all believe in this ritual thing. And if no earthquake and tsunami happen, feel free to take credit for saving the planet. But, as far as I'm concerned, I plan to organize a tsunami emergency response plan at the commune. That way, even if nothing happens right away, the commune will have a plan of action in case it ever does."

Ceil leaned over towards Summer, and said, "I knew you'd be an asset to the commune. We've sorely needed someone like you who knows how to make plans and manage projects."

Kate grinned. "Yup, Mom's your woman. If there's one thing she does exceedingly well, it's managing things."

Summer felt the sting in Kate's words, but she didn't care because it was true. She was a planner and a capable manager and always had been. She felt relief, too, because she desperately needed something useful to do at the commune, or she'd go nuts.

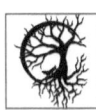

Chapter 21

Summer's Tsunami Emergency Response Plan

Love & Peace Commune, Brookings, OR
Tuesday, August 13, 2019, afternoon

Summer decided she'd begin by getting the lay of the land, and she knew Archer was the person she needed to see. She headed behind the greenhouses to look for him.

To Summer's right was a line of five small bunkhouses and several one-and two-room cabins that house the crew of itinerant workers when it was time to harvest in the fall. Farther on, at the edge of the field, was the forest. It was there she would find Archer. His small stilt-house was camouflaged among the enormous trees, but she still knew the way by heart.

Just as she had when she was a child, Summer slowed her pace as she reached the edge of the forest and moved as silently as possible. She knew Archer would be pleased that she hadn't forgotten. Even at forty-two, Summer wanted to please her old mentor. Soon she glimpsed his little house, paused beside one of the great trees perhaps fifty feet from the ladder. She sensed it was empty. Where was he?

"Hey," the voice came from right behind her. She jumped and spun around.

Archer stood before her with a silly grin on his face. "Princess Rain, finally, you're here."

"You were expecting me?"

"Of course."

"You snuck up on me, Archer. I guess I'm out of practice!"

He nodded. "You didn't have a chance. I have eyes in the skies now."

"What is that?"

"Follow me," he said as he turned around and headed into the forest. She noticed as he turned that he was wearing a backpack that appeared to be heavy and full. Of what, she had no idea. With Archer, she knew it could be anything.

Suddenly, Archer came to a stop and put his hand up. Then, he placed one finger over his lips to indicate silence.

She glanced around but waited patiently.

"We've had some visitors in the forest recently," he whispered.

Summer frowned. "Visitors? Outsiders, do you mean?"

"I've been keeping an eye on them, of course. Two guys with fancy vests full of knicks and knacks. They wander around the forest, busy and officious, poking and digging. Sometimes they stop and record stuff on their devices."

Summer wondered who would be wandering around their woods. It was private land, even if it wasn't well marked.

"Come on, I want to show you my viewing nest," Archer said. He leaned back and craned his head to look up, and so did she.

Summer noticed ropes dangling down the side of the enormous tree. "Up there?"

"Up there, for sure." He pulled off the backpack and set it on the ground. Opening it, he took out two climbers' safety helmets and several sets of coiled rope. Next were the saddles and harnesses, climbing line, and other climbing gear.

"I'm not dressed for a tree climb, Archer," Summer said.

He looked at her jeans and t-shirt. "You're fine. I've got some micro-spikes you can put on over your hiking shoes, and everything else we need is here."

She sat down to stretch the micro-spikes over her hiking shoes. Next, she put on the helmet, making the strap snug under her chin. It'd been decades since she'd climbed one of the big trees, but she knew the drill. She felt a thrill of excitement mixed with fear as she pulled on the harness and hooked herself up, double-checking everything carefully. Archer watched her, inspecting her work, and nodded. "You remember, huh?"

She nodded, but her heart was racing.

He set up his line launcher, and after a single attempt, he looped the line over the lowest branch of the huge tree, a hundred feet off the ground. Soon he had the throw line and climbing ropes dangling down next to them. He glanced at Summer and nodded. She reached up and took the rope, ensuring her harness was correctly connected to the pulley. She began her vertical climb up the side of the tree, using the friction hitches and remembering the instruction she had received so many years ago to climb slowly and keep her sights on what was ahead, not looking down. Archer would spot her until she reached the first set of branches. Then he would free climb and follow her up.

Her first steps up the tree felt tenuous, and her heart thumped in her chest. She closed her eyes for a second to focus and mentally reset herself, and when she opened them again, she felt ready. The only sound was her breathing, as she sucked air in and blew it out. Her sole thought was of the next foothold, the next pull on the friction hitch line, the winding sound of the line moving through the pulley as her feet braced against the bark, and she bounced gently in her harness with the friction hitch lines grasped firmly in her hands. She was surprised when the first branches came within reach.

From there, it took longer to get further up into the canopy, where the tree's newest growth flourished. The top of a sequoia redwood tree, hundreds of feet in the air, contains a miniature forest of berry bushes, ferns, and even a layer of soil made of decayed ferns, redwood leaves, and bark. Archer had built his nest platform tucked away within the canopy, and the view from up there was breathtaking. Once Archer reached the canopy, the two sat next to each other, not saying anything as their breathing returned to normal, and they looked around at a world of treetops. A salamander skittered across a branch next to Summer.

"I'd forgotten about the salamanders up here," she said.

"Crazy that they can live up here, huh?"

Summer remembered her teen years when the commune set out to protect the redwoods from the timber companies. She'd spent many a night sleeping hundreds of feet in the air in a hammock slung off the side of giant old-growth trees. It had been a lark to climb one of the great sequoia redwoods and a badge of courage to spend nights sleeping in the canopy with the older tree-sitters.

It was odd but she never shared the memory of tree-sitting with Peter. Of course, she knew he would've been appalled at that kind of illegal activism, so she kept it to herself as one of her private triumphs. It was a treasured memory that had nothing to do with her parents, the commune, or even Archer; it had to do with herself and her personal measure of courage. For her, climbing to the canopy and tree-sitting was more like a vision quest that young Native Americans go on or the first bear kill of a young warrior. Tree-sitting was that same sort of coming-of-age marker for her.

"So?" she finally said, glancing at Archer.

He had a dreamy expression as he gazed at the fat clouds drifting across the blue sky. He glanced over at Summer quizzically. "Oh, yeah. The guys." He reached into a hole that seemed to be dug into the tree bark and pulled out a small pair of binoculars. "I come up here regularly these days to check what's going on in our neighborhood," he said. "A couple of weeks ago, I saw these two guys step out into the open over there–see that small ridge and the clearing between those two trees?"

She followed where he was pointing and nodded.

"I watched them for a while, but of course, once they moved back into the forest, I couldn't see through the understory. I ended up climbing down and tracking them on foot."

"What were they doing?"

"Not sure. Up to no good, I'd bet," Archer answered. "They belong to your Uncle Spencer, you know."

Summer looked at him in surprise. "Really? Are you sure?"

"Yup. he was out there with them the week before your grandma died. Sneaking around, pointing to this and that, and he was nodding with that shit-eating grin he has." Archer stopped and shook his head. "Sorry, but I don't like your uncle. I wouldn't trust him as far as I could throw him."

"So, did you tell Ceil and Sky?"

Archer nodded. "They said to keep an eye out and to let them know if I see them in our woods again."

"It's worse than you think," Summer said, the anger rising in her voice. "Spencer seems to think he's going to inherit the commune's land now that Grandma Esther is gone."

"What?" Archer said vehemently. "No way!"

"We'll know more after the meeting with the lawyer on Friday."

"We have to stop him, Summer Rain! He can't waltz in and take our land; not without a fight!"

"We will, Archer. We will."

Chapter 22

Spencer at the Commune

Love & Peace Commune, Brookings, OR
Wednesday, August 14, 2019, morning

The following day was clear and bright, and everyone seemed to be up at first light. Revelers had been trickling in for days, and Ceil knew that there was still much to get done in preparation for the Woodstock Reunion, which would begin the following evening. Before that, though, was Esther's funeral which was unfortunately also set for the next day. A funeral and a wild party on the same day was not ideal, but neither event could be changed. So, they would just have to deal with it.

Breakfast was in progress at the lodge. The coffee urn had already been refilled twice. Ceil made a mental note to check on it again before she headed into the kitchen. She was pulling a gallon of milk from the refrigerator when there seemed to be a change in the volume of sound emanating from the dining area. During a momentary lull in the swell of voices, she heard the double doors of the lodge creak open followed by an odd quiet.

She came around the butcher block counter to find out what was happening, and that's when she saw her brother and two other men standing just inside the doors. Spencer was dressed in khaki slacks with a light blue oxford shirt. The other two men wore blue jeans, and one had a fishing vest over his shirt with pens, pencils, and a thick industrial tape measure sticking out of the pockets where the fishhooks and lures would typically be. All attention was on the men.

A chair squeaked as it slid back from a table, and Sky stood up. He walked over to the men and put out his hand. "Spencer. It's been a while," he said with a careful smile.

Spencer took Sky's hand. "Hello, Skylar."

"I'm sorry for your loss."

Spencer's eyes widened for a second. "Thank you, Skylar. I appreciate the sentiment. My mother was a formidable woman."

Seeing Spencer, Ceil grimaced but pasted a tight smile on her lips before heading toward her brother.

She leaned in and hugged him. "Hello, Spencer. I'm glad you're here. I assume you want to discuss the arrangements for tomorrow."

Spencer patted her shoulder. "Sure, we'll get to that, Ceil. But I'd like to get my guys here started on scoping things out first. I'm paying them by the hour," he said with a smile that didn't reach his eyes.

Ceil nodded to the two men. "Scoping out what exactly?" she asked her brother.

Spencer's eyes narrowed. "Mineral deposits, oil, I don't know yet...but I'm interested in finding out whatever possible development potential there might be."

"Development of what, Spencer?"

He spread his arms. "All of this, Ceil, my dear. This property could be put to so much better use than a hippie commune."

"Uh, Mr. Rodgers?" the man wearing the fishing vest interrupted. "How about if Russ and I wait for you outside." He nodded to Ceil, "Ma'am." He turned, and the two men, Mr. Fishing Vest and Russ left, closing the lodge doors behind them.

Ceil watched them leave and then turned back to Spencer. "So, you've been sneaking around in the commune's woods behind my back?"

He looked at her coolly. "Ceil, we both know that when the will is read on Friday, the title to these 25 acres will be mine. And since I don't have a lot of time to spend out here, I hired these consultants to check the place out so that they can let me know what sort of potential we're sitting on."

"Are you kidding me?" Summer interrupted.

Spencer looked at her for a long moment. "Summer," he said with a nod. "So, I assume you're here for your grandmother's funeral. It's good to see you again."

Summer's eyes narrowed. "Uncle Spencer, you don't own this place. Not yet. So, I suggest you send your lackeys home until you do. I can't believe you'd pull this literally the day before Grandma Esther is laid to rest."

"Honey," Ceil started to say.

Summer cut her off, "Ceil, he doesn't have the right." She turned to Spencer. "You know we could call the police and charge those guys with trespassing, don't you?"

Spencer's face slowly turned an angry red. "I'd hoped we could at least treat each other amicably, particularly in light of our recent loss," he said, looking from Summer to Ceil. "Apparently, being a family doesn't mean much to either of you."

Summer rolled her eyes. "Or could it be that 'family' means something quite different to you than it does to us?"

Spencer stared down at her but didn't reply. He turned to Ceil. "The reading of the will is Friday. You can expect my guys back here Friday afternoon."

Ceil frowned. "Oh, I doubt you'll want them here then, Spence. There will be over two hundred hippies here celebrating our Woodstock Reunion Weekend."

"Woodstock?" Spencer looked at her incredulously. "Are you kidding me? So THAT's how you're treating our mother's death, Ceil?"

She shook her head. "I wish I could take credit for the timing, but we celebrate our Woodstock Reunion weekend every year, August 15th to 17th. So, I guess you'll have to blame Esther for her timing."

"You're blaming our mother for dying?" Spencer's voice rose. "God! Where is your shame, Ceil?" He started towards the door, then turned back for a final shot, "I'm looking forward to clearing your freeloading friends off this land. I'm sure the state of Oregon will thank me for doing them a service."

He slammed the door. The sound echoed in the silence of the room. Ceil let out the whoosh of a long-held breath. She looked around at the faces turned towards her, then she glanced at Summer and Sky and said in perfect deadpan, "That went well, don't you think?"

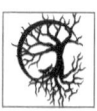

Chapter 23

Summer gets Ceil ready for Esther's funeral

Love & Peace Commune, Brookings, OR
Wednesday, August 14, 2019, morning

Spencer's arrival had been an uncomfortable start to the day, but Summer felt proud that she had spoken up to him. She was feeling almost cocky in this newfound persona. Being back at the commune had somehow given her a sense of freedom and permission.

As the daughter of a couple of hippies, the bar had been set pretty low for her as far as career or life goals. If she wanted something more than living on a commune, she'd get no help from them. All they wanted was for her to have a happy life and what did that really mean anyway?

After she left and headed East, especially after she met and married Peter, she spent the next twenty-something years living a somewhat circumscribed life. It had all revolved around Peter and protecting his precious position with the law firm. He made it clear from the beginning that it was her job to support and further his interests. She was glad that chapter of her life was over.

Summer had been busy all morning as she started working on an emergency plan for the commmune. She met with Sage in the greenhouse to ask questions about the business, the state of the harvest, and what it would take to protect it against a possible disaster.

Afterwards, she found Ceil sitting in front of her computer at a small table in the corner of the dining room. Summer stopped a few feet from her, brows furrowed as she looked Ceil up and down. She sighed loudly. "Come on, Ceil. I can see we need to go and find you some decent clothes to wear to Esther's services tomorrow."

Ceil was studying a spreadsheet, and numbers filled the screen. She looked up at Summer and frowned. "What do you mean? What's wrong with my clothes?"

"Really? You want me to say it out loud?" She planted her fists on her hips, leaned in."OK, woman, you asked for it. What's wrong with your clothes is the same thing that's been wrong with them since I was twelve and began to notice. You dress like a homeless person, and, I might add, you're not a young one." She paused and then added in an earnest, almost pleading tone, "Ceil, people are going to see you at Esther's funeral services tomorrow, and you need to look like one of the sane members of this family. God knows that Uncle Spencer and his wife will be decked out."

Ceil looked grim for a second, but then nodded. "Yeah, Spencer likes to be the center of attention. He turns into a regular peacock when there's an audience."

"So, you need to step up your game. That's all I'm saying. And I'm going to help you. Dressing for effect happens to be something I know a bit about."

Ceil smiled. "Well, honey, that's certainly true." She stood up and stretched. "OK. So, where to?"

They drove in Summer's car a half-hour south to Crescent City, on the California side of the Oregon-California border. There weren't many shops, but Summer found a decent consignment store on a side street that had Ceil's size, well-made clothes and good prices, too.

After some browsing and trying things on, they found an outfit that they both agreed looked good on Ceil. While Ceil changed back into her raggedy jeans, Summer paid for the clothes with her credit card. Putting the card away, she wondered when Peter would start refusing to pay her credit card bills? After the last big fight over an account he had closed, he hadn't said a word about the other ones, and the couple of times she'd checked, they were all current. Summer guessed she should just be thankful because if he ended up marrying the new girlfriend, things would surely change. She sighed. She hated still being dependent on Peter.

The divorce was much harder on her than she'd anticipated, even though she'd seen it coming. How come her mother hadn't warned her about the dark side of marriage?

Immediately, the question made her smile. How could Ceil give her advice when she had never been in a traditional marriage herself?

As they stepped out of the store, Ceil studied her daughter and asked, "Hey? What are you thinking about, kiddo?"

Summer had always found Ceil's searching look disconcerting; invasive even. She shook her head and glanced away. "Just thinking about Kate and wondering what's going on with her."

"What has she said to you?"

Summer frowned. "You mean beyond this crazy out-of-body thing she claims she experienced?"

"Well, that...you know, that's not crazy. I was wondering if she'd said anything more about her and Cody?"

Summer shook her head. Ceil looked thoughtful for a moment but didn't say anything.

Summer stopped and took Ceil's arm. She leaned in. "Ceil. Please don't do anything crazy at the funeral, OK? Spencer and Audrey would love it if we come off as a bunch of vagrant hicks and I really don't want to give them that satisfaction."

"Why should we care what they think? Besides, what kind of crazy thing would I do?"

Summer shrugged. "I don't know. You do say some really off-the-wall things some times." She unlocked the car and they got in. She settled into the driver's seat and looked down at her cell phone. "Kate texted me while we were in the store that she's found you a hair salon," she said and started the car.

"Kate?"

Summer nodded. "She wanted to help out, so she made some calls while we were down here shopping for an outfit. She just sent me directions, and we'll meet her at the place she found in Brookings."

The salon was on a side street and Kate was standing out front when they drove up.

"Hurry, the hairdresser is squeezing you in between two other appointments," Kate said as Summer and Ceil got out of the car.

It didn't take long for a shampoo, trim, and blow-out.

Ceil's eyes lit up when she looked in the mirror at her long gray hair straightened and glimmering in the hair salon's lights. "Oh my God!" she breathed. "I look like one of those cool hippies in advertisements. Long gorgeous hair streaming down her back; clean, trendy clothes...It's just a bunch of bullshit, but oh my, look at me!"

Kate nodded. "You do look pretty awesome, Grandma Ceil. Your hair looks great!"

Ceil smirked. "Who knew? Right?"

"Wait, I didn't mean that it doesn't always look beautiful..."

Ceil touched her hand. "I know, Kate. But now I'm frickin' gorgeous, huh?"

"You are."

Summer smiled too. "Just another great idea of mine. So you're welcome, MOM."

"Mom?" Ceil repeated, with an odd look on her face. "Remember when you tried calling me that when you were... what?...fourteen?"

Summer growled, "And you wouldn't answer...."

"Because I never realized you were referring to me, honey. Honest."

"Yeah, right," Summer answered, but without any bitterness. It had been a different lifetime ago, although she recalled how it had smarted.

Summer wanted to make things right between herself and her mother and with Sky's illness and poor prognosis, she was running out of time. It meant delving into her mother's secrets, but to do that, she had to get Sky's permission first. If she wanted to talk to Ceil about Zeke, Sky would need to be forewarned. She took a deep breath. She vowed to talk to him today as soon as they returned to the commune.

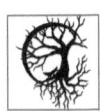

Chapter 24

Summer & Sky talk

Love & Peace Commune, Brookings, OR
Wednesday, August 14, 2019, afternoon

When they got back, and the three women went into the lodge. Ceil and Kate headed for the kitchen to see whether Nia needed any help with dinner. Summer spied Sky sitting in the loft above, and she took it as a sign that now was the time to talk to him.

He smiled warmly as she came up the stairs. "Archer told me you two have been busy developing emergency evacuation plans for the commune."

She nodded. "Hopefully, we'll never need them. It's hard to believe I'm doing this on the word of a couple of New Age soothsayers."

Sky nodded. "We've missed your clear-eyed skepticism around here, Summer."

"It's what's always been missing at the Love & Peace Commune."

He laughed appreciatively as he turned his attention to the laptop on the table next to him. It sat next to the machine that controlled the wifi speakers around the commune.

Summer watched Sky for a minute or two. She took the opportunity to really study his face and posture. She needed to talk to him before he got any sicker, and she needed to do it now, before she lost her courage.

She sat down next to him. "Sky? Do you remember the summer when I turned thirteen and Zeke showed up for a visit?"

She felt Sky tense next to her and noticed a look of wariness on his face. He squinted speculatively and nodded his head.

"I think it's time we talked again."

He studied her for several seconds. "Maybe we should take a walk, OK?" He closed the application on the laptop and stood up slowly.

Summer saw the look of concentration on his face and wondered if he was in any pain, but she said nothing as she stood up too.

She followed him down the stairs and they walked companionably towards the door. Ceil stuck her head out from the kitchen area with a questioning look on her face.

Sky put his hand up. "We're just going for a walk around the compound. Be back in a little while."

She nodded and disappeared.

As Sky and Summer walked along the worn dirt pathway, she thought about what she wanted to say and wondered how to say it.

Sky glanced over at her. "Want to go to the riverbank or into the woods?"

Summer saw that people were putting up a tent at one of the campsites along the river. She decided it'd be more private to go into the forest. "Let's sit under Ceil's Goddess Tree, OK?"

"Ceil would like that you think of it as her tree."

Summer paused and let him go first on the labyrinth trail. As they walked, she noticed that his gait seemed off but knowing that he didn't like to talk about how he was feeling, she hoped he'd let her know if he wasn't feeling up to a walk today.

They walked in silence and when they reached the tree, Summer found a soft spot away from the path between the ferns where they could sit with their backs against the trunk.

She looked up and was, as always, mesmerized by the sheer enormity of the tree and its spreading green canopy far above. She felt her heartbeat return to a calm resting rhythm.

Finally, she looked at Sky. "I think it's time you told Ceil about your mumps."

His eyes widened. "My mumps? But why now?"

"You once said that secrets between people who love each other aren't a good thing. And I think we have too many secrets that have grown out of your mumps."

"How do you mean?"

"First, I've never been able to admit to Ceil that I know Zeke's my biological father, so there's always been this unsaid thing between us. And then there's Zeke. Although he's reached out to me many times over the years, there's always been a gulf between us because I can't acknowledge out loud what I know about our relationship. And, last, there's Kate. I want her to know the truth about Zeke, but how can I tell her if it's a big secret?"

Sky's head drooped. "You're right, Summer. I guess I just figured after all this time, what did it matter?"

"The truth always matters."

"I can't argue with you about that," he said with a sigh. "I'm just afraid it will change things between all of us."

"I suppose it will change things, but maybe it'll be a change for the better. The truth is pretty powerful."

He took her hand and squeezed it. "I will always be your dad, Summer."

She looked into Sky's eyes and held tightly to his hand. "I know, Sky, and I will always be your daughter. Always."

After a moment of silence, he added, "I'll talk to Ceil. I promise. I just have to find the right time and the right words."

Chapter 25

Ceil at Esther's funeral service

Church, Brookings, OR
Thursday, August 15, 2019, morning

The following day was Esther's funeral, which was held at the small church in Brookings. When Ceil entered, she saw a small group of mourners already inside. Spencer, his wife, Audrey, and their two boys were seated in a front pew. Ceil recognized a few staff and residents from the nursing home huddled together in the row behind Spencer's family. There was also a row of older people whom Ceil assumed were neighbors and friends from Esther's past when she lived in Rosalie's big house on the hill overlooking the harbor. Ceil nodded to them as she, Summer and Kate made their way down the center aisle to their places in the pew opposite Spencer.

It was quiet and a little humid in the church and Ceil was soon squirming in the skirt she and Summer had picked out. She should've practiced sitting in it, she realized. And the damn pantyhose! She couldn't recall the last time she had worn pantyhose. Lord, she'd forgotten how uncomfortable they were. She rubbed her legs together in frustration.

Summer nudged her, leaned over and whispered fiercely, "What are you doing?"

"Sorry," she mouthed and grimaced, patting Summer's arm lightly. She heard her daughter release her breath, and that made her want to giggle, but she held back the urge. There was no sense in getting Summer upset, and besides, even she had to admit giggling would be unseemly at her mother's funeral.

She wished Sky was there with her. She ached for his reassuring presence. But he hadn't been feeling great that morning, so she told him to rest up for the party instead. It's not like he was crazy about Esther, anyway. Besides, she wondered if it would've just been a depressing reminder of his own mortality. And neither of them wanted to dwell on that.

The priest came out and led them in a few prayers and gave a sermon about God's welcoming old souls into heaven. Ceil only half listened. She'd always liked the quiet of churches, the moments between the priest's words where she could begin to sense the shape and deep silence of a sacred peace. She wished he'd stop talking so she could contemplate that holy peace some more.

Then suddenly he did stop. But it wasn't a quiet peace Ceil heard; it was more of a deafening silence. She looked up and saw the priest lowering himself into a chair at the side of the altar. He calmly nodded, obviously waiting for the family's eulogy part of the services to begin. She waited too.

Spencer leaned over and whispered her name and, when she looked at him from across the aisle, he nodded, indicating she should go up to speak. Wait! He had never mentioned that she was to give the eulogy! Her shoulders slumped slightly. She glanced at Summer and saw she had a stunned expression on her face. Well, at least, she wasn't alone in her surprise. She sighed and rose to her feet and smoothed her skirt.

It was so quiet that she could hear the echo of her footsteps as she walked to the podium at the side of the altar. She turned and faced the congregation and saw there were only about four or five rows of people. The rest of the church was empty.

The priest nodded to her. It crossed her mind that he looked sadder than she felt, and she wondered if he had known Esther personally? Perhaps he had visited her when hospice was called in? It reminded her how little Spencer had told her about the details of the funeral arrangements he had made.

Even so, she was glad that Spencer had taken care of talking to the priest. The thought of meeting with a priest after all this time? That would've felt awkward. She was spiritual and as faithful to her own beliefs as any Christian was to theirs, but organized religion had long since left her cold. She felt that whatever essential good there may have once been in the Church, it had been tainted by the human beings running it. Now it was a shell of itself, or was it a shell game, where believers had to find where God was hiding in all the catechism and interpretation.

Ceil needed to get on with the eulogy. She cleared her throat. "Hello," she said, testing the mike. She smiled. "Thank you all for coming. I'm Ceil Rodgers, Esther's daughter." She paused for a long second. "I'm sorry that I haven't prepared any formal remarks. To be honest, I assumed my brother, Spencer, was going to take care of memorializing our mother." She smiled dryly. "After all, he was her favorite." No one even cracked a smile at her wisecrack; all she saw before her was a sea of blank faces staring up at her. She heard the faint sound of rustling as a few people changed position in their seats.

She began again. "When someone close to us dies, we want to remember why they were important in our life. In that vein, I would like to share a few thoughts with you about my mother."

She paused and continued, "My mother gave me life, so if for no other reason, I am grateful to her for that. She raised me and my brother, Spencer, as best she could under extraordinary circumstances," Ceil said, remembering. "Not that we were poor or homeless or anything like that. I say 'extraordinary' because my father presented her with a challenging life as a military officer's wife, where she had to be ready to move from army post to army post every two years as he rose in the ranks and took on more and more responsibility. He was a West Point graduate and an Army aviator during WWII. Part of the 'Greatest Generation' as they call them now. Personally, I'm not certain they were the greatest generation, but they were raised to care about their country, and he willingly chose the life of serving in the military. He was promoted to Lt. Colonel before his early death at the age of fifty-seven." She paused again.

"My mother never had a career of her own; as was common in her day, she chose my dad, for better or worse, and made the best of the life that went with it." Ceil smiled. "Don't get me wrong. My mother was very good at being an officer's wife. As the Army promoted him, her responsibilities in supporting his career increased, as well. For instance, she was in charge of helping his subordinates' wives and families acclimate to whatever post in whatever foreign country they lived. She was expected to volunteer–to run the Officers' Wives Club, put together fundraisers for the orphanages they sponsored, plan events, and even drive the General's wife around because the woman was afraid to go off the base by herself and she didn't trust the Korean driver assigned to her. So my mother drove her around." Ceil rolled her eyes.

"My mother did a lot of good in the many countries my father served, and she deserves to be recognized for her devoted service. America should have a special medal for women like her, don't you think?" Again, Ceil smiled and paused for a response. She heard a chuckle or two and she saw a few of the mourners nodding their heads. She should end it there, she thought. But she looked out and saw her audience listening, waiting for her to continue. So, she asked herself what she was thankful for when it came to her mother?

She cleared her throat. "The truth is, the thing I'm most thankful for when it comes to my mother is that through her, I came to know her mother, my Grandma Rosalie. I remember how lost I was when I arrived back in the States for college. I'd flown halfway around the world—from Nairobi, Kenya. I got off the plane in Portland, and Grandma Rosalie was there waiting for me at the airport. She took me in. I spent nearly all my college vacations with my grandmother here in Brookings. She was truly a godsend in my life." Ceil nodded as if to affirm the sentiment.

"Grandma Rosalie accepted me for who and what I was and let me know that it was alright to be liberal and independent as long as I stayed true to myself. As a female, I don't remember ever getting that message in childhood from my mother—I mean, that it was OK to be true to my own nature. My grandmother enabled me and made me the person I am today," she paused and added, "whoever the heck I am. So, I am thankful—ever so grateful–to my mother for giving me Grandma Rosalie."

Ceil lowered her head and paused as if in prayer. She sneaked a look, and although she couldn't read their reactions, she knew her audience appeared confused or possibly appalled; she wasn't sure which. Oh, God, let this end, she thought desperately. Please, God, let this end.

Then an odd thing happened. God heard her. Of course, He did. She was in church, wasn't she? The doors at the rear of the church creaked open. A beam of light shot through the opening door, and people—her people—started streaming in. She blinked and then smiled in recognition. The people of the commune and a host of weekend visitors poured in and started filling the empty pews.

They filed in, wearing jeans, wild tie-dyed t-shirts, and crazy headbands. Some had flowers in their hair and beads clicking around their necks. They were dressed for the Woodstock Reunion and looked like the cast of Hair. Somewhere in the rear, a tambourine or two were being struck in time to the steps of the people entering. They filled most of the pews behind the funeral guests, and after they were settled, the tambourines stopped, and Nia—lovely Nia—stood up. She briefly nodded to Ceil and, without accompaniment, started singing a sweet and stunningly beautiful, "Ave Maria."

The entire church and congregation sat in mesmerized awe as her voice grew full and rich with the moving hymn.

When Nia ended the song, Ceil realized her own cheeks were wet with tears. She wiped at them, sniffed, and smiled her thanks to her friends and her commune family. "God bless you," she whispered as she returned to her seat.

Nia, still standing, then started singing the first words of "Amazing Grace," and she gestured for everyone—communards, visitors, and funeral guests alike—to stand up and join her in singing the hymn together.

Ceil saw Spencer rise awkwardly to his feet, looking confused and somewhat embarrassed. Ceil felt his eyes on her as she returned to her seat and she was sure he was wondering if she had planned this hippie invasion. *So, let him! It serves him right!*

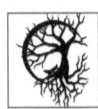

Chapter 26

Zeke arrives

Church, Brookings, OR
Thursday, August 15, 2019, morning

"Well, that was an interesting memorial to...uh, who was that again? Grandma Rosalie, was it?" Summer murmured to Ceil as they left the church.

"Huh?" Ceil answered.

"You realize you just gave a eulogy that was more of a tribute to your grandmother than to your mother, right? Why?"

"Honey, even though Esther was my mother, she did nothing but tear me down, belittle my dreams, and show disdain for every choice I made. The best thing she ever did was to let me spend time with Grandma Rosalie. It was Grandma Rosalie who built me up, made me dream bigger, and encouraged me every step of the way. I meant what I said."

"Esther was your MOTHER, Ceil," Summer hissed. "You should give her some credit. After all, you turned out well. Don't you think she had SOMETHING to do with that?"

"Aw, you think I turned out well. Damn! I never thought I'd hear you say those words, honey."

"Shut up!"

"No, really, Summer. I'm seeing a whole new side of you." She paused and changed her tone, "You have to understand that my mother was jealous of me because of the attention my dad lavished on me... I am pretty sure I'm right about that. Spencer was her perfect child, and she let me know that she favored him. He was better than me, smarter than me, bigger, taller, and way more worth her time and effort. But you know what? I had something that Spencer didn't have. I had the GIFT."

Summer made a dismissive 'tsk' sound.

Ceil paused and studied her daughter for a second. "Will you give me credit when I die?"

"What?"

"Are you going to give me credit for how well you turned out?"

Summer stared at Ceil for a second. "Wait! Are you manipulating me here?"

Ceil patted Summer's arm. "That's my girl."

Summer pulled her arm away and frowned angrily. Just as she was going to respond, there was a voice behind them.

"Ceil?"

Summer and Ceil turned around and Zeke was standing there.

"Zeke!" Summer exclaimed. She wasn't exactly sure how she felt now that he was standing in front of her, but she felt a bubble of excitement begin to fill her chest.

Zeke took two steps toward her, pulled her into his arms, and hugged her. "Summer, it has been such a long time!" He held her back at arm's length and looked her up and down. "Well, you don't look any the worse for the wear. Divorce becomes you." Then he turned to Ceil. "Hey," he said softly. "How's my other best girl?"

"It's so good to see you, Zeke."

He nodded. "You, of anyone, know I couldn't miss this reunion. Plus, with Sky..." His eyes clouded for a second. "Anyway, I got in this morning and went straight to the commune. Sky told me about your mother. I'm sorry, Ceil," he touched her hand. "Anyway, when some of the others said they were coming here to liven up the services, I tagged along. I heard the tail end of your eulogy, babe. You nailed it."

Summer's eyes met Ceil's for a second then she turned to look around for Kate.

Ceil said, "Thanks, Zeke. You know how complicated things have always been between my family and me."

Just then, Kate appeared. "Hey, where did you guys disappear to?" she said as she walked up to them.

Zeke smiled. "You must be Kate."

Kate eyed him for a second. "And you must be the infamous Zeke."

He reached out and pulled her in for a hug. "Infamous, am I?"

Summer pulled her car keys out. "We need to get back, so let's hold off this reunion until later. Do you need a ride, Zeke?"

"No, I'm riding with Nia."

Kate got into the backseat. "Come on, Mom, Grandma Ceil, let's get going. See you later, Zeke."

He waved at the three women and then turned to catch up with the rest of the raggedy group of hippies getting into an assortment of vehicles, including painted VW buses and a couple of ancient pickup trucks.

"Okay, Grandma Ceil," Kate said in a whisper. "I get what you see in him."

Ceil blushed. "He is still a good-looking man, isn't he?"

Summer started the car. "Oh, boy. This is going to be some reunion."

Chapter 27

Ceil & Sky after the funeral

Love & Peace Commune, Brookings, OR
Thursday, August 15, 2019, late morning

With Esther's funeral over, Ceil, Summer, and Kate drove back to the commune in Summer's rental car. Ceil couldn't wait to get into the lodge to take off their funeral garb and change into something more comfortable; something appropriate for the beginning of the Woodstock Reunion.

It was August 15, and time to start the party of all parties. They were celebrating the day when more than 400,000 young people attended the Woodstock Festival on Max Yasgur's alfalfa farm in Bethel, NY. The commune's plan was to keep to Woodstock's original schedule and play all the music, or as much of it as they had accumulated over the years, in the order it was originally played. That meant the first of the playlist would start at 5:07 p.m. and would, of course, be Richie Havens singing "From the Prison." Then the music would continue through the next two days ending on Sunday morning, the 18th, with Jimi Hendrix's final set.

Their goal was to play all the music from the original Woodstock Festival weekend. But, unfortunately, they didn't have every song because some of the songs were covers of Beatle songs and were never recorded under the band who sang them at Woodstock. "With a Little Help from My Friends" was sung more than once by multiple groups at Woodstock. And many of the original recordings turned out to be not very good. But Sky and Zeke did their best to play the music pretty much as the original attendees heard it.

This year would be particularly auspicious because, unlike the original Woodstock, this August 15th night in Oregon would have a full moon shining down on them and not a hint of rain in the forecast.

When Ceil got to her room, she tugged off the pantyhose and tossed them in a corner. If she never had to wear another pair of those, it would be too soon. Next, she carefully hung up the skirt and top that Summer had bought for her. Already Ceil felt a bit sentimental about them. They looked great on her, and she had so few dress-up clothes—well, none, actually. It hadn't occurred to her until she walked up and down the racks at that consignment store the other day that maybe she'd grown frumpy looking.

What could she wear tonight that would make her look good and maybe a little younger and appealing to Zeke. She noticed the interest in his eyes when he looked at her in the church parking lot. She couldn't remember the last time a man had looked at her like that. She would never expect it from Sky these days. They'd been together too long and she was pretty sure he didn't notice how she looked anymore. Besides, with his illness, he had no libido left.

But Zeke was the first man in a very long time who had looked at her with...what? Desire? Her heart skipped a beat.

She put her hand on her chest, closed her eyes, took a deep breath, and when she opened her eyes, she looked in the mirror above her bureau. She sighed. Yes, there was still an old woman looking back at her. Her hair, which once was a sandy brown, was more gray than brown, and her eyes were surrounded by crow's feet and wrinkles. Dammit. It sucked getting old. Inside, she still felt 25...OK, maybe 39, but certainly not over 60, heck, nearly 70, for God's sakes.

She dug through her bureau and found the long-sleeved deep purple blouse she hadn't worn in years. As soon as she pulled it out, she knew it'd look just right. She'd find her tight black jeans and wear the blouse loose and flowy. It'd be a warm night, but it'd be nice to have the silky soft sleeves against her skin. Having Zeke around filled her with anticipation; something she hadn't felt for a long, long time.

Sky. The thought of him filled her with guilt. She and Sky had so much good history, and she didn't want to let him down now. To placate her conscience, she decided to see how he was doing. She hurriedly pulled up and zipped her jeans and slid on a pair of sandals. She looked in the mirror and ran a brush through her hair. It might be gray, but it still looked good, thanks to Kate and the hair salon.

She found Sky in the bedroom next door, sitting up in bed. "Hi," she said, knocking as she walked in.

He looked up from the book he was reading, slid his glasses off, and set them on top of the book's cover. "Hey, Ceil. Boy, you look great! How did the services go?"

She sat on the bed next to him. "Well, Summer said I made a mess of the eulogy. Apparently, I talked more about Rosalie than I did about Esther. But then, Nia showed up with the rest of the gang, and she sang beautifully! 'Ave Maria' and 'Amazing Grace'!

It took my breath away." After a pause, she asked, "So, how are you doing?"

"Getting rested for the first night of the Reunion, of course. And I feel good."

Ceil looked at him but didn't say anything.

"Hey, I DO feel good, Ceil. And I am going to the bonfire tonight, and I will sing along with Tim Hardin and Arlo Guthrie, just like always."

"You won't be up late enough to sing along with Arlo Guthrie. Probably none of us will. He didn't come on until midnight."

He smiled. "Maybe...maybe not. We'll see."

"I heard you saw Zeke."

"Yeah. He stopped by before he went to the funeral services. Great seeing him again, huh?"

"Sky, you should've seen his face when he caught sight of Summer and Kate!"

He nodded. "I would've liked to have seen that." He studied her face.

She looked at him quizzically and shook her head. "So, what's the strange look for?"

"Ceil, I probably never would've brought it up, but yesterday Summer told me that I need to tell you about something that happened a long time ago."

Ceil tilted her head as she waited.

"So here goes before I talk myself out of it. When Summer was thirteen, she saw you and Zeke in the woods kissing."

Her eyes widened, and she grew still.

"Afterwards, she came to me all outraged and out for blood. So, I sat her down, and she and I had a talk about it. I told her that there was more to the story that she needed to know."

Ceil whispered, "More to the story?"

"Yeah, You see, I told Summer I had the mumps when I was a freshman in college."

Ceil looked confused. "I don't understand what that has to do with...."

Sky put up his hand. "A few months later, the doctor did a test on me and told me that probably because of the mumps, I was sterile." He stopped talking and waited for her to say something.

Ceil stared at him. "Sterile? But..." Then she put her hand up to her mouth and closed her eyes. There were several long moments of silence before she said, "So, you...always knew that Zeke was Summer's biological father?"

He nodded.

Ceil stood up, unable to sit quietly as her mind spun out of control. She started pacing, trying to catch up with all her tumbling thoughts. Then she stopped and looked at Sky. "You know that mumps thing—that it causes sterility, I mean—it's an urban legend. They've proven that it isn't... So, wait a minute! Summer knows about Zeke?" she said, half a question and half a stunned realization.

"We both know about Zeke," Sky answered.

Ceil looked at him, and her shoulders slumped. "Oh, Sky, I'm sorry. I've wanted to tell you. You...I...When I realized I was pregnant, Zeke was already talking about going back to Hawaii. Plus, I knew he wasn't ready to be a father, and I knew you would be a great one," she stopped. "I was right about that, by the way. But I should've told you; I should've told both you and Zeke the truth."

Sky looked at her in surprise, "Wait. Are you saying that Zeke doesn't know?"

She shrugged. "I never told him. You didn't, did you?"

"Babe, Zeke and I are best friends, but I can't imagine having that conversation with him."

Ceil sat down next to Sky again. She reached out and touched his temple with her fingers. "I love you, Sky. And, if I had it all to do over again, I'd still want you to be Summer's dad."

He smiled wistfully. "Yeah, I've always thought it worked out well. But I should've told you about the mumps. Summer is right. There shouldn't be secrets between people who love each other."

"I'll have to set this right with Summer."

"And Zeke?" Sky asked.

Ceil looked at him and finally nodded. "And Zeke."

Chapter 28

Ceil finds Zeke in the forest

Love & Peace Commune, Brookings, OR
Thursday, August 15, 2019, late morning

Ceil was anxious to see Zeke alone. She wanted to get this confession over with before she lost her nerve. She knew he was planning to help Sky set up the music for the party after lunch, and she wanted to talk to him before he got involved.

When she came down the stairs from the loft, she was momentarily stunned by the volume of noise in the main room of the lodge. Normally the place was quiet and serene. It was chaos now. New arrivals were streaming in, and there were loud explosions of voices, as people recognized each other and hollered over the crowd to get the other person's attention.

She smiled and nodded to people as she passed but didn't stop to talk. It was hot outside, but there was a breeze moving the leaves in the trees.

She walked towards the river, trying to remember which of the cabins Zeke would be staying in. She saw Nia coming towards her.

"I'm looking for Zeke. Have you seen him?"

"He was heading towards the woods a little while ago. He said he wanted to walk the labyrinth to get his head in the right place before he helped Sky with the music."

Ceil shook her head. "That's so Zeke, huh?"

Nia laughed. "Do you remember how he used to complain about all the work we had to do to set up that labyrinth trail? How he hated laying each of the border stones just right to make the path nice and smooth?" She shook her head. "Now he can't wait to walk it. How things change, huh?"

Things do change, Ceil thought. When she remembered her early twenties before coming to Oregon and setting up the commune, what she recalled was how exciting life had seemed to her then. Every day was dripping with tantalizing possibilities. She never knew what would happen next or where she would end up by nightfall. She practiced spontaneity by feverishly saying "yes" to every new experience and shutting off the rational voice in her head that wanted to analyze everything and hold her back. Watch the dawn from the middle of the Golden Gate Bridge? Sure! March against the war at the state house in Sacramento? Definitely! Get stoned while watching the sun sink into the Pacific from a clifftop in Carmel? Count me in!

She saw the look of bemusement on her friend's face. "Oh, yeah, Nia, I think it's us that changes."

Ceil entered the forest and began walking. She noticed it was much cooler among the trees, and she reveled in it. When she reached the Goddess Tree, as usual, she paused to reach out and lay her palm against the rough bark.

"Hey," a soft voice came from her left.

Ceil smiled and breathed his name, "Zeke," even before turning to face him.

He stepped out from behind the tree and took her in his arms.

She hugged him tightly and leaned up to kiss him. Afterward, she pulled away. "It's been a while, Zeke."

He nodded. "Sorry about that, C. I didn't want...you know, I never wanted to...be the third wheel. You and Sky..."

"I know. But I'm glad you came this summer."

"Because of Sky?"

"He's not going to be around too much longer."

Zeke furrowed his brow. "Yeah, I noticed how much thinner he is, and there's a sort of world-weariness that wasn't there before, you know? What do you think? How long does he have?"

"Sky's doctor said it could be soon." She shrugged. "I'd say maybe a month, possibly two. Probably not too much more than that."

Zeke stared at her for a long second. "God, I hate that this is happening to him. Is he in much pain? I asked him earlier, but he didn't answer me."

"Some, I think. But you know Sky. He doesn't complain. He's tired a lot; I've noticed he keeps to himself a lot more than he used to. He's slowing down and doesn't have as much energy as before."

"What about you? How are you handling it?"

Ceil looked at him and tears welled in her eyes. She couldn't speak; she lifted a shoulder and glanced away. They were quiet for several minutes. Then he took her hand and they walked slowly towards the labyrinth path.

After a while, Ceil said, "Zeke, I came out here looking for you because there's something I need to talk to you about."

"Uh oh," he said. "This sounds serious."

"Kind of," she said. "Zeke, did Sky ever tell you he had the mumps when he was a freshman in college?"

Zeke looked surprised and then amused. "That's what you want to talk about?"

"It's part of it. Sky told me that he was tested a few months afterwards and found out that he was sterile. The doctor said it could be from the mumps, although these days doctors don't think there's a cause-and-effect relationship." Ceil stopped talking when she realized she was starting to blabber. She waited for him to react.

He looked confused for several seconds, but then he smiled. "Ah, so that's what this is about! You're finally going to tell me."

It was Ceil's turn to look confused. "Wait. Tell you...You mean you knew Summer wasn't Sky's?"

He nodded. "You never said, but I wondered even back then. Besides, did I ever show you pictures of Janine?"

Ceil looked baffled by the turn in the conversation. "Janine? Your sister?"

He nodded. "If you put pictures of Summer next to ones of Janine at the same ages, you'd swear they were twins. That sort of confirmed it for me."

Ceil looked down. "I'm sorry I didn't tell you, Zeke. I should have. And you should've had a say in the decisions I made."

"No, you made the right decisions. Summer was lucky to have Sky for a father."

"There's something else," she said and paused. "Sky told me that Summer knows."

Zeke looked stunned. "Really? How did she find out?"

"It turns out she saw you and me kissing out here when she was thirteen, and she immediately ran to Sky with her outrage. So, he told her."

"You're kidding!"

"I had no idea about any of it. Sky only told me about his being sterile earlier today."

"It would've been so much easier if we'd all just been straight with each other from the beginning, huh?" he said reflectively.

"Back then, I just wanted to do the right thing for my baby, but I shouldn't have done it in secret. I'm sorry, Zeke."

"No need to apologize. You were right about me. I wasn't ready to be a father." He grinned and studied her. "It's always been complicated between you and me, hasn't it?"

"Yeah. I was greedy. I wanted both you and Sky."

"It's because of him, I met you," Zeke said. "God, you were so beautiful. So warm and funny." He leaned down to kiss her, but she moved away. "What's wrong?"

"Zeke, you know how I feel about you, but right now...I don't want Sky to feel like I'm abandoning him."

"He's worried about you too, you know. He thinks that you're going to fall apart when he's gone."

"He told you that?" She let out a breath, then nodded. "Of course, he might be right. I can't imagine life here without him. But then again, I couldn't imagine life here without you once, and I seemed to have managed just fine."

"I'm here now," he said, moving closer to her. "Ceil, if you want me to, I'll stay..."

"This time?" She finished and then shook her head. "Zeke, I'd love it if you stayed, but not because you think I'm going to fall apart, OK? Because I won't. And besides, you have your business and life in Hawaii. I know that."

"I'll be retiring next year, Ceil. I'm turning the business over to Kai. Once I do, I'll have nothing to hold me in Hawaii. My sons are grown up, and my ex-wife is happily remarried."

"How about we talk next year after you retire then," Ceil said, smiling at him. "Deal?"

He stared into her eyes for several long seconds. "OK, deal."

They were quiet, and then Zeke asked, "What about tonight?"

"Tonight?"

"Date in the treehouse?"

"Zeke, I...I don't think we should."

"Come on. I think Sky expects you and me to get together and maybe even wants it to happen. It might take a load off his mind, you know."

"Really? Or are you saying that to make yourself feel better?"

"I'm hoping to make you feel better," he said teasingly, pulling her in for a long deep kiss.

When she pulled away, she moaned. "Zeke..." She kissed him once more and then stepped back. "Z, let's remember that this is Sky's big weekend. We should do everything we can to make it the best one yet for him."

"His last Woodstock Reunion, huh?"

"Speaking of which, there's still a lot to get done." She turned to leave. "Are you coming?"

"You go ahead. I'll be right behind you. I want to soak in this place for a little longer."

She nodded and moved away.

"See you later, babe," he said after her.

She waved and then headed out of the forest.

As she walked, she thought about Zeke and Sky. She remembered the early years and the way it had been. Of course, she hadn't known about Sky's mumps. Once the group had settled on the commune land, all the women seemed to be getting pregnant except her. She had longed for a baby, and yet, she remembered how shocked she'd been when she discovered she was pregnant. She had been twenty-seven at the time and one of the oldest first-time mothers in the place. Ironically, it happened just when she'd finally accepted that she would be childless.

She had known from the beginning that Zeke was the father, but it was Sky whom she told. He had been so excited by the news that she didn't have the heart to tell him that the baby wasn't his. But, of course, as it turned out, he had always known that.

Zeke and Sky. These were the two great loves of her life. She didn't think her love for one took anything away from her love for the other. While Sky had been her partner for over four decades, they had never pledged to be faithful to each other. It was never that type of relationship. They loved each other and respected one another, but the relationship had always been very outwardly focused—on managing the commune and its people and when Summer was little, on raising her; it was rarely ever solely about the two of them as a couple.

And it wasn't just her and Zeke. Sky wasn't always faithful either. There had been a woman named Dove who had turned Sky's head. She was a wild, dark-haired young woman, at least eight or nine years younger than Sky. She'd arrived alone at the commune a couple of weeks after Ceil had given birth to Summer, and she had stayed for a few months.

Those were dark days for Ceil, but it had nothing to do with Sky and Dove. For the first few months of Summer's infancy, the world had been a confusing blur of exhaustion and frustration as she tried to figure out how to take care of a colicky infant. For weeks, Ceil had been a bundle of neediness and overwhelming fatigue. She depended on Sky's help to care for their difficult infant. She struggled to manage motherhood and everything else—staying on top of the commune's business and maintaining her healing practice.

For a while, she had become convinced that Summer was allergic to something in her breast milk, and it was making the baby squirm and cry in pain for hours on end. Little by little, she had begun eliminating foods from her own diet—whole grains, fruits, honey, and so many vegetables—that finally, she was walking around ravenous as she grew cranky and thin. She craved everything that she forbade herself, and she found herself resenting Summer and feeling so terrible about it that she'd scold herself for being such a lousy mother.

Then one evening, Ceil suddenly realized that Summer hadn't been colicky for a whole day. Hardly believing her good fortune, she had brought Summer into bed with her that night, fed her, and they both had their first full night of sleep since Summer's birth. However, when Ceil had awakened in the early dawn and reached out, she discovered that Sky's side of the mattress was cold. He hadn't come to bed.

He confessed later that he'd been with Dove. But oddly, Ceil didn't remember feeling jealous. Instead, she only felt a little forsaken and sorry for herself and cheated at not being able to share with Sky the joy of Summer's sleeping through the night that first time.

So, his new interest in Dove made Ceil feel less guilty about how little attention she was giving him. And eventually, things fell into place. Summer grew into a happier baby, and Ceil gradually adapted to the demands of motherhood. Then after a couple of months, Dove found someone else, and she left the commune for Portland or Vancouver. Life went back to normal for Ceil and Sky, and to her delight, Sky loved being a father. It was clear that although he might leave Ceil someday, he would never leave Summer.

Over the years, she and Sky had become a fixture as a couple, and they had settled into an unplanned monogamy in their relationship. But it wasn't from exclusiveness or any commitment they'd made to each other. Truthfully, there just hadn't been anyone else around that either of them was attracted to. That is until Zeke came back on his occasional visits. But he didn't return often, and Sky had always seemed to accept her attraction to Zeke. Ceil believed Sky knew she was where she wanted to be. Didn't he?

She turned it over and over in her mind as she walked back towards the lodge. The one thing she was sure of was that she didn't want to hurt Sky.

Chapter 29

Tsunami evacuation preparation

Love & Peace Commune, Brookings, OR
Thursday, August 15, 2019, late morning/early afternoon

Ceil walked back to the lodge passing near the grills that were now set up along the side of the lodge where Nia and her crew were preparing lunch. The skewered meat of the shish kabobs smelled good, and Ceil inhaled deeply as she walked by. The picnic tables were covered with bowls of vegetables and marinating meat, and Kate, Fern, and Jade were gathered around preparing the skewers. Nia was hurrying back and forth between the picnic table and the grills, taking the skewers as soon as they were ready.

Ceil waved to Kate. "Where's your mom?" she asked.

Kate pointed to the lodge.

Ceil found an assortment of people sitting around the tables, talking, and laughing. The tabletops were covered with an assortment of coffee mugs and empty beer bottles. She spotted Archer and Summer standing at the head of a table in the back. They were gesturing and pointing at a large map taped to the wall behind them, and the people around the table were listening intently and nodding.

"What's up?" Ceil asked Summer when she got closer.

"We've started making our evacuation plans. We've decided that the best way to protect the commune is to evacuate everyone up into the trees." Summer waited for Ceil's reaction. The others at the table stopped talking and turned to look at Ceil, too.

"Wait. Into the trees? Seriously?"

Archer spoke up. "Look, Ceil, we admit it sounds a little crazy, but if you think about it, it would be the fastest way to evacuate the commune at short notice. Those trees aren't going anywhere. They've survived tsunamis and earthquakes for centuries, and they can again, God willing. Plus, most of us who have lived here know how to climb those trees. We'd only have to instruct the newbies and give everyone else a refresher course."

Ceil put her hand to her forehead. "What would we need to do that?"

Archer nodded. "We've already started thinking that through. First, there's the old canopy platforms in the trees that need to be checked and maybe reinforced."

"The old canopy platforms?"

"Yeah, remember? We created a bunch of canopy nests back when we were tree-sitting to protect our trees from the timber companies. I got the idea of fixing them up when I saw your brother and his consultant creeps sniffing around in our forest. At the time, I thought we might have to go back into the canopies for tree-sitting like we did before." He paused. "So, I climbed up and checked them out over the last couple of days, and I discovered that most of them are still in decent shape." He turned to point to a diagram he'd taped to the wall behind him. "All told, there are eight platforms—one in the canopies of each of our eight largest redwoods. So, our first step would be to beef them up and get them ready."

Ceil nodded. "And what sorts of supplies would we need if we evacuated to the trees?"

Summer chimed in, "We would need to store enough food and water, blankets, and medical supplies for everyone, as well as some tools and equipment."

"Tools and equipment?"

Vijay, who sat across from Ceil, said, "Equipment like extra rope and guide lines, harnesses, and some basic tools like a hammer, screwdriver, nuts and bolts. That sort of thing."

Ceil nodded.

Archer added, "Once we have the canopy platforms ready, we will need to get all the supplies up in the trees. It'll take some time and muscle, but we have enough people here this weekend to really get things rolling, so I think it's very doable." Archer was quiet for a few minutes as a few people nodded and others looked thoughtful. Then he broke the silence, "But, Ceil, it's not just the evacuation into the trees that we need to be thinking of."

"I'm listening. What else?"

"If we're talking earthquakes and tsunami flooding, we need to figure out how to save our greenhouse operation, too. The commune would be done for if we lose our produce business." Archer paused and put his hands on his hips letting his statement sink in. Then he continued, "Now, I know this may sound even nuttier than the tree thing, but hear me out, OK?" When Ceil nodded, he asked, "What if we bind all the table flats together inside the greenhouses? I know we're expecting a tsunami. But, this far inland, it probably won't be a giant wave crashing down on us; it's more likely to be the river rising quickly and flooding the area. If the table flats hold together, they will float. And we could add ballast underneath them just to make sure, as well as to stabilize them, so they don't tip over. We'd also need to secure them, so they don't float away."

Ceil nodded. "Ah! I see where you're going with this. You mean, build an ark?"

Archer grinned. "Yeah. Kind of. But filled with plants instead of animals. We need everything to ride on top of the water for just a little while. After the tsunami flood hits—depending on how bad it is—the water should recede fairly fast. And, if the ark idea works, there's a chance we won't lose everything we've worked so hard for."

"Yeah, but don't forget we would still lose all the produce in the fields," Ceil added, looking somber.

"It's true there'll be some losses."

Zeke had joined the group while they were talking, and after listening in, he interrupted. "What if we go ahead and pick whatever's in the fields now? Heck, we could bag the produce and store all of it up high, out of range of any flood waters."

Summer added, "We have lots of people here this weekend. We could organize groups to go out in the fields to pick."

Sky spoke up, "But what if we're preparing for something that doesn't happen for a week or a month, or heck, until next year? Do we want to pick all the produce in the fields now?"

Ceil bit her lip. "That's true. If we pick everything in the fields now and nothing happens...we'll have to sell or give the food away quickly or schedule a crazy amount of canning next week. But, heck, we were planning to harvest soon anyway."

Sky nodded. "True. So, I suppose it can't hurt much to go ahead and harvest now. Let's say that anyone who's not helping with reinforcing the platforms in the trees should go into the fields to pick."

Summer turned to Vijay and asked, "You work in the greenhouse, Vijay, right?"

Vijay nodded.

"Could you organize people into groups of pickers? Give them some instructions on what to do?"

"Sure, no problem," he said excitedly. "We can even get some of the little kids working too. You know, there are a ton of baskets and hemp bags in the worker cabins from last year's harvest. We can hand them out to the pickers."

"That's great, Vijay!" Summer said, turning back to the group around the table. "Archer, how about if you take the rest of the group here to the trees to show them what needs to be done for the canopy platforms." She looked around at the faces turned towards her, and continued, "I can start working on the list of supplies we'll need. Once the canopy platforms are ready, we will be able to start storing all the non-perishables in the trees."

Ceil turned to Summer, "How many people can we fit in the trees? I mean, we have more than a hundred people here already with more coming. Would there be room for all of them ?"

"Wait until you see what Archer has come up with! First off, the eight canopy platforms will each hold five or six people. Then we have tent pods for small family groups. These pods hang off the side of the tree under the canopy platform and each can hold two adults and up to three small children. If we need even more space for people, we can use individual climbing harnesses temporarily. It might be tight, but we've calculated that we can fit around ninety to one hundred people, maybe more. Of course, we'll need an accurate head count on who needs to be accommodated."

Ceil looked impressed. "It sounds like you and Archer have worked out a pretty workable strategy for evacuating the commune. How do we get everyone prepared for it?"

Summer looked thoughtful. "We will need to train people on how to use the equipment and practice getting up and down the trees. Once we get some of the tent pods set up, maybe we can get the families with little kids to test them by sleeping in the trees overnight."

Ceil looked at the crowd around her and shook her head in amazement. "I can't believe we're going to do this."

Zeke nodded. "It's insane, but you know, I think it's also an awesome solution."

People made eye contact and there were a few nervous nods of agreement.

"Let's get to work," Archer said like a general leading his troops. He looked over at Sky and Zeke, "You boys should get the music set up for the party. Maybe you could put on some motivating tunes this afternoon to get people working harder. What do you say?"

Sky nodded and turned to Zeke. "Wait until you see what I've rigged up this year. Bluetooth speakers in the trees!"

The two of them headed up the steps to the loft where the computer and audio equipment were set up. Ceil watched them for a second, her heart swelling a bit at the sight. "Like brothers," Zeke had often said. She glanced over and saw that Summer was watching her. Ceil asked, "Do you think this will work, honey?"

Summer nodded. "We're pretty confident it can work, at least for a short-term evacuation. And Rob says the waters should recede quickly, so we'll only need to stay up there for a day, maybe two at the most. I guess it all comes down to getting everything ready."

Ceil thought about that. "OK, tell me what do you need me to do."

"Help me with the list of supplies. You can tell me what is available here and where it is. Then, if we need to, we can go into town to pick up anything we are still missing."

Ceil nodded. "Want to walk through the pantry and storeroom out back?"

"Let's make a list first, and then we can check what and how much we have."

Ceil studied Summer. "Kate was right. You are good at this sort of thing."

Chapter 30

Sky's Woodstock Playlist
Richie Havens, August 15, 1969, 5:07pm to 6:00 pm
Opening song: "From the Prison"

The Beginning of the Woodstock Reunion

Love & Peace Commune, Brookings, OR
Thursday, August 15, 2019, evening

Lunch came and went, and all afternoon the commune hummed with activity. In the storeroom, Summer and Ceil found several climbers' hammocks and hanging tents refitted with new ropes, carabiners, and clips. They carried them out to the grove to add to the growing pile of what Archer had begun calling "the useful stuff."

"Where did all this equipment come from anyway?" Kate asked as she walked with Summer and Ceil around the grove, observing the different activities and the progress made.

Summer simply answered, "Archer."

"Archer?" Kate repeated.

Ceil explained. "Archer was going to start a tree-camping business a year or two ago. He thought it might be a side hustle that the commune could try out. When he was researching equipment, he found an arborist business down in California that had gone belly up, and he bought all their supplies for pennies on the dollar and he sent one of our trucks down to pick it up. It's true the guy is by nature a packrat, but that's been lucky for us!"

"Wow. Perfect timing too," Kate said.

Ceil nodded. "The Universe always knows what's going to be needed."

Summer rolled her eyes. "As if!" she responded derisively.

Kate chimed in, "And yet, Mom...it happened, didn't it?"

Ceil chuckled. "Leave your mom alone. She's one of those folks who needs to be hit over the head with the supernatural to believe there's something to it."

"Hey," Summer said, looking from one to the other. "I'm doing all this, aren't I? And all on the off chance that we might experience an end-of-the-world apocalypse. So obviously, I've already been hit over the head."

"Whatever it takes," Ceil said with a laugh.

As they walked, they watched as ropes and pulleys hoisted planks up into the canopy of one of the redwoods that needed a platform to be rebuilt. They could hear the distant tapping of hammers way above them. A little further down the labyrinth path, training was being conducted in groups of six, explaining how to use the climbing harnesses and saddles and getting folks comfortable with hanging from the side of a tree. Finally, they stopped and watched Taj as he organized a team to put together scaffolding that resembled a window washing platform on a tall building. It was attached to a simple pulley system with a small boat motor and could raise and lower several people at a time, including the younger children who were too young for climbing harnesses but too big to be carried easily. They started referring to the device as a 'family lift.' They'd make one for each of the platform trees.

After their tour, the three women headed back to the compound to help out with dinner. As they passed the fire pit, they saw that someone had assembled a giant pile of fire logs, ready to be lit for the big bonfire that evening. Under the bleachers were additional logs to be used for the fire throughout the next few days. They wouldn't run out, although they'd have to pay close attention to the weather and the wind. They couldn't take the chance of setting off a wildfire, especially this late in the summer.

Just as they reached the lodge, Rob and Sowi came walking up.

"I was afraid we might be late," Rob said. "To be honest, I have no idea what time Woodstock started."

"5:07 p.m., to be exact," Ceil said with a laugh. "That's when Richie Havens came on stage and sang 'From the Prison.' So, you'll hear it soon. Sky is good at getting this thing off to a perfectly timed start."

"I read that Richie Havens wasn't supposed to be the first act," Kate said.

Summer glanced at her in surprise. "When did you get interested in Woodstock?"

"I dunno. I noticed it's sort of a 'thing' around here, you know?"

Ceil said, "You're right, Kate. The band, Sweetwater, was actually supposed to open the festival, but they got stuck in a traffic jam trying to get there. And they weren't the only ones. Many performers were brought in by helicopter because of the incredible traffic jams."

"I remember hearing about that," Sowi said. "That, and the mud," she added with a laugh.

"Mud's not going to be a problem for us here this weekend," Rob said.

"Well, I think that depends on the tsunami, doesn't it?" Ceil said with an arched eyebrow.

"Yeah, when and if...."

Ceil put up her hand. "OK. This is a good spot to stop and wait."

"Wait? For what?" Rob asked.

"You'll see," Ceil said with a smile.

People started congregating in front of the lodge as it turned five o'clock. Soon everyone was looking up at the loft window where Sky and Zeke could be seen, their heads nearly touching as they conferred with each other about something.

Finally, Sky looked down at the crowd. "OK, folks! It's almost time," he hollered.

Everyone grew quiet.

"5...4...3...2...1...." Sky said in a voice loud enough for the crowd below to hear. Then the first chords of Richie Havens' guitar could be heard throughout the compound from the speakers mounted in the trees as he started singing the opening line of his song "From the Prison."

"Powerful!" Rob said. He whistled appreciatively.

"Perfect!" Sowi added.

They all listened for a while, then Rob took Sowi's hand and pulled her away so he could show her around the compound. Ceil noticed Kate's eyes following them as they walked away together. *Was something going on between Kate and Rob?*

They turned and headed into the lodge to begin preparing for the dinner buffet. Ceil went into the kitchen to help Nia out, while Summer and Kate started cleaning off tables and putting salt and pepper shakers and a napkin dispenser on each table. When some of the other people in the lodge saw what was needed to be done, many happily joined in to help out.

Chapter 31

Sky's Woodstock Playlist
Swami Satchidananda, August 15. 1969, 6:00 pm to 6:15 pm
Gave the invocation for the festival

Cody shows up

Love & Peace Commune, Brookings, OR
Thursday, August 15, 2019, evening

After dinner, Kate watched as groups started heading to the bonfire area in the center of the compound. She knew people were tired. Many had worked hard picking vegetables, others were exhausted from tying the flats together in the greenhouses. Several canopy platforms were rebuilt in the trees, and harnesses and saddles were prepared and tested with new carabiners and lanyards. While they had accomplished much, Kate had taken a close look at the to-do list that her mother and Archer had put together, and she knew there was still much left to complete.

She wiped down the last table and pushed her hair out of her eyes with the back of a wrist. She looked up to see Archer at the lodge door, glancing around the room, and when he spied her, he made a beeline over.

"Hey, cutie-pie, did you know a young man is looking for you outside?"

"A young man? You mean Rob?"

Archer shook his head, "Nope, Rob and Sowi are at the bonfire. No, this kid said his name's 'Cody.' Friend of yours?" He watched her expression change. "Oh, I see you know the guy then, huh?"

"Cody?" Kate said in a cry mixed with a laugh. "Oh my God! He's here?" Her eyes met Ceil's from across the room for just a second, then she quickly headed for the door.

She hurried across the compound towards the lit bonfire. It was crackling with twigs, fast-burning pine, and a few under-seasoned fat logs. She could see sparks being carried upwards into the early evening sky. The benches were already filled with a cohort of colorfully dressed people and behind the benches there were a group of over-excited children chasing each other with high-pitched squeals and laughter as one or more of them got tagged.

A few guitars were being strummed in unison, riffing together the chorus of an old folk song. She scanned the faces. So many new people had arrived in the past two days.

"Kate?"

She whirled around, and there stood Cody. His beard was a bit fuller, and he appeared dirty and tired. But he looked absolutely wonderful to her. He seemed hesitant as if he wasn't sure she'd welcome him. She grinned and threw herself into his arms. "Oh, my God! I'm so glad you're here, Cody! So, so glad!"

His body felt stiff to her, and she immediately noticed the lack of welcome in his arms. "I didn't know how to get in touch with you," he said tensely. "You didn't answer any of my texts."

She let go of him and glanced at him in confusion, feeling her pockets. "My phone...." Then she put her hand over her mouth and let out a laugh. "Oh my God. You won't believe this! I don't have my phone.... I mean, I...Wow! I must have left it up in my room at the lodge. Me without my phone. That's a first, right?"

Cody looked at her, and he frowned. "Are you OK, Kate? Are you like high or something?"

Kate shook her head; adrenalin and a crazy happiness coursed through her veins. "Of course not. Hey, why would you think that anyway?"

"Because you're acting so weird."

"Oh, Cody, you have no idea! The past week has been incredible. This place." She threw her arms out. "This place is amazing."

He reached out and took her shoulders in his hands, holding her still. "Cut it out, Kate. You...you're acting like a...like a ten-year-old."

Kate's smile faded. "I don't get it. Cody, what's wrong?" she finally asked.

He let go of her and turned slightly. "Nothing's wrong with ME. I was worried about you. I've been worrying about you for days now. And you never answered any of my texts! So, I didn't know what to think."

"But you knew where I was. I told you I was coming down here to see my grandmother...."

"You left with some Indian guy in a car, Kate. Then I couldn't get a hold of you. I was worried. I didn't know what had happened to you."

Rob walked up to them just then. "Hey! It's Cody? Right?" Rob said, putting his hand out to shake Cody's.

Cody stared at him. Kate could see it register on his face who Rob was. His eyes turned cold.

"You're the guy who gave Kate a ride...."

Rob grinned. "Yup, that's me."

"I thought you said you were headed to Port Orford," Cody said.

Rob's eyebrows rose, he glanced at Kate, and she shrugged ever-so-slightly. "Uh, yeah, man. I'm renting a cabin north of Gold Beach near Cape Bianco."

"But you're here now with Kate," Cody said. His jaw was set and his lips barely moved.

"Wait a minute," Kate interrupted. "You've got it all wrong! Rob wanted to meet my grandmother, so he drove me to the commune. That was last weekend. Now he's back for the party. So, what's the big deal?"

Rob moved away, returning to the bonfire, to give them some privacy.

"The big deal is you've been unreachable for the past week, and now I'm beginning to understand why," Cody glowered.

Kate stared at him in dismay, and then anger started boiling up in her. "Really? And what did you think? That I'm sleeping with Rob now?" She paused as he just stared at her, not blinking. "Fine, Cody. If that's how little you think of me, then you can go to hell." She spun around and hurried away.

When she turned to look back, he was gone.

Chapter 32

Sky's Woodstock Playlist
Sweetwater, August 15. 1969, 6:15 pm to 7:00 pm
Opening song: "Motherless Child"

Kate talks to Nia

Love & Peace Commune, Brookings, OR
Thursday, August 15, 2019, evening

When she got to Nia's cabin, Kate knocked and called out, "Nia?"

Nia appeared on the other side of the screen door. "Katie Rose! You look upset. Come on in."

"Do you have a few minutes to talk? I know you're probably getting ready for the bonfire."

"Aren't you going?"

"I'm not sure."

"Is this about your hiker friend? I saw him wandering around earlier. Cody, right?"

Kate met her eyes. "Yeah. I don't know what's got into him."

"Come on. You can have all the minutes you need, sweetie."

The cabin was tiny, about the size of a hotel room, except it had a small loft bedroom above the kitchen that could be reached by a ladder secured to one wall.

"I'll put on some coffee. Or would you prefer tea?" Nia asked.

"Uh, tea, I think. I've been off coffee recently. It seems to upset my stomach a bit."

Nia frowned. "That doesn't sound good. You OK otherwise?"

"Oh yeah. I'm great. Just haven't been in the mood for coffee, is all." She looked at the Krishna posters papering the walls, one next to the other like you'd see in a college dorm room. There was also a large fabric orange flag with a huge navy-blue peace symbol slashed across its center. There was also a small altar on a low table in the corner of the room. She went over to it to get a closer look. There was a brass statue of a multi-armed Hindu goddess. In front of it were several colored candles and a dish of incense ashes. "Which one is she?" Kate asked, nodding at the statue.

Nia said, "That's Devi. She's the goddess of Shakti, the power that underlies the female principle. As I understand it, she's the mother goddess, the source of all energy, strength, and creativity. Don't you just love all her arms? Think about how much we could get done with eight arms!"

"Many hands make light work? Or is it too many hands in the pot spoil the sauce?"

Nia patted the seat of the tall chair, which was pulled up to the butcher block island separating the kitchen area from the tiny living room. "Come on, sit. Let's talk," Nia beckoned.

Kate took a seat and watched as Nia filled the teapot with water from the sink and placed it on the small stove to boil. "Tell me about this Cody person."

Kate sighed. "I was so happy to see him when he showed up, Nia. You have no idea. But it turns out, he just came to vent his anger at me. I can't imagine what I did to make him that mad."

Nia studied her. "What did he say exactly?"

"That he'd been trying to get in touch with me. That he hadn't heard anything from me since I came to the commune, and he was concerned."

Nia's eyebrows rose. "Well, that doesn't sound bad. It sounds like he was worried about you...."

"But then he accused me of sleeping with Rob."

"Is something going on between you and Rob?" Nia asked.

Kate shook her head. "We're just friends. He gave me a ride down here last week."

Nia nodded.

"Anyway, how did I know Cody was suddenly worried about me? When I left him on the trail, he'd just had a tantrum when I told him I wanted to come down here. And then when I tried to set up some way to get in touch with him, he said to just leave him a message on his cell, and when he got the chance, he'd check his messages."

"So, did you leave him any messages?" Nia asked.

Kate shook her head. "I...I was going to, but there never was anything definite to tell him. He'd want to know how long I planned to stay, and I didn't know."

The teapot whistled and caught Kate by surprise.

"These misunderstandings happen all the time between people who care about each other. You two just haven't figured out each other's emotional language."

"Each other's emotional language? What is that?"

"Everyone's different. Our emotional makeup is as unique as we are. We assume everyone speaks their truths the same way we do, but that is rarely the case. You develop your way of expressing your emotions based on how you were raised, how your parents interacted with each other, and how they interacted with you. You know, the weight they put or didn't put on emotional communication. For example, some parents express themselves with a lot of touching and few words; others are all words and minimal touch. And even within that communication is how they use touch, what words they speak, and what they mean by them."

Kate shook her head in confusion.

"Let me give you an example: Do you 'make love' or do you 'have sex'?"

"What?"

Nia laughed. "Oh, no, I'm not asking that as a question. I meant, do you call the act 'making love,' or do you refer to it as 'having sex'? Or, God forbid, do you say 'hooking up'? There's a difference."

Nia stood up, put one of the steaming cups in front of Kate, and then took the other one. She swished the teabag around by its string and then lightly tapped it against the rim of the mug before tossing it in the trash bin nearby. Kate cupped her hands around the mug, feeling the moist steam with its distinct herbal aroma rising into her face.

"Well, 'making love' does sound more romantic."

"Agreed. So, if you call it 'making love' but your partner refers to it as 'having sex,' you might feel resentful. You may feel that somehow, he's not feeling towards you what you're feeling for him. That may or may not be the truth. But the point is, you have to learn whether that's just his way of expressing himself, or if indeed, he calls it 'making love' when it's with someone else, but 'having sex' when it's with you," Nia said with a twinkle in her eye.

"I see what you mean."

"It takes time, sweetie, and with some men, it takes a LOT of time to get on the same wavelength."

Kate grimaced. "I thought Cody and I were on the same wavelength. I've been with him for over a year, and we usually get along great."

"So, what's changed?"

"Me," Kate answered, a little surprised by how quickly the word came out of her mouth.

"Ah," Nia said, taking a sip from her mug and then blowing on it. "And how do you think you have changed?"

"Well, it began when I had the timestream experience...after that, I just felt like a completely different person."

Nia nodded. "Your grandma has that too. That...uh...'Gift.' Personally, I'm glad as hell I don't have it. It would scare the shit out of me. No, thank you."

"But it's more than that. I'm seeing everything with new eyes now. After being here at the commune, the world looks different to me. Things that weren't important before are important now."

"In just a week?"

"Even in the first couple of hours. I felt like I was changing as soon as I walked into the lodge. And, Nia, the labyrinth! Every time I walk it, I'm...made better."

"And you don't think Cody will appreciate the person you are becoming?"

"It almost doesn't matter what he thinks. I'm not sure he fits with this new me."

"I know what you mean. For over fifty years, I've been looking for someone who fits with me. Unfortunately, I doubt the guy exists. Maybe I'm too picky, but I'm OK on my own. I have lots of close friends here – men and women. And after all this time, I don't think I've left a space in my life for a partner. Maybe I could've accommodated someone when I was younger, but not now."

"Never?"

"Well, never say 'never,' but I'd be mighty surprised to find that kind of relationship at this point in my life."

"I know I'll have to talk to Cody eventually, but Nia, I'm not ready yet. Not yet."

"OK, fair enough. Just don't leave Cody out of any ... uh, big decisions, OK?"

"Big decisions? Wait. What has Ceil told you?" she asked suspiciously.

"Nada. I'm just sensing some things about you, Kate. I don't have your family's crazy gift thing, but you're giving off some strong signals these days."

Kate sighed. "Is it the coffee thing that gave me away?"

"Coffee?" Nia asked, puzzled for a second, and then she grinned. "Oh, I see. Switching to tea. Yeah, that might be a give-away."

"Really? Coffee?"

"It's a good thing, sweetie. It's your body taking care of you, making everything perfect for what comes next."

Kate looked at her for several long seconds, then closed her eyes. "Ceil gave me a pee stick, which was pretty definitive."

"Do you know when your last period was?" Nia asked gently.

Kate shook her head. "It's been pretty unreliable for the past couple of months, especially once I was on the trail. I figured it was messed up from all the strenuous hiking, long days, different food, and all."

"Weren't you on the pill?" Nia asked.

"Yeah, but sometimes I'd forget a day or two, and then I'd take three of them when I remembered. I know, it was dumb."

"Yup. And it just proves you're pretty much a typical twenty-something." Nia sighed.

Chapter 33

Sky's Woodstock Playlist
Bert Sommer, August 15. 1969, 7:15 pm to 7:45 pm
Opening song: "Jennifer"

Ceil & Sky at bonfire

Love & Peace Commune, Brookings, OR
Thursday, August 15, 2019, evening

On her way to the lodge, Ceil stopped to admire the deepening colors of the glorious sunset spreading across the sky beyond the vegetable fields. As the colors slowly darkened, twinkling stars began to appear. First, just one or two broke through the deepening blue of the night sky, then there was a scattering of pinpricks of light. Eventually, when night had settled around them, the Milky Way would fill the sky with bands of clustered stars. Then, just before nine, a full moon was due to rise. The earth at night was a magical place.

It was dark when Ceil turned towards the bonfire. Several guitars and a tambourine played along with the music of Tim Harden's "If I Were a Carpenter," one of Ceil's favorite love songs. She paused for a minute and closed her eyes to listen and hum along.

Finally, she moved through the darkness to the lodge hoping to find Sky there. The main floor was empty now, but she could hear some rustling from the loft above. She went up the stairs and found him alone, staring out the window at the crackling bonfire in the distance. In the corner near the window was the computer controlling the night's playlist, and the screen cast an eerie bluish light through the room while the audio equipment nearby vibrated, and tiny green and red lights blinked.

It was funny that even though she and Sky had been together for such a long time, and fundamentally agreed on most things, there were topics that they didn't broach. Mostly they avoided discussing messy private things, like commenting on how much alcohol or weed the other person consumed, or noticing how the other person was spending or not spending their time. It was judgmental and, for both of them, crossed an invisible line. After all, they were adults and they should treat each other as adults.

Over the years, though, Zeke had become one of the messy subjects that they avoided. And now that Zeke was back again, Ceil knew she needed talk to Sky about him.

The three of them had such a long history. From the beginning, they had embraced the freedom of the sixties in their open attitudes towards love and sex. But now that she was older, she recognized their naïveté in willfully ignoring the fundamental truth about human love and relations. While you can certainly love more than one person, sex brings with it a desire for exclusivity. It takes a big heart not to feel excluded or jealous when you're the third person in the relationship. She knew she would have to broach this messy subject.

She went over and stood beside Sky, and after a moment, he looked up at her and smiled. "Hey," he said.

She smiled back. "Hey."

"There's going to be a full moon tonight," he said.

"It's a perfect night, huh?"

"It is."

"Did you see all the people at the bonfire?"

"Just from the window up here in the loft. I was thinking about going down to listen to the rest of Tim Hardin's set. It's too bad that Ravi Shankar comes up after Hardin, though, because sitar music puts me to sleep. You want to go with me?"

"Yeah, but I thought maybe we should talk first," Ceil said.

"About Zeke?" he asked.

She nodded. "I talked to him this morning and it turns out he had guessed he was Summer's father. She looks exactly like his sister Janine, and he put two and two together."

"Huh. Smart guy." Sky paused. "Is that what you wanted to talk about?"

They looked at each other for a long moment. "Sky...you know how I feel about Zeke, but I love you, OK? I don't want things to start getting weird between you and me because of him. You and I have always been a good team."

"Yeah. A good team," he repeated. "Was that enough for you?"

"Mostly. I mean, I don't have any regrets about the life we've made here together."

He nodded. "Yeah, me either. But, Ceil, we both know what's coming for me...for us. I don't want you to face it alone."

"Alone? Are you kidding? I live in a god-damned commune, remember? Anyway, I'm stronger than you think." She studied him for several seconds.

Finally, he nodded. "That's true. You are one of the strongest people I know."

"Are we good?"

He smiled and reached for her hand. "How about you and I go check out the bonfire together?"

"I'd love to," she said.

They walked hand-in-hand towards the laughter and singing coming from the bonfire area. The stars were full out now, and they glimpsed the full moon through the branches of the trees as they walked.

As they drew closer, they could hear the crackle of the fire as it burned through the logs, and tiny sparks flew up and winked to black as they floated back to the ground. Tim Hardin's "Snow White Lady" was playing from the speakers in the trees, and someone on the other side of the fire pit was strumming a few chords on a guitar along with Hardin's tune.

Sky stopped and looked at the scene and sighed. "I'm really going to miss all this."

Ceil looked at him in surprise. He never mentioned his illness or his mortality. "You OK, Sky?"

He shrugged. "Mostly, I'm just bone-tired all the time. I feel nauseous sometimes. But I guess it could be a whole lot worse."

She stared at him. The reflection of the firelight played across one side of his face; the other was in shadow. Sky rarely admitted to feeling poorly. This was something new. *What did this mean?* "Is there anything I can do for you, Sky?"

He shook his head.

"Best Woodstock Reunion ever!" Zeke said from behind them. He placed a hand on each of their shoulders and pulled them into a three-way hug.

Summer came out of the darkness, then, and stood next to him.

Zeke turned to her. "Summer, can you drive me down to the airport in Crescent City tomorrow? My guy, Kai, will be flying in tomorrow, and I need to pick him up."

"Sure, Zeke. We're going to the lawyer's office for the reading of the will first thing in the morning, but I can drive you down right after that. Will that work?"

"Perfect."

Ceil felt Sky take her hand and squeeze it. She glanced at him and saw that he was looking at Zeke and Summer. He was smiling.

Chapter 34

Sky's Woodstock Playlist
Jefferson Airplane, August 16. 1969, 8:00 am to 9:40 am
Opening song: "Volunteers"

Ceil at the reading of Esther's will

Crandall Law Office, Brookings, OR
Friday, August 16, 2019, morning

On Friday morning, Ceil and Summer walked into the law office of Larry Crandall in Brookings. It was a low building on a hill overlooking a panoramic view of the Brookings Harbor, marina, and the Pacific Ocean beyond.

The receptionist came over, nodded to them, and looked out the front window too. "Incredible view, huh?" she said as if she was just noticing it for the first time herself.

"I bet you never get tired of it," Ceil commented.

The woman nodded. "You're here for the reading of Esther Rodger's will?"

Ceil said, "We are. I'm her daughter, Ceil, and this is my daughter, Summer."

The receptionist smiled at her in greeting. "I'm Anna. Mr. Crandall and your brother, Spencer, are already in the conference room."

Ceil felt her stomach muscles clench. "We need to wait just a moment for my granddaughter. She's parking the car."

"Ah. Parking is a nightmare around here," the woman said with a grimace. "We certainly appreciate having the lovely view but wish the building came with more parking out front."

Kate opened the door just then, a little out of breath. "Sorry, I finally found a spot a couple of blocks away."

They followed the receptionist down the hall to the conference room, and as the three women entered, Spencer and Larry Crandall stood up. The lawyer came forward with a smile and extended his hand. "Ceil, good to see you again," he said, shaking her hand. Next, he turned to Summer and Kate. "Summer, it's been a long time. And you must be Summer's daughter, Kate."

"Yes, I am."

Ceil nodded to Spencer as she took the seat opposite him. "How are you, Spencer?"

He studied his sister for a moment, then said, "Fine, thanks, Ceil. Audrey and the boys flew back to New York this morning."

"Sorry we didn't get a chance to catch up with them," Ceil said.

"Quick trip," he replied off-handedly. "They had to get back. The boys are off to Maine for two weeks of camp and Audrey needs to drive them up there from New York tomorrow. They'll be a day late, as it is."

He settled into his seat and regarded Ceil. "Your friends pretty much took over the funeral services yesterday. Did you plan that invasion?"

"No, that was as spontaneous as it gets, Spencer."

"It certainly livened things up," Crandall said. "And that woman, Nia – what a voice she has!"

Ceil nodded. "She does, doesn't she? 'Ave Maria' was one of Esther's favorite hymns."

Spencer choked back a laugh. "Like you would know what her favorite hymn was."

Ceil glared at her brother. "As it happens, I do, Spencer. Don't forget I was the one visiting her every week at the nursing home these past two years. She mentioned it on a couple of different occasions."

"Sure, she did," Spencer shook his head slightly, unconvinced.

Ceil gave him a dismissive wave of her hand and turned away.

Summer and Kate took seats next to Ceil.

Crandall, seated at the head of the conference table, leaned forward, looking a little uncomfortable at the exchange between Spencer and Ceil. He cleared his throat. "Now then, are we ready to look at Esther's will?"

All nodded, and he took his reading glasses from his shirt pocket. He perched them on the bridge of his nose and began reading the document in his hand, "I, Esther Golden Rodgers...."

His voice droned on reading the sterile legal language, verbatim. But in the end, the will was relatively short and straight forward. Esther left her jewelry to Ceil, although Ceil knew there was very little of it left that Esther hadn't already given away. Everything else went to Spencer: the family home in Brookings, an apartment in New York, all funds remaining in her bank accounts, and lastly, all her land holdings in Oregon, which turned out to be a cattle ranch near Klamath Falls and the 25 acres outside of Brookings. The commune's land was Spencer's.

Ceil's looked at Crandall in shock. "But...that can't be...!"

Summer leaned forward, "Mr. Crandall, we all know that Great Grandma Rosalie meant for Ceil to have the commune's land. It wasn't Esther's to give!"

Crandall shrugged. "Don't forget, Summer, that Rosalie died without a will. Therefore, everything she owned was passed down to her only surviving child, Esther. It was solely Esther's to do with as she pleased."

"But..." Summer started to say.

Ceil interrupted, taking one of Summer's hands. She drew a deep breath and looked at the lawyer. "So, you're saying that Esther had the deed all along?"

He shook his head. "No, I don't think so. We got a certified copy from the county register of deeds. Esther never mentioned having the deed."

Spencer let out a breath and sat back with a satisfied smile on his face, his hands were clasped behind his head as he looked over at Ceil. "I can't believe you're putting on this big act, Ceil, like this is a huge surprise! I tried to warn you last week that you should start making some plans. But all you could talk about was your hippie party."

Kate looked from one person to the next—Crandall to Spencer to her grandmother and finally to her mother sitting next to her. Finally, she asked, "What will happen to the commune?"

Chapter 35

Sky's Woodstock Playlist
Quill, August 16. 1969, 12:15 pm to 1:30 pm
Opening song: "They Live the Life"

Summer & Zeke pick up Kai

Love & Peace Commune, Brookings, OR
Friday, August 16, 2019, late morning

When they returned to the commune, it was mid-morning, but the music of the second day of the Woodstock Reunion—in keeping with the 1969 schedule of events—wouldn't begin until just after noon with the rock group Quill's forty-five-minute set.

Kate parked behind the lodge. The three women sat in the car for several long minutes without speaking.

"Now what?" Summer said aloud.

"Yeah, do we tell the others?" Kate asked, looking over at Ceil in the passenger seat. She glanced up, met Summer's eyes in the rearview mirror, and Summer lifted her eyebrows.

Ceil looked out the car window. "The last Woodstock Reunion," she said. She looked at Kate and shook her head. "No, not yet. Let's make this a great party tonight. The best one ever. For Sky's sake," she added.

Summer and Kate followed Ceil into the lodge to change out of their somber business clothes.

When Summer came downstairs again, Zeke was there talking quietly to Ceil. He saw Summer and waved her over.

"Are you ready to head to the airport?" she asked him.

He nodded, turned back to Ceil, and hugged her. He whispered something in her ear, and she smiled and nodded. Then she headed upstairs. Sky had decided to sleep in late, and Summer assumed Ceil was going to see if he was up yet.

Summer and Zeke went outside and walked around to the back of the lodge, where they'd left the car earlier.

"You want to drive?" Summer asked, dangling the car keys in invitation.

"Sure!" He went to the driver's side while she took the passenger seat.

"I'm looking forward to meeting Kai," Summer said. "Ceil mentioned you're thinking of retiring and turning your surfboard business over to him next year."

"He's worked with me since he was a kid. There's nothing Kai doesn't know about building surfboards, and he's got a real knack for it. Plus, he spends hours researching the latest techniques and tools. He went to college nights to get a degree in Business Marketing. Kai's a real smart guy."

"What will you do then?"

"Actually, I'm thinking of moving back here. What do you think of the idea?"

He pulled onto the state road that would take them along the Chetco River into Brookings, where it would meet up with the coastal highway, Route 101, south across the California border to Crescent City.

"I thought you didn't like living in the commune," Summer said non-committally.

"True. I didn't when I was younger. I wanted my own business and to feel like I was growing something and that everything I earned was mine. Back then, I believed it'd be suffocating to live in a small community like the commune, cut off from the rest of the world. It turns out I was wrong."

Summer glanced at him in surprise. "Really? How so?"

"When I left the commune, I returned home to Hawaii and started my own business just like I'd planned. I discovered that when things are going well, it is a huge ego trip just as I thought it would be. But when it isn't going well—and Summer, nothing ever goes right forever—it is scary as hell! I had people—my family... my wife and two boys—that were completely dependent on me. If I screwed up and the business didn't do well, they could suffer."

"Yeah, I know what you mean."

"That's the benefit of having a community support system like the commune. The rest of the community is there for you and your family. They have your back. So now I think that the classic American story about the individual making it all on his own is pure horseshit."

"You sound like a communist," she teased.

"No, the truth is, the story is bogus. Even back in the cowboy days, frontier towns had churches, and communities that people relied on for support. Bad harvest? Neighbors helped you out. Broke your leg? Your church fed your family until you were back up and around. We've lied to ourselves about how everyone can pick themselves up by their bootstraps. Which, if you think about it, can't actually be done." He chuckled. "It's physically impossible to pick yourself up by your own bootstraps. I don't know how someone came up with that saying in the first place."

Summer laughed. "That's true, isn't it?"

"Anyway, I learned the hard way that it's better to sacrifice some ego to gain a little security; give a little, get a little. It's just a better way to live your life."

"It's worked for Ceil," she said.

"Yeah," Zeke smiled and nodded. "There's Ceil. Another good reason for me to come back."

"Figured."

They were quiet for a few minutes, enjoying the morning views as they drove along the river. The sun reflected off the water, as a couple of kayakers paddled their way through a calm stretch of water.

"So, what about you?" Zeke asked.

Summer sat up a little straighter in her seat. "Me? I'm...I'll be fine. I just need to figure out my next step, I guess."

"Was your divorce bad?"

"I can't explain it, Zeke. The whole thing took me by surprise, I think."

"You didn't see it coming?"

"Well, sure, in retrospect, there were signs that pointed to big problems. Peter was working late, not coming home, and all the rest. It was a classic situation. I discovered he was sleeping with his assistant when I stumbled across some text messages on his phone. We fought, and I told him to leave, and to my amazement, he happily grabbed his stuff and left. Poor Kate was the collateral damage. She had a pretty awful senior year. Once she left for college, she wouldn't come back even for holidays."

"Is she OK with the divorce now?"

Summer nodded. "I think so. It was hard when the three of us were going through it all in Boston, but once she put some distance between herself and us, she said it got easier to deal with. What about you and your divorce? How'd it go for you?"

"My divorce was much simpler than yours," Zeke said with a laugh. "The boys were in elementary school, and after many years of complaining about my never being there for her, never around, always putting work first, Lani finally 'suggested' we do a trial separation. She ended up moving down the block from me so the boys could walk between the houses whenever they wanted. We both liked the arrangement, so we stayed like that until the boys graduated high school. We only got the divorce because she met someone, and I guess our relationship was too hard to explain to the new boyfriend. They're happily married now, by the way."

"That sounds so perfect. So...mature!"

Zeke laughed. "She was the mature one; I was just a dumb workaholic."

They were quiet for a while, then Zeke said, "There's something else I think we should talk about."

Summer looked over at him. "What's that?"

"Ceil told me that you saw us together in the forest back when you were 13."

"Ceil told you that?" Summer said in genuine surprise.

He nodded. "She apparently heard the story from Sky."

"Oh, so he's talked to her already," Summer said and nodded. "I told him that it was time to get rid of all these secrets between us."

"And you're right. Thank you for that, Summer." He paused, then continued, "But Ceil's reasons were honest. She wanted you to have the best father she could give you. Back then, that guy was Sky."

"I know. But, Zeke, I'm still waiting for Ceil to tell me. She still hasn't said a word to me about any of this."

"She will."

"Are you sure?"

He glanced at her and then back at the road. After a pause, he nodded and repeated, "I'm sure."

"OK." Summer studied him for a minute or two. "You and I are good, though, right?"

He grinned. "We're good."

She was quiet, then added, "I think you would've been a great father, too, Zeke."

"Thanks, Summer. There's no one else I'd rather have for a daughter."

When they arrived at the Crescent City airport, Zeke parked the car in the small lot out front, and the two went inside. The plane from Oakland had just landed and was taxiing up to the back of the terminal. Pretty soon the passengers were streaming into the building carrying their luggage that they had picked up from a baggage cart near the passenger boarding stairs.

Kai caught sight of them and waved. "Hey! Zeke!" he said excitedly.

Zeke pulled him into a warm hug and grinned. "Aloha, Kai! Welcome to the Mainland." He turned. "Hey, man, I want you to meet Summer."

Summer put her hand out, but Kai reached out and hugged her. "It's good to finally meet you, Summer. I feel like I already know you."

Chapter 36

Sky's Woodstock Playlist
Country Joe McDonald, August 16. 1969, 1:30 pm
Opening song: "Janis"

Summer & Ceil discuss the commune land

Love & Peace Commune, Brookings, OR
Friday, August 16, 2019, afternoon

When Summer, Zeke and Kai returned to the commune, the second day of the Woodstock Reunion was fully underway. The rock group, Quill, was the first group to play on that second day of Woodstock in 1969, starting in early afternoon. Country Joe McDonald followed Quill.

Zeke took Kai for a walk to show him around the commune and find him a place to sleep for the night. Summer watched them walk off with Zeke pointing here and there, while Kai glanced around with interest, shifting his backpack on his shoulder.

"Is that Kai?" Ceil asked as she approached from the direction of the greenhouses.

Summer nodded. "Really nce guy," she added. "By the way, Ceil, I think we need to talk."

Ceil studied her face. "About what?"

Summer let a breath out and said, "About the commune land, of course."

Ceil nodded. "OK. Let's talk in the lodge."

Summer followed Ceil to her small office area.

Just then Kate was coming down from the loft. When she spied them, she wandered over and pulled up a chair next to Summer.

"Tell me again what you remember?" Summer said to Ceil and furrowed her brow.

Ceil paused and then said, "Well, let's see. Sky and I hitchhiked from the Bay Area and were camping on a beach just north of Brookings. We'd been squatting in a vacant house down in San Francisco with a bunch of other kids, our first commune experiment. That didn't last long because we were routed out of the place by the cops... 'pigs,' we used to call them..." She giggled at the memory.

Summer gave her a disapproving look.

"Anyway, when we got up here to Oregon, I remember that Grandma Rosalie asked Sky and me to lunch. Her house was so lovely! There were lilac bushes all around it. They smelled heavenly and her house was always so serene."

"So, what about the land?"

Ceil continued, "So, anyway, we told her we had come north with the idea of forming a commune up here in Oregon. You know, do the whole back-to-the-land thing. It was a huge movement at the time."

Summer interrupted, "Ceil, come on. Get to the part about the land, would you?"

"Summer, I AM getting to the part about the land," Ceil said as she looked at Kate who was grinning as she glanced from her mother to Ceil and back again. Ceil pursed her lips for a second and said, "While we were having lunch, Rosalie asked what we would need to form a commune."

Ceil saw Summer roll her eyes. "Honey, you need to bring it down a notch, don't you think? You could use some of Grandma Rosalie's serenity, that's for sure!"

Summer leaned forward. "I'd be serene if I could get a straight answer from you. I asked you a clear-cut question about what Grandma Rosalie told you about the land, and you're talking about squatting in buildings in San Fran, camping on Oregon beaches, and smelling lilacs, for God's sakes."

"And yet, I AM getting to the heart of it."

"And I am listening."

"Rosalie said she knew the perfect spot for a commune. It was 25 acres back along the edge of the federal forest land. It wasn't good for much because it was such a small patch of land surrounded by federal and state land, so there was no chance of adding to it. However, there was a dirt track that led to it from the state road and a feeder stream from the Chetco that ran through it, and there was even a short bit that bordered the river itself. You know, down where we have our little beach, although 'beach' is bit of an exaggeration, don't you think?" Ceil glanced at Kate who smiled.

Summer said, "OK, so she offered you the land. Was there a title? Did she sign anything over to you?"

Ceil shook her head. "No. I'm sure there was a title somewhere, but I never saw it personally. Grandma Rosalie just said, "Go out and take a look. If you like what you see, you and your friends can settle there." Ceil looked thoughtful. "She said, 'It's a sacred place.'"

"A 'sacred place'?" Kate repeated. "What did she mean by that?"

Ceil studied Kate. "At the time, I assumed she was just saying that it was a special place to her. But now I believe she was talking about the trees; the big sequoia redwoods in our labyrinth."

Kate nodded. "It does feel like a sacred place out there. Especially when you're walking the labyrinth."

Summer interrupted, "So, getting back to Grandma Rosalie...."

"How is this going to help, Summer?" Ceil asked. "Spencer has the title. We all saw it this morning."

"I'm going to do some research into Oregon real estate laws. There may be something we can do to fight this."

"Really?" Kate sat up with interest.

"It's not over until it's over," Summer said. "But right now, we need to prevent him from doing anything rash, like open-pit mining, fracking, or who knows what else he has up his sleeve. He could easily destroy the place long before we get our day in court."

"The trees," Ceil said, looking suddenly pale. "He'd fell our trees, wouldn't he?"

The three were silent.

"We won't let him," Summer said flatly. She looked at Ceil. "We are doing a lot of work in the canopies of the trees right now. If we have to, we can just start doing our tree-sitting protest thing again."

Ceil nodded and smiled at Summer. "We got the lumber companies to leave our trees alone. Although it wasn't just the tree-sitting that turned the tide. Do you know what did?"

Kate and Summer both shook their heads.

"The Northern Spotted Owl," Ceil said. "When the bird was listed as a threatened species under the Endangered Species Act, it saved what was left of the old-growth groves that were its habitat, and it pitted the lumber industry against environmentalists which still goes on today."

"I didn't know that," Kate said. "I mean about the owl. Wow!"

"Well, my point is that we need to prevent the trees from being chopped down," Summer said. "Owl or no owl."

"So, in addition to all the tsunami preparations, we will need to think about scheduling round-the-clock tree-sitting to protect our trees, huh?" Ceil asked.

"Hey!" a voice said from the doorway. It was Archer. "Speaking of protecting the trees, those guys are back. They're out there walking around in our woods again."

Summer stood up. "The same guys?"

"Yup! Those couple of doofuses with the cameras and calculators," he said derisively. "They sure ain't part of our crowd."

"Spencer's guys," Summer and Kate said in unison.

"Oh, no," Ceil said, shaking her head. "I thought he'd wait until Monday, at least."

Summer looked at Archer. "We may need to start that tree-sitting thing sooner than we thought."

"No problem. We'll be ready."

Chapter 37

Sky's Woodstock Playlist
Keef Hartley Band, August 16. 1969, 4:45 pm to 5:30 pm
Opening song: "Spanish Fly"

Summer & Kai team up

Love & Peace Commune, Brookings, OR
Friday, August 16, 2019, evening

After leaving the lodge, Summer ran into Kai in the compound and invited him to come along with her to help out. They spent the afternoon in the forest together while the music of Santana, John Sebastian, and the Keef Hartley Band played throughout the compound. Their first job was to help test the lifts to be used to raise and lower the tent pods containing small groups of people—

families primarily—up into the canopy of the trees. There would be twelve tent pods in four groups with no more than three pods to a tree, and when they were in place, they would hang just below the canopy of the redwood. The pods would be watched over by a canopy team on the platform, composed of a captain with four or five other communards. Archer had designated the eight largest sequoia redwoods to hold the hanging pods and they were spread throughout the forest.

Archer assigned people to the different tree teams and the communard families to specific tent pods. Summer took notes and organized the list of names and which tree they were assigned to so that everyone would be accounted for. All afternoon they practiced going up and down the trees and getting comfortable with their new sleeping arrangements.

"This is pretty crazy," Kai said as he followed Summer out of the forest and back towards the compound at the end of the day.

"What? Spending the day building nests in the trees?" she asked.

"The whole idea of evacuating people up into the canopy of redwood trees! It's just nuts."

Summer nodded. "It is. And hopefully, all this preparation will end up being for nothing. I mean, there's no guarantee that there will be an earthquake or a tsunami, or if there is, when it might happen."

Kai shook his head in wonder. "And yet, everyone is working like crazy, as if it definitely will happen."

"Communes are funny places," Summer agreed.

"I sort of like it," Kai said after a moment. "I like the way everyone comes together as a community and gives one hundred percent, even if the effort may turn out to be unnecessary."

"If you live in a commune, you have to believe that the 'we' of community is more important than the 'I' of the individual. You learn to put the community's needs first," Summer explained. "I have to admit that I had a problem with that concept growing up here. But in the past week, I find that I'm starting to appreciate the benefits."

They were quiet as they came out of the forest. They stopped at the point where the path split. To the right, it headed towards the cabins along the river; to the left, it continued into the compound. Summer looked down at her hands and wiped them on her jeans. "I don't know about you, but I could use a shower."

"Me, too." Kai nodded. "What's the plan for tonight?" he asked.

She glanced at him speculatively. "I'd say first, a shower, then dinner with everyone at the lodge, and later there will be more music and the bonfire."

"Mind if I tag along with you?" Kai asked.

Was he flirting with her, Summer wondered. And almost immediately the image of being in the shower with him, naked and wet, came to mind. *Oh, Lord, Summer! What's wrong with you?* He was just being friendly. She had to admit, though, that she enjoyed the fantasy, and heck, it was nice being around a decent guy for a change. "Sure," she said. "Dinner usually starts around six, so come over to the lodge when you're ready. I'll keep an eye out for you."

He grinned. "Great! Sounds like a plan. I'll see you at the lodge for dinner." He waved and headed off towards his cabin by the river.

Summer watched Kai walk away. She liked him, she thought. He was funny and easy to be with. They could be friends, right? It'd been years since she had a guy friend. *Yeah, but could they be more?*

Chapter 38

Sky's Woodstock Playlist
Incredible String Band, August 16. 1969,6:00 pm to 6:30 pm
Opening song: "Invocation"

Summer's legal research

Love & Peace Commune, Brookings, OR
Friday, August 16, 2019, evening

At dinner Summer had intentionally steered Kai to a table with several communards   because she wanted the distraction of eating with a group. She realized that she and Kai had spent most of the day together and she was starting to feel a little unsettled by the idea of them pairing off. She was glad he seemed to enjoy the banter at the table and was curious about the communards and their life on the commune. When everyone got up and indicated they were heading to the bonfire, Kai glanced at Summer, and she realized he was waiting for her to decide if they were going with the group. The realization made her freeze for a second.

"Uh, Kai, why don't you go ahead to the bonfire with the others. I have a few things to take care of here first. OK?"

He looked momentarily perplexed but smiled genially. "Sure, no problem, Summer. I'll see you later?"

"Sure. Of course. See you later."

When he was gone, she plopped back down in her seat.

"What's up with you?" a voice asked.

She looked up and saw that it was Fern, picking up some condiment containers and the salt and pepper shakers from the long table.

"Hi, Fern. I'm just feeling a little confused, I guess." Then, not wanting to discuss it, she asked, "Do you need any help?"

"Nah. We've got this under control. You should go out to the bonfire and enjoy all the great music. Canned Heat is next up and then Mountain. The Grateful Dead's set starts at 10:30 p.m. You won't want to miss that!"

"I'll keep it in mind. But actually, I have something I need to do here first."

"Oh, OK," Fern said. "But it's a beautiful night out there, Summer. There's a full moon. Don't waste it all inside."

Summer turned on the computer, and waited for it to boot up. Now was as good a time as any to get some answers to a few questions she had about the Oregon state real estate laws. She knew this was just an excuse, though. She was feeling uncomfortable with her growing interest in Kai.

As she read through the various statutes, her mind kept drifting back to Kai and her earlier shower fantasy. She admonished herself, but decided she'd see if he wanted to hang out together tomorrow.

Chapter 39

Sky's Woodstock Playlist
Arlo Guthrie, August 17. 1969, 1:45 am to 2:15 am
Opening song: "Coming into Los Angeles"

Summer tells Ceil & Kate about her research

Love & Peace Commune, Brookings, OR
Saturday, August 17, 2019, morning

"Where were you last night, Mom?" Kate asked when she saw Summer after breakfast. "Kai was asking about you."

"I was busy doing some research online to help save this place, while you were all out there getting stoned at the bonfire."

Summer raised her eyebrows. Seeing that both Kate and Ceil were grinning, she shook her head disapprovingly. "Drugs don't help you get things done, you know. Drugs make you forget and become lazy. When are you people going to realize that?"

Ceil said, "I'd have to say...I hope never! Besides, weed gets you into the flow of things. It syncs you up with the people around you. It's just a different kind of getting things done, Summer. That's all."

Kate leaned forward. "So, Mom, what did you find out in your research?"

"I discovered something interesting! Oregon has a real estate statute called 'adverse possession.' It's sort of like squatter's rights, or the idea that 'possession is nine-tenths of the law'."

"Huh? What does that mean?" Ceil asked.

"It's the presumption of ownership. If an occupant of a piece of property can establish a pattern of ownership for an extended period of time, then the presumption is that that person owns the property. The burden of proving the property has not been used exclusively would then shift to the landowner, in this case, to Spencer."

"So, we could be presumed to own the land?" Ceil clarified.

Summer nodded. "Yes, but there are some things you'd have to prove—like that you've used it continuously for at least ten years and that you had the honest belief that it was yours."

"Is that legal?" Kate asked. "How do you know all this, Mom?"

"I worked as the personal secretary for a big-shot real estate lawyer in Boston years ago. I always found the subject interesting, so I've read a lot on my own about property law since then."

"So how do we prove any of this?" Kate asked "Do we have to take Uncle Spencer to court?"

"Absolutely!" Summer said. "And Ceil, one more question: who paid the property taxes on the land?"

"We did, of course," Ceil said. "I couldn't let Rosalie pay if we were the ones living here."

"Do you have proof? Maybe some canceled checks?"

"I suppose. But the bank that keeps the commune's retail account would have a record of it."

Summer shot her fist in the air. "Perfect. Then the next step is to find us a real good Oregon real estate lawyer. We're going to fight this. I mean it, Ceil."

Chapter 40

Sky's Woodstock Playlist
Joe Cocker & the Grease Band,
August 17, 1969, 2:00 pm to 3:25 pm
Sky's favorite song: "Just Like a Woman"

Kate's father & Cody arrive

Love & Peace Commune, Brookings, OR
Saturday, August 17, 2019, afternoon

Kate joined Ceil, Nia, and Summer, moving from group to group, helping the last-minute arrivals find a place to park their car or to pitch a tent, explaining what was going on with the building of platforms in the trees, picking produce from the fields, and turning the greenhouse buildings into floating arks.

In the forest, the last of the tree platforms were rebuilt on the ground and then lifted by ropes into the trees. Workers assembled the last of the hanging tent pods to be used by small family groups. The pods were now hung under each of the eight redwood canopies.

In the greenhouses, groups of volunteers bound the tables together so that they would ride out any potential flooding.

In the fields, dozens of young children and their parents filled baskets and backpacks with ripened corn, beans, tomatoes, lettuce, cabbage, peas, and even hemp and marijuana. Then the greenhouse staff processed the harvest by carefully packing the vegetables and crops into containers and hoisting them into the air-cooled loft area of the greenhouses.

Surrounding the activity and giving it a rock concert feel was the soundtrack of Woodstock playing in the background from speakers wirelessly connected throughout the commune. The music at the actual Woodstock Festival for August 17th had a gap from 3:25 p.m. when Joe Cocker and the Grease Band finished, to 6:30 p.m. when Country Joe and the Fish began their hour-and-a-half set. Sky and Zeke decided to fill the three-hour gap with music from the bands that had played from midnight to 6:00 a.m. the previous night.

They figured that most people had probably been asleep and would have missed some great groups, like Credence Clearwater Revival, Janis Joplin, Sly & the Family Stone, and The Who. Sky and Zeke made a greatest hits playlist to fill the three-hour gap and the music played throughout the compound and in the forest as more people arrived for the big last night finale of partying planned for that evening.

Kate stopped mid-afternoon to survey the compound as she took a long swig of water from her water bottle that hung from her belt.

Ceil came over. "What do you think?"

"This is amazing. Everyone that arrives just seamlessly merges in and goes with the flow. No hesitation at all, just joining right in the work. I've never seen anything like it."

"Keep in mind that most of the people who come to these reunions used to live here at one point or another. So, they already know how things work on a commune like ours."

They both turned when they heard a car pull to a stop near the lodge. Ceil did a double take. "Is that your father?" she asked Kate.

Kate's eyes grew large, and she cringed slightly. "Oh, boy, this can't be good," she muttered. She forced a smile on her face and walked towards the man who had just emerged from the silver Lincoln Continental sedan. He looked around with a bemused expression.

"Dad?" Kate said when she got closer.

He spun around, a look of relief mixed with aggravation on his face. "Kate!" He hurried over to her and hugged her.

Kate pulled away after a second. "What are you doing here?"

"Cody said you were here..." he started, but she cut him off.

"You talked to Cody?" Kate couldn't keep the steely edge of anger out of her voice.

Peter pointed to the car, and Kate turned to see Cody stepping out from the front passenger side of the vehicle.

She walked over but stopped a few feet from him, staring at him coolly. "So? You left here Thursday night without saying goodbye, and now you turn up with my father? Really, Cody?"

Cody squinted and ran his hands through his hair. "I didn't exactly feel welcome here. I ran into your father in Brookings. He asked about you, so, of course, I told him where you were."

Kate said nothing; she gave him a withering look before turning back to her father.

Ceil came over and put out her hand, "Hello, Peter. It's been a long time."

He took her hand, shaking it awkwardly. "Hello, Ceil. I understand Summer is here too."

"She is," Ceil replied. "Is that why you're here?"

"No, actually, I came for my daughter. I was just surprised to discover that my ex-wife was also here."

"You wasted a trip, Dad," Kate interrupted. "I'm staying here."

Peter pressed his lips together. "You broke your promise to me, Kate. You promised me you would stay away from this place."

Kate lifted her chin. "I needed to talk to Grandma Ceil."

"About your vision of some dire future?" he asked. "Cody told me all about it."

Kate glanced at Cody and then back to her father. "Did he? What could he possibly know about what I saw? He never even asked me about it."

Peter let out a breath in exasperation. "Look, Kate, whatever you said or didn't say to each other is between you two. Cody said you had a hallucination or a bad dream and suddenly had to come running down here to get an interpretation from your hippie grandmother."

Kate noticed a smile flicker across Ceil's face.

Peter continued, "Your mother always said you were a smart girl and would see through all this hippie hogwash. Apparently, she was wrong....once again."

"Really?" Summer said from behind him. "What was I wrong about, Peter?"

He spun around, then snorted. "I see you dressed down for the occasion, Summer. Joining the tribe, are you?"

"How would that be any of your business?" Summer asked coolly. "I see you, on the other hand, went with your summer whites for this little showdown. Interesting choice."

Peter smiled, ignoring the comment. "I heard you sold our house."

"My house," Summer corrected.

"I can't imagine what you were thinking. You could've made a fortune on that place if you'd kept it for a couple more years."

"It's none of your business, Peter. Besides, how do you know I didn't make a fortune on it?"

"Real estate transactions are public record, Summer. Remember?"

Kate put up her hands. "Could you two just stop? I'm staying here, Dad, so you should probably just go."

He stared at her. "I advise you to think that decision through, honey. You're only a year from graduation, and you'll be throwing away a college degree." He turned to Summer. "I know you agree with me about this. So, are YOU going to pay Kate's tuition from that fortune you made on the house?"

Summer rushed forward, her hands balled into fists and her body tense.

Peter took a step back.

"She will get her degree, Peter, and I think the person who should be thinking this through is you. Would you cut your daughter off because she wanted to spend time with her grandmother? That should make you a father-of-the-year, huh?"

Peter stared at Summer then turned back to Kate. "I'll check with you tomorrow to see if you've changed your mind. I'm staying at the St. George's Hotel in Brookings tonight."

Peter strode back to the car and got in. Cody opened the passenger door and was about to get in when he noticed Kate's stony stare and he paused. Then he shrugged and climbed into the car. No one spoke as the doors clunked shut and the car started up.

Kate, Summer, and Ceil stood elbow to elbow as they watched the car back up and then disappear down the dirt track heading towards the state road.

"Well, that was interesting," Ceil said. "There's no accounting for families, huh?" she said. "Hippie grandmother! I loved that part!"

As they returned to the lodge, Joe Cocker's cover of "With a Little Help from My Friends" played from the speakers.

How apropos.

Chapter 41

Sky's Woodstock Playlist
Country Joe and the Fish, August 17. 1969, 6:30 pm to 8:00 pm
Opening song: "Rock & Soul Music"

Ceil & Kate's disaster prediction

Love & Peace Commune, Brookings, OR
Saturday, August 17, 2019, evening

Sky and Zeke were up in the loft together, setting up extra speakers inside the lodge to continue the Woodstock Festival music soundtrack, day three. They debated, not for the first time, how long Country Joe and the Fish's set lasted and when exactly Ten Years After started with their classic, "Spoonful." But one thing they could agree on was that this would be a great night of music.

At Woodstock in 1969, the music played on through the night: The Band from 10:00 p.m. to 10:50 p.m., then Johnny Winter from midnight to 1:05 a.m.; Blood, Sweat & Tears from 1:30 a.m. to 2:30 a.m.; Crosby, Stills, Nash & Young from 3:00 a.m. to 4:00 a.m., and Paul Butterfield Blues Band from 6:00 a.m. to 6:45 a.m. It would go on all night here too. The last night of the three-day festival had been a Sunday night in 1969, but it was a Saturday night this year. The perfect party night!

Ceil glanced up at the loft and watched Sky and Zeke as they huddled in the alcove above, occasionally raising a teasing voice or a laugh, obviously enjoying each other's company. Watching them together, she felt good, contented even. She would do whatever she could to bring some extra love and happiness into Sky's waning days. And she knew it helped him having family and close friends nearby—working together, living together.

"Hey, you look happy," Kate said, sitting beside her.

"I am. Even with all the crap at the reading of the will and preparing everything here for a disaster. Even so. I feel grateful. You're here, Summer's here, Zeke is here, and thank God, Sky is still here."

Kate hesitated and then said, "Grandma Ceil? Do you feel it too? It's going to be tonight, isn't it?"

Hearing the serious tone of her voice, Ceil turned and studied Kate's face before replying. She sighed and gave a nod. "Yeah, I think so, honey. I think so."

"Me too."

"You too, what?" Summer said as she sat down next to Kate. She glanced from Ceil to Kate and back again.

"We think it might be tonight," Ceil said.

Summer let out a sigh and slumped. "Oh, Jesus!" She frowned, looking from her mother to her daughter. "Wait a minute. I thought you guys said you couldn't predict when something would happen...."

Ceil said, "True. It may not happen tonight. But...."

Summer combed her fingers through her hair. "Ah, geez."

Kai grinned as he sat down next to Summer. "What's up?"

The three women looked at him, and his smile faded when he saw their serious expressions.

Summer leaned over. "You know the tsunami that we're all talking about?"

He nodded.

"They think it could be happening tonight."

He glanced from Ceil to Kate and then back to Summer. "Are you shitting me?"

Summer said, "Unfortunately, we have some consensus on this from our New Age seers here."

"Well, I hope you guys are wrong then."

"Me too," Summer agreed. "But, just in case, I plan to sleep in the trees tonight."

Kai nodded. "Good idea! I'm with you, Summer. Running and scaling a 250-foot tree in the dark? No, thanks, that's not for me. So, let me know when you're ready. I'm coming with you."

Summer felt a jolt of satisfaction go through her. She reached over and put her hand on top of his. "Thanks, Kai. We make a good team."

"We do," he agreed.

Zeke came down the stairs and over to the table. He glanced at Ceil. "So, babe, what's up?"

Summer answered, "Earthquakes, tsunami, and devastation... according to these two tonight may be the night."

Zeke sat down next to Ceil on the bench and took her hand, placing it between his two hands. "We're going to get through this thing, babe. We're ready for it." He squeezed her hand lightly. "Right?"

She turned and stared into his eyes. "Yes, Z, we will, and yes, we are." She let out a breath. "I guess it's just the waiting."

Chapter 42

Sky's Woodstock Playlist
Ten Years After, August 17. 1969, 8:15 pm to 9:15 pm
Opening song: "Spoonful"

Summer & Kai

Love & Peace Commune, Brookings, OR
Saturday, August 17, 2019, evening

It was after 8 p.m. when Summer saw Archer come into the lodge. Ten Years After had just started playing "Spoonful," and she was sure that the crowd outside in the compound near the bonfire were dancing and singing along to the song. The music had such a driving beat that the overhead speakers in the trees buzzed with heavy bass. Alvin Lee on vocals and guitar was magical, not to mention Leo Lyons on the bass guitar. How could you not want to sing and dance when music like that was playing?

Archer looked around the room and when he saw her and Kai, he nodded and came over.

"I heard Ceil and Kate think things are going to start happening tonight, so I took one more look at our plans. I think we're in good shape," Archer said. "Canopy nests are all done; supplies are stored in the trees. Pods are hooked up. Harnesses are ready. Zip lines are in place. After the bonfire, we'll start moving folks up in the trees for the night. We have a few families already up in the tent pods. They wanted to get the little kids to bed, so we helped them ascend early to settle in."

"Any problems?" Kai asked.

"We did have some folks look up at how high the pods were and decide they prefer to leave tonight after the bonfire."

"It's probably not a bad idea," Kai said. "Particularly, if they have a thing about heights."

Summer said, "Yeah, I can see that might be an incentive to get out of here."

"I just hope if we do get a tsunami tonight, those people head inland and don't stop along the coast," Kai said.

"That's what I've been telling them: head inland to Grants Pass or Medford. Better safe than sorry."

"What about you? Where are you going to be sleeping tonight?" she asked Archer.

"In the Western Tree platform over on the other edge of the forest, near my treehouse. It's the big redwood I took you up the day after you got here. Nia said she wants to come up with me, and we'll have Fern, Remi, and Aspen, too. I have enough room for maybe eight; it'd be crowded with more than that, but we could probably squeeze in a few if we have to."

"Sky has the local wireless network set up, and he found a communication app that will work on our phones even if they are offline. Did you have any trouble downloading it?" Summer asked.

Archer took a cell phone out of his pocket. "Damn devices," he said in disgust. "I wish I had time to hook up walkie-talkies between the trees."

"This will be better," Summer said. "We can do group calls with it. That way, we can all be on at the same time. Can't do that with your walkie-talkies."

Archer nodded. "That's true enough. Maybe CBs then. I just hate being dependent on these damn things," he said with a shake of his head. He turned on his phone to check it and nodded again. "Yup, it's all set up and charged. And I have your number and the others on speed dial."

"Good," Summer said. "I have the list you gave me of everyone who will be in the trees, so we can do a headcount later on, if we need to double-check that we have everyone accounted for."

"And where will you be?" Archer asked, looking from Summer to Kai and back.

"Kai and I will be in Peace Tree 1. It's in the center of the labyrinth trees near the peace sign. Kate, Rob, and Sowi plan to be in Peace Tree 2, nearby in the same grove."

"And Ceil, Sky, and Zeke will be in the Goddess Tree at the beginning of the labyrinth trail," Kai added.

"Funny to have the three of them up there together, huh?" Summer said.

Kai looked at her questioningly, "Why is that?"

"Well, they're an interesting threesome. Lots of history."

"Love to hear that history." Kai laughed. "I've only heard Zeke's side of things. I'm sure there's more to it than he lets on."

"Oh, way more." Summer glanced over at Archer, "Right?"

He snorted. "There isn't anybody in this commune that doesn't have an interesting backstory, and an intertwined one, to boot. So, I'm not saying a word."

"Speaking of backstories," Summer said, looking at Kai. "I've been wondering. Is your brother in this surfboard business with you and Zeke?"

"My brother?" Kai said, shaking his head. "I don't have a brother. I was an only child."

Summer looked at him in surprise. "I'm sure I heard Zeke say he has two boys."

Kai nodded. "Oh, yeah, he does. Koa and Lui. Koa is a video game designer, and Lui is thinking about becoming a doctor. He's in college at the University of Hawaii."

Summer stared at him. "But...I thought..."

Archer looked at her expression and laughed out loud. "Oh! I see! You thought Kai was Zeke's." He clapped his hands.

Kai looked at her in surprise. "Oh, hey, no. Zeke and my dad were buddies beginning in the second grade. Then, when I was ten, my dad got sick, and Zeke promised he'd keep an eye on me. So, when my dad died, Zeke gave me an after-school job at his surf shop. I've been there pretty much ever since." Kai paused, and then grinned. "Yeah, I can see why you might think that, though, because he's always been like a father to me."

Summer suddenly felt a weight had been lifted from her shoulders. For the past twenty-four hours, she had been struggling with the thought that she was becoming attracted to her half-brother. She grinned at Kai. "Well, all I can say is, that's good news."

Kai looked at her and winked.

Chapter 43

Sky's Woodstock Playlist
Blood, Sweat & Tears, August 18. 1969, 1:30 am to 2:30 am
Opening song: "More and More"

Ceil & Zeke

Love & Peace Commune, Brookings, OR
Sunday, August 18, 2019, early hours

Ceil knew they should be up in the Goddess Tree right now. She felt it in her bones that time was short. They'd stopped at Zeke's treehouse to get his backpack. When they got inside, he paused as if deciding something then sat down on the small futon and patted the spot next to him. "Sit. We need to talk, babe," he said.

Ceil looked wary. "Now, Zeke? I mean, we really should get to the tree."

"We will. But this might be the last chance we have together alone for a while."

She studied his face. "And?" Her stomach knotted as she waited for him to speak.

"I think you've been wavering about what you want. Look, I know I said we could talk about it next year, after I retire, but I can't go back to Hawaii not knowing whether you and I have a future together."

"Zeke...But, Sky..."

"Yes, I know," he interrupted. "Sky's dying." His mouth twisted and she could see the pain in his eyes.

He grimaced. "Geez, don't you think I feel like I'm stabbing him in the back even thinking about life after he's gone? But, Ceil, I have to know I'm not going to lose you too." He reached over and took her hand in his, searching her face for reassurance.

Sadness clouded her features. "Zeke, you know I love you, but I can't make plans for after-Sky. It's...it would be like I'm giving up on him."

His head jerked up. "Wait! Do you think there's any hope of him surviving?"

She sighed and shook her head, but then she shrugged. "But miracles happen. I have to believe in miracles, Zeke."

"Miracles?" His expression dulled as he let out a breath.

Ceil let go of his hand and stood up, but it made her dizzy. It felt like the whole room was moving. She glanced around and her face turned ashen. "Oh, my God, Zeke... it's happening...."

Zeke looked up at her in confusion. "What?"

"The earthquake. Don't you feel it?" She felt her knees buckle as the room swayed more strongly.

Zeke jumped up and grabbed her to steady her. His eyes were wide. "Oh, my God! This is it, isn't it?"

"I think so," Ceil said, her voice shaky. "Zeke, we've got to get up into the trees. And fast!"

"How much time do we have?" he asked, reaching for his backpack hanging from a hook by the door.

"Rob said probably fifteen minutes...maybe twenty. But first, we need to sound the alarm."

"Alarm?" he repeated, looking confused. "What alarm?"

"The speakers! We need to go to the lodge, cut into Sky's playlist, and put out a warning through the speakers, just in case there are others in the compound."

"Alright," he said. Then, at the door, he pulled her into an embrace and kissed her deeply. "I love you, Ceil."

"I love you too, Z. Now, let's go!"

They climbed down the ladder and ran across the compound towards lodge. The music of Blood, Sweat & Tears was playing from the speakers.

Ceil tripped when another strong earthquake rippled through the ground below her. It was like running on shifting soil.

Zeke grabbed her hand as she stumbled beside him.

"Shit!" They heard someone scream. "What the hell is going on?"

They stopped and looked around. "Hey! Who's here?" Zeke hollered. They could see the firepit still glowing, but the flames were out.

"Hey, man! It's me, Arlo. What the fuck is going on?" Arlo came out of the darkness rubbing his head and trying to shake himself awake.

"Arlo, it's an earthquake! A big one," Ceil said. "You need to get to the trees. There may be a tsunami soon, and it will flood this area."

"What? That's happening tonight? You mean now?"

"Yeah," Zeke yelled. "It's happening, man! So, get moving!"

They watched Arlo run towards the forest.

Zeke and Ceil turned and raced towards the lodge. Ceil pushed the double doors open. It was dark inside but there was a light on in the loft area.

"What's going on?" a voice asked from above them.

Zeke and Ceil looked up to the top of the stairs and saw the silhouette of Spencer standing there. "Holy Christ! Spencer? Is that you?" Zeke said.

"Spence, what are you doing here?" Ceil asked.

"I was sleeping. When I got here a while ago, there was no one around! What's going on? Where is everybody?"

"But why are you even here at the commune?" Ceil asked again as she and Zeke hurried to the stairs.

"I was supposed to have a meeting with my consultants earlier this evening, but my car broke down out on the state road. I had to hike in the dark. It was late by the time I got to the lodge, but no one was here. I was hoping to use your phone to call a tow truck. My cell phone wouldn't work."

Zeke said, "Yeah. It's a huge dead zone out here. There aren't any cell towers in this part of the forest. The commune uses satellite internet connections."

Spencer frowned. "No cell towers?"

Zeke and Ceil climbed the stairs to where Spencer was standing.

Ceil said, "We've just had an earthquake. Didn't you feel it?"

"Yeah. It practically threw me out of bed. I was afraid the building would collapse."

"Spencer, we think it might be The Big One," Zeke said.

Zeke and Ceil headed into the loft area, and Spencer followed them. Zeke knelt in front of the computer and searched around for the microphone. He found it and switched off the music playlist. Then he cleared his throat and tapped the mike with his fingers. An echo of the tapping thump-thump-thump reverberated through the speakers outside. Finally, he spoke into the mike, "Attention! Anyone who is still in the compound, please head to the grove. I repeat: head to the grove now! There's been a major earthquake, and we think a tsunami is coming. Please go immediately to the grove!"

Spencer said, "I'm going back to bed. Don't worry. I'll be out of here in the morning." He turned to go back down the hallway.

"No, Spencer," Zeke said, taking his arm. "You need to get to the trees with us."

Spencer looked confused. "What are you talking about?"

"We just had a massive earthquake, and there's a good chance that a tsunami on the coast will follow it," Ceil explained. "If that happens, it could send a huge wave up the Chetco River and flood this whole area."

Spencer's eyes grew large as he looked at Ceil. "Are you out of your mind?"

Zeke said. "Seriously, man."

Ceil added, "Come on, Spence; we've got to get going."

Spencer glanced at Ceil and then at Zeke. "Let me get my shoes on." He disappeared into one of the bedrooms.

Soon the three of them were moving quickly across the compound. Several after-shocks caused them to stagger, but they regained their footing and continued.

"How do you know there will be a tsunami?" Spencer asked, breathing heavily as they ran.

"Kate saw it in the timestream," Zeke replied.

"The...time...stream," Spencer repeated, a breath for each word. "Summer's daughter Kate?" he asked, looking from Zeke to Ceil.

Ceil nodded.

Spencer didn't say anything for several seconds as he sucked in air and blew it out. "Wait, so Kate has that crazy gift thing, like you and Grandma Rosalie?"

Ceil nodded again.

"God help us!"

Chapter 44

Kate in Peace Tree 2

Love & Peace Commune, Brookings, OR
Sunday, August 18, 2019, early hours

When the first earthquake started at around 2:00 a.m., Kate woke with a start in Peace Tree 2 as it swayed back and forth, rocking her like a tippy canoe. The movement made her nauseous. She grabbed at the dark outline of the rope swinging above her but couldn't reach it. Then she remembered she'd strapped herself into a harness before going to sleep. Thank goodness she'd thought to do that. It had been an afterthought the night before. But, without the harness, she might have rolled out of her sleeping bag, slipped under the tarp, and fallen to the ground hundreds of feet below.

The tree creaked as it swayed, and the branches rustled as if in a windstorm. Finally, she heard the ominous thud of the hanging tent pods as they knocked against the trunk far below her.

The families. "Hang on," she yelled to the unseen people inside the pods. "It's an earthquake, but the pods are secure, and you will be fine. Just make sure everyone is in a harness and the ropes are fastened tight. There may be a tsunami on its way."

She heard frightened murmurs from below and a child crying.

Rob pulled aside the tarp that Kate had rigged up next to her sleeping bag to give herself a little privacy and stuck his head in. "Hey, Kate! Are you OK?" he asked as he shined his small flashlight towards her. She instinctively put her hand up to block the light.

"I'm fine, Rob. Hopefully, the folks below are OK, too." She leaned over the side but it was pitch black and she couldn't see anything except a bobbing flashlight beam inside one of the pods.

"This is crazy, huh?" Rob said in an excited whisper. "That was the third one in the last fifteen minutes!"

"Hey, is everything OK with you guys?" Sowi asked from behind Rob.

Rob turned. "Kate's fine. We should check in with Summer."

There was a beeping sound coming from Kate's sleeping bag. She reached over and felt around until she uncovered her phone. She picked it up and peered at the screen. "Mom?" she said into the phone, putting it on speaker.

Summer's voice came over the phone, "Hi Kate. I'm checking in with all the tree nests. Everything OK on Peace Tree 2?"

"Yes, we're all OK. We'll double-check the pods in a minute."

There was a scratchy sound, and then Archer's gruff voice came in. "Hey, Summer Rain! Everything's OK over here on the western side of the grove. A few kids are crying, but no one's hurt. Just a little shaken up!" he said, paused, and then laughed. "Shaken up, did you get that one?"

"Archer, that's not funny," Kate scolded.

"Yeah! Not funny," Summer's voice chimed in. The phones were synced, so there was now a party line among the tree canopy nests.

"Hey, Ceil!" Summer said. "Is everyone OK in the Goddess Tree?"

Instead of Ceil, it was Sky's voice that responded. "Ceil and Zeke aren't up here yet," he said, worry evident in his voice.

"What? Where are they?" Kate asked.

"Hold on," Summer said and then came back on, "Arlo is here with me, and he says he saw them earlier, just after the first earthquake. They were heading to the lodge to broadcast the warning over the speakers."

"OK," Sky said. "We'll keep an eye out for them. But for now, Summer, is there anything we need to do?"

"First, we need to find out if a tsunami is on its way. Rob? Can you find out what the official line is on the earthquake?"

"I'm linking to the commune's wi-fi connection right now so I can use it to call my professor," Rob said. "Hang on. If I can get through, I'll be able to find out what the Oregon statehouse is saying about all this."

Kate turned on her electric lantern to a low setting. It shed enough light so that she could now see Rob's face as he waited, his phone pressed to his ear, a deep crease furrowed across his brow. She found it comforting to have the light.

"Hey, it's Rob," he said into the phone as he gave a thumbs-up to Kate. "I'm currently a few miles east of Brookings, at the Love & Peace commune near the Chetco River. We're getting some pretty strong seismic activity here. What's the official line on this?"

He listened for a minute, nodding, then said, "Yes, sir. Text or call me at this number. I'll be here."

He looked over at Kate. "Summer? Sky? Archer? Can you guys in the other trees hear me, OK?"

Several confirmations could be heard coming through Kate's speakerphone.

"My professor says a major earthquake was centered one hundred miles off the coast, within the subduction zone. They are zeroing in on the exact location and will have more information shortly. The state has already issued an alert along Oregon, Washington, and northern California coastlines to begin immediate evacuations."

"Oh, no," Kate whispered, sat back on her knees, and closed her eyes. She remembered the towering wave rising at the horizon she'd seen in the timestream.

She felt Rob's hand on her shoulder and looked at him. He studied her face. "You OK, Kate? We have a lot ahead of us, I think."

"I'll be fine, Rob. Just give me a minute."

He patted her shoulder. "I know. It can be disconcerting when something in the timestream suddenly becomes a reality." He paused. "Kate, we have things under control here. We're all going to be fine."

She stared into his eyes and saw the well of deep assurance he was offering. Whether it was true or not, she accepted it with gratitude. If Rob said they would be fine, she would believe him. "Thanks, Rob." She took a deep breath and let it out slowly.

"Good. That's what I want to hear." He turned as Sowi lifted the tarp and came in.

Kate picked up her phone. "Mom, you seem to be running this show. Is there anything you need us to do?"

"Yes. First, let's check on everyone. Get a status from each canopy and a list of who's here. In case something happens, we need to know if anyone is missing. I have the master list Archer drew up on who was assigned to which tree, so I need each tree captain to let me know who's in the tree, how many tent pods are attached, and who's in the pods. I'll update the list if needed."

"OK," Kate responded.

"When we know everyone is fine and accounted for, the next thing we'll need is to get intel as to what people can see from their vantage points. Rob, do you want to tell everyone what to expect?" Summer asked.

"Sure," Rob said, as he took Kate's phone from her and held it closer to his mouth. "We're most concerned about a tsunami coming up the river. If that happens, we'll have sudden flooding below us, and later on, we'll want to know how deep it is so we can figure out when we'll be able to descend again. So, everyone, keep your eyes peeled once the sun comes up." He raised his voice, "Come on, gang, we've got this!"

Kate heard voices on her phone and said, "Granddad?"

"Katie," Sky said. "How are you doing, love?"

"I'm OK. Any sign of Zeke and Grandma Ceil?"

"Not yet. I'm sure they're headed this way, though. I'll let you know the minute I hear anything."

"OK," Kate said. She pulled her knees up, and hugged them, putting her forehead against her kneecaps. Her head swam for a moment. Then, she opened her eyes and moved her head back and forth to clear her thoughts.

"You alright?" Rob asked.

She looked up at him. "Yeah. Just worried about Zeke and Grandma Ceil, is all."

Rob nodded. "Yeah. Me too."

Chapter 45

Sky's Woodstock Playlist
Crosby, Stills, Nash & Young, August
18. 1969, 3:00 am to 4:00 am
Opening song: "Suite: Judy Blue Eyes"

Ceil, Zeke, & Spencer head for the trees

Love & Peace Commune, Brookings, OR
Sunday, August 18, 2019, early hours

Back in the compound, Ceil, Zeke, and Spencer jogged past the tent sites along the river to the path opening into the forest. Spencer suddenly came to a stop. He bent over, his hands on his hips, breathing heavily. When they realized he wasn't behind them, Ceil and Zeke stopped and turned around.

"Come on, Spencer!" Zeke yelled.

Spencer shook his head and waved them on, "You guys go on! I need to stop and breath. I'll catch up."

They jogged back to where Spencer was standing. Zeke took his arm, "Come on, Spencer! We need to get up in the tree as quickly as possible."

Spencer looked at Zeke, then over at Ceil, and frowned. "Wait a minute! Did you say UP in a tree?"

"Geez, where did you think we were going?" Zeke asked incredulously.

Spencer shook his head. "I don't know. Maybe to one of those treehouse places you have out here...."

"They aren't high enough," Ceil interjected

Spencer bent over again. "No, no, I can't go up a tree!" He looked at Ceil, his eyes wide with terror. "Ceil, I can't!"

She patted him on the back. "Come on, Spence! We'll help you. But we have to hurry!"

Spencer kept shaking his head, his eyes roving back and forth in panic.

Zeke put his arm under one of Spencer's armpits, and tugged on him. Ceil took Spencer's other arm. Together they pulled and half-dragged her brother down the dark path towards the Goddess Tree. There was a full moon, and rays of moonlight occasionally filtered through and were caught and reflected by the white rocks that bordered the edges of the labyrinth path.

Ceil could feel Spencer's heartbeat racing under her fingers, and she could feel tremors passing through his body, making him shake uncontrollably.

"No, no!" Spencer said, trying to dig his heels into the ground. "Stop! Ceil! I think I'm having a heart attack."

"You're not having a heart attack, Spencer," Zeke shouted. "You're having a panic attack. You need to calm down. We're almost there."

When they reached the tree, Ceil and Zeke were breathing hard. They let go of Spencer and he dropped into a heap at the base of the tree. Ceil looked upward, but all she could see were a few dim lights far up in the tree's canopy.

"Now what?" Spencer whimpered.

Ceil pulled out her phone and switched on the flashlight. She saw that several ropes were dangling down from above, and nearby was a large cardboard box which she assumed would contain harnesses, saddles, helmets, carabiners, pulleys, hitches, and everything they would need to climb the tree.

She nodded her head towards Spencer, "What should we do about him?"

Zeke shook his head. "Pulley him up like a sack of potatoes?"

"Well, I like the sentiment, but whew, I'm pretty sure the two of us couldn't do it. He's no lightweight." She pressed the speed dial on her phone. "Sky?"

"Ceil?!" Sky answered immediately, the relief palpable in his voice.

"It's OK, Sky, we're down here at the base of the Goddess Tree. Zeke and me," her voice dropped, "and Spencer."

"Spencer?" Sky repeated incredulously. "What's he doing here?"

"It's a long story. Any suggestions on how we can get him up the tree?" Ceil asked. "He's pretty terrified. He's afraid of heights."

"Figures," Sky responded.

"Ceil, is that you?" Summer's voice broke in.

"Yes, honey! We're at the base of the Goddess Tree trying to figure out how to get your Uncle Spencer up into the canopy. Any ideas?"

"Well, we have the 'family lift,' that motorized pulley contraption that we used to get the little kids up in our tree, but it's over here in the middle of the labyrinth. If you can bring him here, we might be able to winch him up in that."

"Do we have enough time?" Zeke asked over Ceil's shoulder.

"Let me check with Rob," Summer said. "Rob?"

Rob's voice came on, "So far, so good. The folks in the eastern tree haven't seen any rise in the river. But you should try to get over here as quickly as possible."

Ceil looked at Zeke and then over at Spencer, who was curled against the base of the tree with his eyes closed. "The two of us can't pulley him up. He's about 180 pounds of dead weight. We'll have to get him over to you folks. Summer, can you send someone down to the ground who knows how to work that 'family lift' contraption and have it ready for us when we get there?"

Summer's voice came back on, "Will do. We'll have everything ready for you."

"Thanks, Summer," Ceil said. She looked over at Zeke. "OK, let's get going."

Zeke bent over Spencer and patted him on the shoulder. "Hey, Spencer, you OK, man?"

After a moment, Spencer moved and slowly raised his head to look at Zeke. "What?" he asked in a soft, defeated voice. He was still visibly trembling, and there was a glean of sweat at his temples and above his lip.

"We got to go, man," Zeke said. "To the Peace trees. There's a...uh...an elevator there to take you up the tree. OK, man?"

"An elevator?" Spencer repeated hopefully.

Ceil suppressed a smile as her eyes met Zeke's.

Zeke leaned down, grabbed Spencer under the armpits, and lifted him to his feet. Although Spencer was upright, he sagged against the tree trunk. Ceil stood on the other side, and linked arms with him. She nodded to Zeke and said in a soothing voice, "Come on, Spence, we've got to get a move on."

They led Spencer along the path with the flashlight from Ceil's phone dimly lighting the way.

About halfway to the Peace trees, Spencer suddenly put a hand in the air. "Hold on," he said, gulping. "I think I'm going to be sick." He abruptly bent over and threw up in the ferns at the edge of the path. Zeke grabbed Spencer's arm to prevent him from toppling over. Spencer straightened and wiped his mouth with the back of his hand. Then, without comment, the three continued on their way.

When they got to the center of the labyrinth, they found Arlo waiting for them as he stood in the dark at the base of the enormous tree.

"Hey, Zeke! Ceil!" Arlo said. He glanced at Spencer curiously. "Is he OK?"

"He will be once we get him up in the tree," Ceil said.

Arlo nodded. He turned on his flashlight, which he shone into a cardboard box next to him. He reached down and took out a helmet. "Here. He'll need to be wearing this. Although if he falls, I doubt it'll help much."

"Here, Spence, you need to put this on," Ceil said, handing him the helmet.

"A helmet?" Spencer said. "I need a helmet to go up an elevator?"

"Yeah. For this one, you do."

"Elevator?" Arlo whispered to Zeke.

Zeke nodded with a smile but didn't explain.

They walked Spencer to the scaffolding platform and directed him to sit on one end.

"You guys have your harnesses and gear, right?" Arlo asked, looking from Ceil to Zeke.

"Huh?" Zeke responded.

Arlo explained, "We built this scaffolding platform to take little kids up. But it can't hold this many adults—too much weight. So, you guys will need to climb. Put on your gear, and we've got a couple of climbing ropes over here that you can use," he said, pointing to the ropes dangling down nearby.

"Shit," Zeke said, looking over at Ceil. Then, he turned to Arlo, "We left all the climbing gear at the Goddess Tree."

"Never mind," Ceil said. "Arlo, take Spencer up and hand him over to Summer, OK? We'll go back to the Goddess Tree."

"We'd better hurry, Ceil," Zeke said.

She glanced at him and nodded.

Spencer was sitting on the platform, and even in the moonlit darkness, Ceil could see the whites of his eyes; they were round with terror. "But, Ceil," he said, "I thought you guys said there was an elevator?" His voice was rising with panic.

"This is an elevator," Arlo said smoothly. "It's called the 'family lift.' Now, Spencer, you just need to close your eyes and keep them closed, OK? I'll let you know when we're there and when you can open them again."

Spencer looked at Arlo, then over at Ceil and Zeke. They nodded to him. He looked back at Arlo and tightened his hold on the scaffolding's rail next to him. Then, after a moment, he squeezed his eyes shut. Ceil let out a breath she hadn't realized she was holding.

She and Zeke didn't wait to watch Arlo and Spencer ascend. Instead, they turned and raced back to the Goddess Tree.

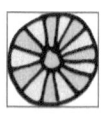

Chapter 46

Sky's Woodstock Playlist
Crosby, Stills, Nash & Young, August
18. 1969, 3:00 am to 4:00 am
Sky's favorite song: "Wooden Ships"

Summer & Kai wait for the tsunami

Love & Peace Commune, Brookings, OR
Sunday, August 18, 2019, early hours

Summer and Kai were huddled together, listening to the chatter coming over the speaker.

"What's going on?" Summer asked into the phone.

"Mom, this is Kate. We just got word from Tripper Jay and Marley over in the eastern end of the woods. They're the ones closest to the river. They just said the river has gone dry below them."

"What?" Summer exclaimed. "Did I hear that right? The river has run dry?"

"Rob says that it's a sign the tsunami is coming. He said it sucks everything out before it surges back in!"

"Holy crap!"

There was a click on the phone. "Sky?" Summer said. "We just got Spencer up here on Peace Tree 1. Arlo said that Ceil and Zeke are heading back to the Goddess Tree. They left their climbing gear there, so they had to go back."

"I know," Sky said, his voice tight with emotion. "They just called from below and said they are getting suited up in their harnesses right now."

"Tell them to hurry, OK?" Rob chimed in. "In fact, everyone should hold on tight. Make sure to tell the pods below you to double-check that they are all harnessed in, and that the pods are securely attached to the tree."

There were a lot of voices and confused chatter over the phone for several minutes.

Archer's voice came on. "Any water over there yet, Marley?"

The others went quiet to listen.

"Oh, dear Lord, you should see it, Archer! We rigged up a searchlight to a harness and lowered it to about thirty or forty feet above the ground. We just saw a huge wall of water come up the riverbed. It's forcing the river to flow in reverse!" She paused. "By the way, The first wave took out our beach and all the tent sites that used to be along the river. I can't see further up the river, but I imagine the cabins are probably floating too."

"What about you guys in the other trees? Can anyone see anything below?"

Several voices came on and said it was too dark to see.

"What's that noise?" Summer exclaimed. She exchanged glances with Kai. It sounded like the turbulent rumble of a waterfall.

He put up a finger and listened. "It's like…oh, wow! Summer! Look down there," he said, pointing over the side of the canopy.

Summer leaned over and strained to see. Kai handed her their powerful torch flashlight, which according to Archer, was more powerful than police flashlights. She switched it on and pointed it downward. Rushing water sloshed around the trunks of the giant old trees in the grove.

She said into her phone, "Kate, tell Rob we have water below us now. A lot of water."

Kai put his arm around Summer's shoulder and pulled her close. At least, she wasn't alone, she thought.

Chapter 47

Sky's Woodstock Playlist
Credence Clearwater Revival,
August 17. 1969, 12:30 am to 1:20 am
Sky's favorite song: "Born on the Bayou"

Ceil & Zeke reach the Goddess Tree

Love & Peace Commune, Brookings, OR
Sunday, August 18, 2019, early hours

At the Goddess Tree, Ceil and Zeke hooked their harnesses and saddles to the pulley and were inching their way up the ropes when they heard the rush of water.

"Look!" Zeke yelled and pointed to the east. An enormous wave was heading towards them.

They both scrambled to get a few feet higher when the surge hit the tree. The dark water splashed and swirled angrily around the base and sloshed against the trunk. Ceil saw the cardboard gearbox lift, float for a few seconds, and then quickly tilt and disappear in the deluge.

"We have to get higher! The next wave could be bigger!" Ceil hollered to Zeke, hoping he could hear her over the sound of the torrent just below them.

They both scooted themselves up, cinching their pulleys, and stretching their feet to bounce up the side of the trunk. After gaining a few more feet, they paused to look down as a second larger swell hit the tree. They dangled in the darkness over the abyss of black water for several minutes.

"Wow," Ceil said.

"I know," Zeke replied. "Holy shit!"

Ceil looked over at Zeke. "I think we made it, Z!"

He looked at her and nodded. "Damn! I think we did."

They continued climbing in silence. Suddenly, Zeke put his hand up to signal for Ceil to stop. "Wait a sec. Do you hear that?" Then he laughed. "I hear Crosby, Stills, Nash & Young playing 'Marrakesh Express.' The playlist must've come back on. Geez, I can't believe the speakers are still working."

"What time does that make it?" Ceil asked.

"I think the group played from 3 a.m. to 4 a.m., and 'Marrakesh Express' was about halfway into their set. So, that would make it around 3:30 a.m."

"Long night, huh?" she said as she started to climb again.

"Yeah, and it's not over yet." Just as Zeke said it, the branches just above them shook and the tree swayed for a second. "Another earthquake?" he asked, his voice tight.

Ceil glanced downward into the pitch dark below. "Probably after-shocks. We'd better keep moving."

Chapter 48

Sky's Woodstock Playlist
Paul Butterfield Blues Band,
August 18. 1969, 6:00 am to 6:45 am
Opening song: "Born Under a Bad Sign"

Ceil & Zeke in the Goddess Tree

Love & Peace Commune, Brookings, OR
Sunday, August 18, 2019, early hours

When she finally pulled herself up and over the platform of the Goddess Tree, Ceil had never been so happy to be in the canopy of her tree. She had been terrified while hanging off the side of the tree in the dark, with the tsunami rushing towards them. But now that they were safe, she had to admit that it had been exhilarating to climb the Goddess Tree with Zeke. It made her feel thirty again with all the heedless energy of youth coursing through her veins. She was amazed and pleased that she had been able to keep up with him over the past hour or so. *Was it just adrenaline?*

After stowing her gear in a backpack hanging from one of the branches, she turned and noticed Sky sitting under the tarp nearby. He was silently watching her. She crawled over to him and sat beside him. "Hey, are you OK?" she asked quietly.

"Ceil, I've never been so scared in my life. I thought I was going to lose you," he said with a shake of his head.

"I'm sorry, Sky. We had to go to the lodge to use the speakers to warn any others who might be in the compound. And, luckily, we did, or who knows what might've happened to Spencer."

"I heard you found him in the lodge," Sky grunted. He shook his head and stared at Ceil. Then, finally, he said in a flat, low voice, "I was worried about you. I thought you might not make it up here in time."

"It was close," she admitted.

He sighed. "Yeah."

Ceil looked up and saw Zeke making his way towards them. He brushed away a branch hanging down from the tarp, and sat down next to Sky. "How you doing, man?"

"Better now that you guys are up here," Sky said. "I thought you weren't going to make it in time."

"It was scary when we were hanging off the side of the tree, especially when we saw that first wave coming through."

Sky shook his head. "It should've been me out there, Z, not you."

"No, man, no way. I was right where I needed to be. And so were you."

The branches vibrated around them and there was the slightest sway to the tree.

"Another after-shock," Ceil said, as if naming it made it less scary.

Sky voice turned morose. "It's all of this! I felt useless while you guys were down there risking everything."

"We don't think you're useless, Sky!" Ceil rubbed his arm. She decided to change the subject. "Did Summer or Rob say what we can expect next?"

"Yeah. We wait and see if there are more earthquakes or tsunamis. If not, then we wait for the water to recede." He yawned. "I'm beat."

Ceil nodded. "That's a good idea. Get some sleep. You can lean against me, Sky. Go ahead."

Zeke stood up. "You guys sleep. I'll take the first watch. I'll wake you if I need you, OK?"

Ceil met his eyes. "Thanks, Z."

Ceil watched as Zeke crawled out of the tarp area, past Stone, who was sound asleep, his mouth agape. On the other side of Stone, Ceil could see a dark mound that must be Pablo.

She heard Zeke whisper something to him and Pablo opened his eyes. "Hey, Zeke."

"Just wanted to let you know that I'm taking the first watch, so you can get some shut-eye. Is everything OK with the zip lines?"

"Yeah. You want to take a look?"

The two men crawled to the edge of the platform and, after a second or two of whispering to each other, Zeke reached down and found the line. "So all we need to do is hook our harness and saddle to the zip line trolley?" he asked.

"Yeah, it's a breeze going downward, but once you get to the junction in that tree over there, it gets a little harder." He pointed but Ceil was too far away to see at what. "From there, you'll have to use the ascender pulley and rope in order to move up the slope of the zipline to the Peace Trees on the other side. It's not as easy as going downward, but it's not too hard."

Zeke clicked on his phone and said into it, "Katie Rose?" After a second, Ceil heard him say, "Pablo has the zip line secured here to the Goddess Tree, so if we need to move between trees for some reason, we should be all set. Could you check the line on your end?"

After a few minutes, Zeke said, "Good. How are you doing?" There was silence for several moments, then he said, "Your dad and Cody are probably fine." There was another second or two of silence. "If you need anything, give me a call. I'm going to sign off now. I'll let you know when someone else takes over the watch here."

Ceil felt the weight of Sky's head on her shoulder and knew he must have fallen asleep. She wondered if she'd be able to fall asleep, too.

Chapter 49

Sky's Woodstock Playlist
Paul Butterfield Blues Band,
August 18. 1969, 6:00 am to 6:45 am
Sky's favorite song: "Morning Sunrise"

Kate in Peace Tree 2

Love & Peace Commune, Brookings, OR
Sunday, August 18, 2019, dawn

Sunday morning's dawn finally lightened the skies at 5:50 a.m. After two hours of tsunami surges overflowing the riverbank, the communards in the trees could finally see through the early dawn light to the ground below. It didn't look inviting. Below them was a moving sea of brown, sludgy water filled with branches, leaves, and a jumble of indefinable flotsam.

"What a mess," Kate said as she laid on her belly and stared over the edge of the platform from the canopy. "Rob, is there any way to tell how deep it is?"

Rob came and sat next to her and looked down too. "Not sure, but we shouldn't attempt descending until we know the flooding is over for certain."

"What about the after-shocks we've had?" Kate asked. "Do they mean more tsunamis and flooding are coming?"

"Not usually. Of course, if we have another massive earthquake, all bets are ...." Rob was interrupted by a scream from below. "What the..."

Kate scrambled to the edge of the platform and peered over. It was Meadow in one of the tent pods. "Dylan!" she shrieked. "Oh, my God! Somebody help!"

Kate stretched further over the platform edge to look at the tent pods below. To her horror, she could now see a child swinging freely under the pod, his harness still tethered to the rope. "Oh, my God! Dylan!"

Her phone beeped, and Summer and several others spoke all at once, "Kate! What's going on over there?"

"It's Meadow's son, Dylan, the four-year-old. He must've fallen out! He's outside the tent pod swinging from his harness." Kate's heart was in her throat. She could hardly breathe.

"What do we do?" Summer asked.

Zeke's voice came on the phone. "Hold on! I can zip line over there. Then maybe climb down and grab him."

Kate looked around at the others in the tree with her: Rob and Sowi, then over at Starr, who was six months pregnant and finally, at Starr's partner, Dune. She knew Rob and Sowi weren't experienced enough to help much; they had made their first ascent using climbing gear only twenty-four hours ago. Starr couldn't do it in her condition, and Dune, unfortunately, was afraid of heights. He hadn't moved from the center of the platform since he came up the night before.

"I'll go down," Kate said, already checking her harness and leaning over the platform. "Meadow!" she yelled down. "You and Gage check your harnesses and carabiners. Then see if you can reach Dylan's rope."

Meadow was sobbing now. She strained to reach the rope connected to Dylan's harness, but it had swung too far out. Dylan struggled in his harness, kicking, and crying with his arms outstretched towards his mother.

"Meadow," Kate said, trying to keep her voice gentle and reassuring. "Talk to Dylan. See if you can calm him down. We don't want him squirming and maybe loosening his harness."

Kate reached out and hooked her carabiner onto the climbing rope attached to the platform. She would use the cam foot descenders to belay down far enough to grab the little boy. It wasn't much of a plan, but it was all she could think of.

"Kate, I can do it," Summer said into the phone. "I've been climbing trees longer than you have, honey."

"There isn't enough time for you to get over here, Mom. It's OK. I'm going down."

Rob touched her shoulder. "Are you sure, Kate?"

They could hear the little boy's shrieks as he swung in a wider arc, together with Meadow's and Gage's voices as they tried to reassure him.

"I've got to," Kate said. She felt butterflies in her belly but nodded to Rob and Sowi, and, before giving herself a chance to change her mind, she stepped over the edge of the platform, and the rope went taut with her weight.

Archer had taught her years ago how to climb trees and belay, and this past week she had learned how to use the foot and knee ascenders which made going up so much easier since it relied on your leg muscles rather than upper body strength. Kate stepped off the Peace Tree 2 platform and began to descend to the tent pod and to the dangling little boy below.

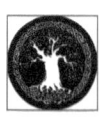

Chapter 50

Sky's Woodstock Playlist
Paul Butterfield Blues Band,
August 18. 1969, 6:00 am to 6:45 am
Another favorite song: "All in a Day"

Ceil in the Goddess Tree

Love & Peace Commune, Brookings, OR
Sunday, August 18, 2019, morning

In the Goddess Tree, Ceil woke up to see Zeke racing over to the zip line. She sat up suddenly and realized that Sky was no longer curled up next to her. She searched around for him frantically. He was gone. But how could that be?

When she heard Zeke curse, she jumped up and ran over to him. He pointed. Dread pooled at the pit of her stomach as she saw Sky zipping over to the junction tree on the trolley.

Zeke was about to clip his carabiner directly onto the zip line when Ceil grabbed his arm. "Zeke, no! You can't go without a connection to a zip line trolley! Besides, do we know if the cable can hold both of you at the same time?"

He looked at her and then out towards the junction tree. Sky was nearly at the junction. "Damn him! He shouldn't be doing this. He may not have enough strength to help them." He saw the look of confusion on her face and he quickly explained what was taking place over on the Peace trees.

"Oh, my God!" Ceil's hand went to her mouth. "Kate shouldn't be doing the rescue!"

"Yeah, and now they'll have Sky to worry about, too," Zeke said with a shake of his head.

Ceil's face fell. "Oh, God! Let's hope that Katie can get to Dylan first."

Zeke put his arm around Ceil's shoulder and said into the phone, "Rob? Sky is on his way over to help if he can. Tell us what's going on over there. Give us a play-by-play."

Rob's voice was tense. "Kate is descending to the level of the pods. She's nearly there." There was silence for several moments. "OK, now she's alongside the tent pod. I'm not sure how she's going to grab him. Dylan's swinging in a wide arc underneath the pod."

Every muscle in Ceil's body tensed as they waited.

Chapter 51

Sky's Woodstock Playlist
Paul Butterfield Blues Band,
August 18. 1969, 6:00 am to 6:45 am
Last song of his set: "Everything's Gonna Be Alright"

Kate rescues Dylan

Love & Peace Commune, Brookings, OR
Sunday, August 18, 2019, morning

Kate reached the tent pod containing Meadow and Gage and their newborn infant, cocooned in a front pack attached to Meadow's chest. Meadow and Gage looked frantic as they watched their son, Dylan, swinging in his harness below them. Dylan seemed to have dropped a bit, but Kate wasn't positive. She hoped it was just the different perspective she had from this height.

"I'm going to go down a little further to see if I can catch him when he swings around this way," Kate said. "Gage, tie this rope to something secure. Once I get to him, I'll tie the other end to his harness so you can pull him up to the pod, OK?"

Gage nodded and took the rope from Kate. She began descending again. In another ten feet, she was nearly even with the little boy. He had his arms outstretched, and his legs kicked in the air. Kate remembered being in the first timestream when she was up in the air with nothing below her except the ruined city of Portland. She shook the thought away.

"Dylan," Kate said as calmly as she could. "Dylan, honey, see if you can catch my hand, OK?"

He looked over at her, and his face screwed up to cry. His chubby little cheeks were bright red and wet with tears. He stopped kicking his legs and watched her as she reached out for him. He did a slow arc towards her, and when he got close enough, she grabbed his leg and pulled his body towards her. When he got close enough, he latched onto her, wrapping his arms and legs tightly around her torso like a baby monkey. He was terrified, and she could feel his heart racing in his chest against her.

"It's OK, baby, you're fine. Shhhh," she said in her most soothing voice. "It's OK, Dylan, I've got you. You're safe now," she said, rubbing his back with her free arm.

She held onto her ascending rope with her other hand, but with Dylan in her arms and him wrapped tightly around her body, she knew she couldn't ascend with them both.

Suddenly, there was a snapping sound, and Dylan's harness rope sailed past them. It was a second before Kate realized that now he was only being held up by her one arm and his tight hold on her. She could barely breathe. Kate heard Meadow scream from above, indicating she also realized what had just happened.

"It's OK, Meadow. I've got him," Kate called up to her, trying to keep her voice reassuring so that she wouldn't frighten Dylan or Meadow any more than they already were.

Kate swallowed and closed her eyes for a second. "Hold onto me as tightly as you can, Dylan. I need to grab your harness cable so I can attach it to my carabiner, and then your daddy will pull you up."

Slowly, she reached out, grabbed the cable, and began hauling it up. When she got to the snapped end, she pulled it through and finally tied it securely to the other rope so Gage could pull Dylan up.

"Gage, I've tied the end of Dylan's rope to the rope I gave you. Pull it up and tie it to something secure in the pod, OK? The other end down here is attached to Dylan's harness. Do you think you can pull him up?"

Gage's eyes widened.

"It's OK," Kate said reassuringly. "He'll also be tied to my harness, so he'll be fine."

Gage looked at her. "Are you sure about this, Kate?"

She looked up at him as best she could to make eye contact. She nodded. "I'm sure, Gage. Dylan will be fine."

"Kate?" Sky said from above her. He'd made it to Peace Tree 2. "How can I help?" His voice sounded gravelly.

"Granddad!" she said with surprise and relief. "Could you come down and help Gage pull Dylan up to the pod?"

"Katie, what about you?" Sky asked. She could hear the strain and worry in his voice.

"I'll be fine. Once I'm not holding Dylan's weight, I should be able to use my foot and knee ascenders to climb back to the platform."

Chapter 52

Sky's Woodstock Playlist
Sha Na Na, August 18. 1969, 7:30 am to 8:00 am
Opening song: "Get a Job"

Ceil checks on Sky & Kate

Love & Peace Commune, Brookings, OR
Sunday, August 18, 2019, morning

"Rob, what's happening over there?" Ceil asked into the phone, unable to keep the anxiety out of her voice.

He answered in a whisper. "Kate's got Dylan in her arms now, but she can't ascend with him because he's too heavy for her to manage it. She's asked Gage to pull Dylan up to the pod, and Sky's going down to the pod to help."

"Sky?" Ceil said. Her heart missed a beat. "Oh, Rob, I'm not sure he has the strength to do that."

"We'll soon find out. He's already on his way."

Ceil glanced at Zeke, grimly.

After several long minutes, there was an explosion of sound over the phone. "Dylan's back in the pod!" Rob exclaimed. "Whew! What an incredible rescue!"

There were cheers from the people in the other trees.

"Rob?" Ceil said earnestly into the phone. "What about Sky and Katie? Are they OK? Is Katie back in the tree with you yet?"

"Kate is slowly making her way back up. Meadow just called in to say she will keep Sky down in the pod with them for a little while to let him rest before he tries climbing back up here to the platform." He paused. "Ceil, I think Sky should probably stay over here and not try to get back to you folks."

Ceil let out a breath. "Thank God he's OK! And yes, I agree. That sounds like a good idea, Rob. Thanks."

Zeke took Ceil in his arms, and they held each other for several long minutes.

Chapter 53

Sky's Woodstock Playlist
Jimi Hendrix, August 18. 1969, 9:00 am to 11:10 am
Opening song: "Message to Love"

Kate & Sky in Peace Tree 2

Love & Peace Commune, Brookings, OR
Sunday, August 18, 2019, morning

All Sunday morning, Kate and the others kept a close watch on the ground below, waiting for the flood water to subside. It would be days before it dried out completely, but they were anxious to descend to check on the condition of the greenhouses, the lodge, the cabins, and treehouses, as well as the fields.

Summer's voice came over the phone, "Rob?"

"Hey, Summer, Rob here. What's up?"

"What's your best guess about how long before the water subsides, so we can descend?"

"Usually, we'd expect it to recede within twenty-four hours, depending on the topography."

Archer's voice came over the phone, "Rob, we've noticed it's already getting a lot lower over here."

"That's good news, Archer! When you can see the ground, you can descend and test it," Rob said. "But wait until you're certain you can see the ground, OK?"

"We'll keep our eyes on it."

"How's everyone else doing?" Summer asked.

"Goddess Tree here," Ceil spoke up. "We're doing fine. We found the stored food and are starting to figure out meals for the day." She paused. "By the way, Summer, how's Spencer doing?"

There was a pause. "Uh, Ceil, he's harnessed himself to the main trunk and it looks like he's put a handkerchief blindfold over his eyes." She snorted. "He's fine. It's the quietest I've ever known him to be."

"At least he's alive," Ceil said.

Sky was in the Peace Tree 2 platform with Kate and didn't need to be convinced not to attempt a return to the Goddess Tree. Kate helped him remove his harness when he finally got back up to the platform and made him comfortable under the tarp. She thought he looked awful. His face was ashen, and he appeared ill.

"You OK, Granddad? How are you feeling?" she asked, touching his shoulder gently. She frowned and placed the back of her hand against his forehead and then against his cheek. "I think you might have a fever. Let's check that, OK?"

He looked at her, and she saw that his eyes were glassy. "I'm just tired, Katie Rose," he said, and with a long sigh, he repeated, "Just very tired." He closed his eyes and leaned back against a rolled up sleeping bag.

She rose and pulled aside the tarp that helped block the warming sunlight. She saw Rob and crawled over to him. "Do we have a thermometer up here?"

He looked concerned and then glanced at the tarp and asked quietly. "Sky?"

She nodded.

Sowi overheard them. "There's one in the medical case over here in our supplies store. Is he OK?"

"He feels really warm," Kate replied, then dug around in the supplies until she found the white case with the red cross on its lid. She opened it and found a digital thermometer. But when she returned to Sky, he was already sound asleep. She decided to let him sleep. She would take his temperature when he awoke, and if he still had a fever, she'd give him some aspirin to bring it down. But she was worried.

She clicked the speed dial for Ceil's number. Her grandmother answered immediately. "Hey, Katie Rose, what's up?"

"Granddad has a fever."

"How high?"

"I'm not sure. I went to find the thermometer in our medical kit, and when I returned to him, he was sound asleep. I thought I'd let him be and take his temperature when he wakes up."

"Yes, that's what I would do too. Keep an eye on him, OK?"

"What should I be watching for?"

"A fever spike would be the main thing, and fatigue, body aches, that sort of thing. He's been through a lot in the past twenty-four hours."

"We all have," Kate said with a grim laugh.

"It should be over soon."

"Rob says maybe this afternoon Archer will be able to descend to check things out. We still have a lot of water below us in the grove."

"Us too."

They were quiet for a few seconds, then Kate asked, "What do you think is happening along the coast in Brookings?"

Ceil sighed. "The tsunami came up the Chetco River, so I imagine the town has probably been hit pretty hard. But hopefully, they were able to evacuate everyone in time."

"Yeah. I hope so."

"I'm sure they're OK, sweetie," Ceil said gently.

"Thanks, Grandma."

Still, the hours crawled by slowly as everyone continued to take turns gauging the receding water below. The sodden muck on the ground was filled with leaves, branches, bushes, and dark, oddly shaped masses of indeterminate debris. Occasionally, they'd see a small tree float by.

About mid-morning, Zeke whooped into the phone, "Hey, everyone! I hear Jimi Hendrix! He's playing 'Foxy Lady' down there." He laughed, triumphantly.

"I can hear it here too," someone else chimed in.

"Katie?" Zeke said into the phone.

"I'm here, Zeke," she answered.

"Is Sky awake?"

"I'll check. Why?"

"Jimi Hendrix was the last act at Woodstock. I just wanted him to hear some of it. That's all."

"Hey, what's that sound," Summer interrupted.

"The music, do you mean?" Kate asked.

"No, no, I think it's a helicopter!" Summer said excitedly.

Kate looked up through the branches and the wisps of moss in the canopy and scanned the little patch of sky she could see from her vantage point. She, too, could hear the thump-thump-thump of helicopter blades, but she didn't see the craft. Was someone looking for them?

She heard Archer's excited voice. "Yes! I see it! It's circling over us, but I don't think they can see us in the trees."

"What should we do?" Tripper Jay asked from the Eastern tree. "Start a fire?"

"NO!" Archer yelled into the phone. "We're not burning down our forest! Remy will climb to the top of the canopy here and see if he can get their attention. If any of you can do the same from your trees, go for it!"

Kate looked up, but there were only scrawny bushes and small branches above her—nothing strong enough to bear her weight.

"I think I can climb higher on the Goddess Tree," Zeke said. "Ceil found an old tie-dye peace flag in our stuff up here that I can wave at them."

After several minutes went by, Summer asked, "Ceil? How is Zeke doing?"

Ceil was laughing as she said, "He's climbing like a monkey up there. I wish you could see him!"

"Ceil! Can you tell if he's got their attention?" Archer asked.

"No. He's on his way back down now. It looks like he left the flag flapping on a branch near the top, so maybe they'll notice it when they come back around again. Keep your fingers crossed."

Sky stumbled out from under the tarp, put his hand above his eyes, and looked up at the sky. "Was that a helicopter?" he asked groggily.

Kate grinned. "Granddad! I think someone's looking for us!"

He nodded, wearily. "That's good news."

She took his arm and immediately felt the fever heat emanating from his skin. "Hey, you should stay out of the sun under the tarp. And let's take your temperature to see how you're doing, OK?"

He looked around, his eyes still glazed.

Kate guided him towards the tarp but felt him resist a bit. "Granddad, Zeke said that Jimi Hendrix is playing on the speakers below. Can you hear it?" she asked, trying to distract him.

Sky's face perked up. "Jimi Hendrix? Oh, my God! He was the last act. Did you know that they tried to make him go on at midnight on Sunday night? But he refused because he wanted to be the last act playing at Woodstock. So, he waited and didn't go on until nine the next morning!"

"It's later than that now," Kate said, looking at her phone. It's past 10 a.m."

"Oh, his set went on for more than two hours."

"But..."

Sky put his finger to his lips, "Shhhh, I want to hear this...."

Jimi Hendrix started in on 'The Star-Spangled Banner' with his guitar, and the sound drifted up to the canopies. Sky closed his eyes and smiled serenely. "Damn, he was good!"

"You ain't kidding!" Zeke said over the phone in Kate's hand. She raised it so Sky could hear Zeke. "Sky?" Zeke said.

"Yeah, Zeke."

"This has been the best Woodstock Reunion EVER!" Zeke said with feeling.

Sky cleared his throat, then replied, "I know, man. I know." He closed his eyes and Kate had to grab him to prevent him from tumbling over.

"Let's get you back under the tarp, Granddad," Kate said, trying to keep the panic out of her voice.

Rob hurried over to Sky's other side and put his arm around the older man's waist, then he helped Kate drag Sky under the tarp.

"He doesn't look good," Rob whispered.

Kate's eyes filled and she nodded. "I'll call Grandma Ceil to find out what we should do."

Chapter 54

Sky's Woodstock Playlist
Jimi Hendrix, August 18. 1969, 9:00 am to 11:10 am
Everyone's favorite song: "The Star-Spangled Banner"

Summer & Kai - receding water

Love & Peace Commune, Brookings, OR
Sunday, August 18, 2019, afternoon

"Hey, everybody!" Archer's voice crackled over the phone. "Remy and I are down. We're back on Mother Earth! Yahoo!"

Summer felt a swell of excitement. "You're on the ground? So, how is it?" Kai leaned in to hear the responses with her.

"Slippery. And everything is covered in god-awful sludge. But, hey, my house is still standing! Well, OK, it might be leaning a bit. It looks like two of the poles underneath it may have snapped."

"Do you want some company down there, Archer?" Jade's voice chimed in.

"Yes, Ma'am," Archer answered. "Jade, how about you and Vijay and Wilder come down. We can hike over to the greenhouses to check on things and look around. Aspen's right behind me. We'll wait for you."

Ceil spoke up. "Archer, there's still water under us, so let us know what you see, OK? I'm dying to know how everything fared and what's left."

"Yeah, me too," Archer responded. "Ugh, this mud stinks, and it's pretty deep in spots. It nearly sucked the boot off my foot a minute ago. We've got to be careful, everyone."

Summer checked in with the other tree captains as they waited for word from Archer and the team on the ground. Kai nodded at Spencer and Summer noticed that although her uncle asked for progress reports he wasn't willing to unlatch his harness from the trunk. She and Kai shared a smile of amusement.

As the minutes ticked by, everyone in the trees waited anxiously for the first words about the commune's greenhouses and grounds. It turned out the first reports weren't about the greenhouses at all.

"Summer? Ceil? Kate? Are you guys on?" Archer's voice queried.

"What's up, Archer?" Summer answered.

"You are NOT going to believe this!" Archer said with a hoot of laughter.

"Is it the greenhouses?" Ceil asked.

"No, we're not there yet. We're just coming out of the forest on the trail not far from my treehouse. We can see the tops of the greenhouses up ahead, and they are still standing but maybe tipping a bit; it's hard to tell from here. We'll know better when we get a little closer."

"Then what is it that we are not going to believe?" Kate asked, confused.

"The helicopter! It's landing just up ahead. We're on our way over to it."

Summer heard a whoop of cheers from the other people listening on the phone.

After a minute or two, Archer's voice came on again, and the others grew quiet to hear what he had to say. "OK, we're out of the trees now. It's me and Jade, Wilder, Vijay, Remy, and Aspen. We're heading towards the helicopter, but we have to wait until the blades stop rotating."

Everyone was quiet. Summer thought she could hear something, but it was too indistinct to make out.

Archer came back on. "The blades have stopped. Two people in jumpsuits just hopped out and set up a block on the ground below the hatch."

"Can you see who's in the helicopter?" Summer asked.

"Well, I'll be damned!" Archer exclaimed.

"What do you see?" Ceil asked impatiently.

"Oh, sorry. Kate's father and Cody just got out of the helicopter."

Kate said excitedly, "Cody and my dad?"

"Peter?" Summer said, stunned.

Archer replied, "Hang on for a sec. I'll put Cody on the phone so you can hear this for yourselves."

Next, Cody's voice came on. "Hi, folks! I was just telling Archer that the pilot had been ready to give up because nothing seemed to be moving below us at the commune. Then, at the top of one of those big trees, we spotted a tie-dyed peace flag." He laughed. "So we knew someone was down here somewhere. We circled back, and that's when the pilot picked up some sounds on the radio.

It was insane! We could hear Jimi Hendrix playing 'The Star-Spangled Banner!' You were broadcasting it. Did you know that?"

Archer got back on the phone. "Did you guys hear that? Cody here says they spotted Zeke's flag, and when they came back around, they could hear Jimi Hendrix playing." He laughed. "Apparently, we've been broadcasting Woodstock to the world!"

Everyone cheered.

After a second, Katie asked, "Archer, is Cody still there?"

"Hi, Katie Rose. He's standing right here next to me. Along with your father."

"Tell them 'Thanks' for checking on us, would you? I'm looking forward to thanking them in person."

"As soon as the water recedes," Archer said.

"How soon, do you think?" Summer asked.

"Well, ours dissipated pretty fast once it started going down. So, maybe, by later this afternoon." He paused. "Listen, everybody, we're heading over to the greenhouses now, and we'll walk around the compound. I'll check in with the rest of you folks again once we reach the buildings," Archer said, and finished with, "Over and out!"

Chapter 55

Sky's Woodstock Playlist
Jimi Hendrix, August 18. 1969, 9:00 am to 11:10 am
Sky's favorite song: "Purple Haze"

Getting Sky down from Peace Tree 2

Love & Peace Commune, Brookings, OR
Sunday, August 18, 2019, afternoon

Kate went back to check on Sky under the tarp, and to tell him about the helicopter, the tie-dye flag, and Jimi Hendrix. As soon as she sat down next to him, she could see he was not doing well.

She reached out and smoothed errant grey strands of his hair from his forehead and felt the heat rising from his skin. There was a sheen of sweat, with droplets running into his long sideburns. Rob came over and pulled back the tarp. She looked up at him and tears welled in her eyes. "He's in a bad way, Rob. We need to get him down and have Ceil take a look at him right away."

He nodded and backed out, lowering the tarp behind him. Sowi sat down next to Rob and put an arm around him as he dialed Ceil.

* * *

A little while later, a feverish Sky was one of the first to be brought down to the ground. He was lowered from Peace Tree 2 in the 'family lift.' Once down, they carried him slowly to the clearing near the greenhouses and there they were able to convince the helicopter pilot to fly him and Ceil over the tops of the trees to the lodge where, mercifully, the upstairs rooms were still intact and unaffected.

Zeke arrived at the lodge later, his legs and the edges of his cut-offs thick with dried mud. The lodge's main floor was filled with a layer of mud and all the tables and benches were strewn across the main hall. When he saw Ceil on the landing of the loft above, he hurried up to her.

"How is he?" Zeke asked, reaching out to pull her into an embrace.

She leaned against his chest and closed her eyes. "He's dying, Z. I called the Brookings Hospital hot line, but there's nothing they can do for him. They're swamped with patients, as you can imagine." A tear ran down her cheek and she wiped it away. "He's going in and out of consciousness right now. But I don't think he has long."

"What do we do?"

Ceil shook her head. "Be with him. I'm going to call Summer and Kate to get them over here...to say their goodbyes."

Zeke looked stricken. Then he nodded. "I'll sit with him. You find Summer and Kate."

Chapter 56

Sky's Woodstock Playlist
Jimi Hendrix, August 18. 1969, 9:00 am to 11:10 am
last song, "Hey, Joe"

Kate down from Peace Tree 2

Love & Peace Commune, Brookings, OR
Sunday, August 18, 2019, afternoon

The rest of the Peace Tree 2 group—Kate, Rob, Sowi, Dune, and Starr—came down mid-afternoon, followed by the families in the three tent pods, who were lowered to the ground in the family lift.

When Kate finally rappelled down, she saw that Cody was waiting for her at the base of the tree.

Archer had given Kate's belay rope to Cody and she noticed that he was careful to keep the tension on the rope in case she should slip, but she was fine. She hopped the last couple of feet and felt the oozing mud give as her boots sank in a few inches.

Cody smiled at her. "Where'd you learn to climb like that?" he asked.

She nodded towards Archer, who was ascending again to assist others down and was already halfway to the first branches above. "Archer taught me to climb when I was little, and he gave me a refresher course this past week when we started preparing the trees for the evacuation."

Cody shook his head in amazement. "Evacuating people to the tops of trees. What a crazy idea! I can't get over it."

"I know; it does sound a little nuts, huh? My mom organized most of it, and the whole commune has been working on the preparations for days." She paused and looked around. "You have no idea how incredible this place is, Cody. And these people are amazing."

Cody looked at her for several long moments. "I'm sorry about the other night, Kate. I was out of line."

She looked at him and could see he meant it. "It seems like a century ago," she said. They were quiet for a moment, then she asked, "So are you planning to go back to the PCT to finish the hike once this tsunami mess is sorted out?"

"Depends. Would you come with me?"

She shook her head slowly. "No, I don't think so, Cody." She looked around. "You can see the commune will need a lot of work. I'm going to stay and help."

"What about school?" he asked, frowning.

"I plan to finish and get my degree. But I may take online courses for a while and maybe return to Eugene to finish up next year. I haven't decided yet. Look, I've got something I need to tell you," she started and when it looked like he was going to say something, she touched his chest with the palm of her hand, "No, please, just listen to me, Cody."

He studied her for a second, then nodded.

"I discovered something this past week that impacts both of us." She paused and bit her lip. "I know this is not the perfect time or place to be telling you this, but I'm pregnant." She watched his face.

He stared at her as if he hadn't quite understood her words.

"I know it's probably a lot to take in for you," she spoke quickly, "but I've had some time to think about it, and I want you to know that I've already made a few decisions. First, I want to have this baby. Second, I'm pretty sure that I'm not ready to get married, OK?" She glanced at him. "And the last thing is that after I graduate, I'm coming back here to live and raise our child."

He asked in a low voice, "But what about us?"

"You could live here too...I mean, if you wanted to be with me...with us," Kate corrected.

"Live in a commune?" he responded with a look of disdain.

Her chin rose, and she nodded, "Yes, live in this commune." Then she smiled and said, "It takes a village, you know?"

"Kate," he started to say, but he didn't continue.

She watched him for several seconds, then lowered her eyes. She sighed, turned away, and started removing the harness and unhooking the carabiners. Finally, she turned back and faced him again and said, "It's OK, Cody. I realize this type of life isn't for everyone." She removed her helmet and shook out her hair.

He reached for her arm, and she looked at him. "I love you, Kate," he said.

She continued gazing at him. When he didn't say anything more, she said, "And?"

He took a breath and shrugged. "And maybe I can stick around and help with the rebuilding."

"What about later? Will you stay?"

"We'll see," he replied. "It's the best I can do for now, Kate. I want to be straight with you. I just don't know if this is for me."

She relaxed and nodded. "OK, Cody. I guess that's good enough for now."

Her phone buzzed in her pocket and she raised it to her ear. It was Grandma Ceil. She listened for several minutes. "OK, I'll try to get there as quickly as I can."

"What's up?" Cody asked.

"My grandfather, Sky. They have him at the lodge. My grandmother says he's dying."

"I'll come with you," Cody said.

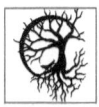

Chapter 57

Saying goodbye to Sky

Love & Peace Commune, Brookings, OR
Monday, August 19, 2019, late afternoon

The lodge building survived the onslaught. It was structurally sound, but the receding floodwaters had filled the first floor with mud and silt that would take days to shovel out. The walls and floors also needed to be scrubbed and everything would need to be disinfected with a bleach solution to prevent mold from forming.

As people made their way to the lodge—and where else would they go? —everyone pitched in to start the cleanup. But a noticeable somberness came over the crowd as they realized that Sky was fading away in the upstairs bedroom.

Nia took over organizing the clean up of the kitchen area. She saw that they would have to replace the ovens, but the stovetop burners had been high enough above the flood that they would be fine once the propane was hooked back up. She was glad to see that the freezers had remained sealed, too, but since the power had been off, and they'd only just started up one of the generators, they'd have to eat most of the defrosted food fairly soon.

When Kate and Cody arrived, most of the furniture—the tables, chairs, benches, and Ceil's desk, and office shelves—had been moved outside to dry after being hosed down.

Kate walked into the main hall and had to step around the piles of mud that several people were shoveling off the floor. She hurried over to the loft stairs.

"I'll wait down here," Cody said. "It looks like these folks can use some help."

Kate nodded and climbed the stairs. She went to Sky's bedroom door and quietly opened it. Ceil and Zeke were side by side in a loveseat bench pulled up next to the bed. Ceil looked up and her expression was calm although Kate could see deep lines etched into her brow. Zeke sat beside her with a stoic look on his face. He was staring bleakly at Sky.

Ceil motioned for Kate to come over to the bedside.

As she moved closer, Kate saw that they'd laid Sky in the bed and covered him with a sheet, but his body was still and his arms lay unnaturally straight along his sides.

She reached for his hand and took it in hers. It was oddly cool to the touch. His arm was slack and his hand didn't grasp hers back.

Her eyes swam with tears. "Oh, Granddad," she said. "I'm going to miss you so much." She turned to Ceil, "Can he hear me, Grandma Ceil?"

Ceil reached out and took Kate's hand and squeezed it. "I think he can hear us, Katie, but I'm not positive."

Just then, Summer entered the room. She looked momentarily surprised to see Kate, but immediately came to her side and put an arm around her and pulled her into a hug.

Kate saw that her mother's eyes were red-rimmed.

"Oh, Mom. I wish he hadn't done the zip line to help me with Dylan," Kate said.

Summer shook her head. "It wasn't your fault. He was just being Sky, trying to take care of everyone."

"We couldn't stop him," Zeke said. "He was halfway to the junction tree before we knew he'd gone. I'm amazed he had the energy to do what he did!"

They were all quiet for a while, then Ceil looked around, shrugged her shoulders and cleared her throat. She gazed at Summer. "Honey, I know this isn't the right time or place, but since Sky's not gone yet, maybe there's still time for me to make things right with you."

Summer looked at her mother quizzically and waited.

Ceil sighed. "There's been a lot of secrets going around among you and me and Zeke and Sky. I want to apologize to you for not talking to you sooner. I took the easy way out, and I'm sorry."

Kate look confused and glanced from Ceil to her mother. She noticed a smile tug at her mother's lips.

"So, Ceil, you're going to come clean finally?" Summer asked.

Ceil nodded. "Sky told me the other day that you already knew about Zeke being your biological father. In fact, he said you've always known. Is that true?"

"Well, not always," Summer replied with a malicious smile. "Just since I was 13."

Zeke smiled at this.

"Why didn't you say anything to me?" Ceil admonished.

"Wait a minute!" Summer put up her hands. "I was the kid in this scenario, remember? Why didn't YOU say anything to me?" Summer folded her arms across her chest as she waited for Ceil's response.

Ceil paused, pinched the bridge of her nose, and finally nodded. "OK, that's fair. But, in my defense, I didn't know about Sky's mumps, so as far as I knew he thought he was your biological father. I couldn't tell you without also telling him, could I?"

"And so, why didn't you?" Summer rejoined, enjoying this even more than she thought she would.

Ceil sighed. "Because, honey, he loved being your father and I didn't want to take that away from him." She shrugged. "I didn't want to hurt him."

Summer saw the truth in that, and she couldn't refute it, so instead she said, "You went to a lot of trouble to keep your secret, and it turned out all of us knew. Zeke said I look just like his sister."

Ceil smiled. "Apparently, you and your Aunt Janine are practically twins."

"I'm looking forward to meeting her," Summer said. "Kai says she's very cool."

Zeke nodded, "You'll like her, and she'll like you."

Kate held up her hands. "Hold on here! What in the world are all of you talking about? What secret? And...Wait a minute! Zeke's your biological father, Mom?" She turned to Zeke. "You're my grandfather?"

Zeke stood up. "Yup. Me and Sky are both your grandfathers, honey."

As Zeke hugged Kate, Summer glanced over at Sky and she could swear there was the trace of a smile on his lips.

Chapter 58

Ceil at Sky's Memorial

Church, Brookings, OR
Wednesday, September 18, 2019, afternoon

A month later, in the little church in Brookings, Ceil rose from her seat and made her way to the podium just to the right of the altar area. She looked out at the crowd that filled the church. Their whole commune family was there, former as well as current members. Sitting in front pews were Summer, Kai, Kate, Cody, Zeke, Nia, Fern, and Archer. Even Spencer had flown in to attend.

Everyone was casually dressed in jeans, long skirts, and such, just as Sky had wanted. Many had donned tie-dye t-shirts that Sky himself may have originally dyed. Ceil smiled at the thought.

She glanced at the pews on the other side of the room. She saw Sky's elderly mother and his younger brother sitting stiffly in their places, stoically holding in their grief, and ignoring the freewheeling casualness of Sky's friends. Ceil nodded to Sky's mother, and the woman visibly relaxed at the recognition, her shoulders slumping as she smiled sadly at Ceil.

Ceil cleared her throat, and the room grew quiet. "I want to thank everyone for coming to this service to send Sky on his way." She paused, looking around. "You know, he would've loved this– his friends and family gathered close. And by the way, he wanted to thank everyone who came for the Woodstock Reunion. He mentioned several times how great it was that so many showed up. I think we can all agree that none of us will ever forget it." There was a titter of laughter throughout the room. "I believe saying goodbye to someone you loved is all about expressing why they meant so much to you personally. Don't you agree? So, today, I want to tell you what Sky meant to me."

Her eyes met Summer's, and her daughter nodded.

"Sky was the father of my daughter, Summer, because I chose him to be. I knew he was meant to be a parent. He had every necessary attribute—wisdom, love, kindness, humility...and most importantly, a sense of humor. If nothing else, he also had the patience for it. And thank God for that! Because we all know I surely didn't."

Her eyes locked on Zeke's for a second. "It's not hard to father a child." She saw a few grins of agreement. "That's the fun part, I know," she said with a smile. She looked at Cody sitting next to Kate. "But it is hard to BE a father, day in and day out, year after year."

She paused. "For one thing, you must be willing to commit to being a parent. You have to stick around and put in the time. Raising the child has to be your priority. And Sky did all that. In fact, he was very, very good at it." She smiled broadly. "My daughter and granddaughter are living proofs of what a good father and grandfather he was. And, for that alone, I will always hold Sky close to my heart."

Ceil paused and glanced around the room. "For the rest of us, Sky was more than just a good father; he was a leader and a guide. The commune wouldn't exist without him."

"You know, he left me his journal and I went back to his entry for August 18th of 1969. It was the last day of the Woodstock Festival in New York state and it said simply, '*The Woodstock Festival was a communal love celebration. I want to live surrounded by Woodstock love for the rest of my life.*'"

"He returned to the West Coast with a mission, and five years later he made that dream come true at the Love & Peace commune. Here he planted the seed of Woodstock love and nurtured it until it flourished in our little community."

After a pause, Ceil continued, "Those first years weren't easy, and the commune would not have succeeded without Sky and his quiet leadership. Thanks to his vision, Love & Peace became a Woodstock village, and he was one of our village elders. That is his legacy."

She was quiet. "So, what is that legacy? Ralph Waldo Emerson once said, '*The purpose of life is to be useful, to be honorable, to be compassionate, to have it make some difference that you have lived and lived well.*' Useful, honorable, and compassionate— there is no better description of Sky. He made a difference, and he left us all the better off for having known him. We will miss him," she said, and added softly, "I will miss him most of all."

The room was silent. Then Nia stood up at her seat and quietly began to sing, "Swing Low, Sweet Chariot." She turned and looked around and one by one others stood and sang with her. Ceil nodded to her friend. It was only appropriate that Nia would sing a song from Woodstock. Sky had loved it when Joan Baez had sung the spiritual well after midnight on the first night of Woodstock. In his journal, he said it was the second to the last song of that long first night and it had helped him to get to sleep.

Chapter 59

Ceil, Summer, & Kate back at the lawyer's office

Crandall Law Office, Brookings, OR
Friday, September 20, 2019, morning

Two days later, Ceil, Summer, and Kate were back at the lawyer's office. It was hard to believe it had only been a month since the reading of Esther's will. The only difference this time was that they were all dressed far more casually than on the previous visit.

Just as before, the three women stood in front of the same window, but now they looked out at a tsunami-ravaged Brookings Harbor. The old marina, with its cabin cruisers and fishing boats neatly lined up, was gone now. All the retail and office buildings that had been on the ocean side of Highway 101, across from the lawyer's office, were also missing. Many had been built a hundred years ago, back in 1906 when the town was founded. There were now just foundation holes filled with mud, sand, and debris, like open wounds lined up along the highway running through town. It wasn't just Brookings, though. The same devastation was repeated up and down the entire coastline of Washington, Oregon, and northern California.

Anna, the receptionist, came over and pointed out the window. "You can see where the marina used to be," she said, shaking her head sadly. "It's just a pile of splintered wood and smashed concrete pilings now. My dad lost his fishing trawler in the first wave. It got crushed up against the seafood restaurant that used to be over there at the start of the docks. He found pieces of the boat two days later and a part of the bow with the name still painted on: 'Dusty Spring.'" She sighed heavily. "Our offices here were lucky, though. We are high enough up the hill that the building was left intact, although we did have some flooding. There was a lot of clean up to do in the basement," she added grimly.

Ceil shook her head in sympathy. "Where were you when the earthquakes started?"

"Home." Anna explained, "I live a little north of here. Luckily, our house is way up in the hills, so the tsunami waves didn't reach us. Plus, it's not too steep, so there were only a few small landslides that closed the road for a day or two. All in all, we were fortunate." She suddenly grinned. "Hey, I heard you folks evacuated into the trees!" she said with obvious delight. "I saw the footage on the news. What an amazing idea!"

Ceil replied, "We had Summer here to thank for that. It was her idea and she organized all the preparations."

"Preparations?" Anna repeated and frowned. "But how could you know it would happen?"

Ceil glanced at Kate and then shrugged. "They've been telling us for years that the subduction zone was due for a release of tension that might set off a tsunami."

Anna nodded. "Yeah, but who really believed it?"

Kate agreed, "True. And then it happened."

The door opened, and Spencer walked in. He smiled, walked straight over to Ceil, and hugged her.

She stepped back in surprise. "You OK, Spencer?" she said with a dubious laugh.

"Never better," he responded. He looked at Anna, "Is Larry ready for us?"

She nodded. "Please go ahead into the conference room. I'll let Mr. Crandall know you folks are here."

Ceil noticed Summer taking a deep breath before the three women followed Spencer into the conference room.

They all took the same seats they'd sat in previously, Spencer on one side of the table and the women on the other.

Larry Crandall came in, and they exchanged handshakes and nods of welcome.

He sat down at the head of the table. Then he glanced from Spencer to Ceil and then to Kate, and finally he looked at Summer. "So, Summer, you called this meeting. What did you want to discuss?"

Spencer interrupted. "Larry, maybe I should go first..." he started to say, but Ceil watched as Summer put her hand up and shook her head.

"No, Uncle Spencer, I've got this," Summer said, pulling out some papers from her purse. "I've contacted Rhymes & Goodwin in Portland–they are an internationally known real estate law firm," she said by way of explanation to the others. "I have discussed the commune land with them and want to officially inform you, Uncle Spencer, that we will take you to court over the title to the 25 acres by proving that Ceil indeed owns the land, subject to the adverse possession statute of the State of Oregon. It requires a minimum of ten years of continuous possession, which the commune more than satisfies. In addition, I have documented proof that Ceil has been paying all the property taxes for the past forty-five years." Summer turned and handed the documents she'd taken from her shoulder bag to the lawyer.

Crandall cleared his throat and nodded gravely as he glanced through the sheets, "Interesting. Very interesting, Summer."

"That is an impressive approach, Summer," Spencer said with a widening grin. "But really, there's no need."

Ceil saw Summer frown and sit up straighter in her chair, but Spencer held up both hands as if to stop her from saying anything more.

"Wait," he said. He reached into his jacket, pulled out an envelope, and tapped it lightly between his fingers. "This is the title to the land." He opened the envelope, pulled the document out, and handed it over to Larry Crandall. "I've already signed it over to Ceil."

They all turned to Crandall, who took Spencer's document, studied it, and then smiled. He glanced at Ceil. "Indeed, he's signed the 25 acres over to you, Ceil. It appears to be yours, free and clear."

Ceil felt stunned and for several seconds she stared at the lawyer, speechless. Then she looked at Spencer for confirmation before she finally smiled. "Thank you, Spencer. I guess I owe you."

Spencer shook his head, "Nope. I'd say we are even, Ceil."

Larry Crandall turned to Summer, "I hope you can get your deposit back from Rhymes & Goodwin. But I want you to know that I'm impressed with your resourcefulness. Have you ever thought of going into real estate law yourself?"

"It's a thought," she said with a nod.

* * *

Summer drove the three of them back to the commune. They didn't talk because Summer had to concentrate on her driving. The state road was still in terrible shape. In several spots, the lane closest to the river had been completely washed away, and the other lane had been covered with small boulders and mounds of mud. It was slow and a bit arduous, but they made it back without incident.

"I don't get it," Kate said as they got out of the car and carefully stepped along the plywood boards that were still serving as temporary walkways over the muddiest sections behind the lodge.

"It'll take a while for this to dry up," Ceil said, taking in the ravaged compound. The bonfire fire pit area was unrecognizable, still filled with a dark sludge mixed with branches, leaves, and rocks. The two bleachers were gone, although the splintered wood was found in the pile of brush and debris heaped at the foot of two ash trees just at the edge of the forest.

"No, I don't mean the flooding," Kate said. "I mean, I don't get why Spencer signed the title over to you without a fight."

Following just behind Kate, Summer said, "He probably realized he didn't have a chance in court."

Ceil shook her head. "No, that's not the reason. He signed the title before hearing about your adverse possession claim, although he deals in real estate for a living, so he probably was already aware of it." She stopped and turned to look at Kate and Summer. "I think he was thanking us for saving his life that night in the trees."

Summer snorted. "He was a mess, wasn't he? First, you and Zeke found him wandering alone around the lodge after the first earthquake; then you took him to the forest and told him he's got to go up into the trees." Summer laughed and shook her head. "Who knew he was so afraid of heights? And you should've seen him after Arlo brought him up in the kiddie lift that night! Arlo had to lead him like a blind man because he refused to open his eyes. And later he tied himself to the trunk, just in case."

Ceil joined in the laughter. "When he was a kid, he wouldn't ride horses because he said the saddle was too high off the ground!"

Kate turned and looked at her grandmother. "So how does it feel, Grandma Ceil? Now that the place is truly yours."

Ceil took a moment to take it all in. "Yes, it's really and truly ours, isn't it?" she said quietly. "Finally."

Chapter 60 - Epilogue

God Speed, Sky

Love & Peace Commune, Brookings, OR
Friday, October 18, 2019, afternoon

A month after the Memorial Service for Sky, Ceil, Zeke, Summer, and Kate slipped away to walk together along the path of the rebuilt labyrinth. In one last act to honor Sky, he had asked them to scatter his cremated ashes on the new peace sign at the grove's center.

They walked slowly, and Kate noticed that Ceil touched the reddish-brown bark of each huge sequoia redwood as they passed. Kate reached out and did the same. It was a gesture of thanks for protecting them and keeping them safe.

After they finished scattering Sky's ashes at the center of the grove, the four of them sat on the ground around the peace sign. They were silent in thoughtful reflection.

Several minutes passed when Kate's thoughts were interrupted by her mother who was swatting at her shoulder. "Ew," Summer said. "Look at all of them!"

Butterflies flitted through the ferns and grasses around them.

"What do you mean 'Ew,'" Kate said with a laugh, "Mom, they're beautiful!"

"They're a swarm of flying insects, and they make my skin crawl," Summer replied, brushing again at her bare arms.

When Kate looked over at Ceil, she saw that her grandmother had risen. She watched, mesmerized, as Ceil then crouched down with her hand held out. To her amazement, Kate saw a single butterfly flutter over to Ceil and gently perch on her outstretched finger.

Ceil glanced at Kate, then over at Summer, and finally at Zeke with a growing smile spreading across her face. Kate could see tears welling in her grandmother's eyes. "Sky promised he'd send me a sign that he is fine...and I think this is it," Ceil said, wiping away a tear.

Kate nodded but she couldn't speak. Instead, she just pointed upward.

Ceil tilted her head and looked up, and her eyes grew round. "Oh Sky!" she said in an awed whisper. Then she laughed aloud and hugged herself. The movement caused the butterfly to lift and flutter around her head, once, twice, and a third time, then slowly it rose to join the hundreds of butterflies swirling in the canopy above.

THE END

About the Author
M.H. Sullivan

Prior to moving to New Hampshire in 1977, the author spent most of the previous 20+ years living overseas. As the daughter of a U.S. State Department diplomat, she lived in Korea, Taiwan, the Philippines, Thailand, and Ethiopia.

After graduating from Boston University, Maureen worked in Washington, D.C. as a travel agent and then as a staff aide on Capitol Hill. After getting her Master's degree from Simmons College Graduate Program in Management, Maureen worked as a technical writer in the software industry and later in the medical devices industry. She moved to NH in 1977, married in 1978, and has lived in NH ever since. She has two daughters and two granddaughters.

Maureen was the publisher of the *Southern NH Children's Directory* and related publications from 1994 to 1999. In 2008, she published her first novel, *Trail Magic: Lost in Crawford Notch* (revised edition released 2026), and in 2010, she published a memoir, *The Sullivan Saga: Memories of an Overseas Childhood*. A second novel, *Jet Trails: Looking for Blue Skies*, was published in 2015 (revised edition released 2026). *Goodbye Woodstock: The Last Reunion*, is her third novel.

Books by M.H. Sullivan:

Trail Magic: Lost in Crawford Notch

The Sullivan Saga: Memories of an Overseas Childhood

Jet Trails: Looking for Blue Skies

Goodbye Woodstock: The Last Reunion

For more information, go to www.romagnoli-publications.com.

www.ingramcontent.com/pod-product-compliance
Lightning Source LLC
Chambersburg PA
CBHW020224260626
47156CB00002B/520